THE GIRL NEXT DOOR

JENNIFER SUCEVIC

The Girl Next Door

Cover Design by Mary Ruth Baloy at MR Creations

Proofreading by Kate Newman at Once Upon a Typo

Home | Jennifer Sucevic or www.jennifersucevic.com

ALSO BY JENNIFER SUCEVIC

Campus Player

Claiming What's Mine

Confessions of a Heartbreaker

Don't Leave

Friend Zoned

Hate to Love You

Heartless

If You Were Mine

Just Friends

King of Campus

King of Hawthorne Prep

Love to Hate You

One Night Stand

Protecting What's Mine

Queen of Hawthorne Prep

Stay

The Breakup Plan

The Boy Next Door

Chapter One

MIA

Summer before freshman year of college...

"Get your butt over here," my best friend squeals from the window where she's taken up sentinel, "you *need* to see this!"

That's a negative, Ghost Rider. I'll take a hard pass. I have zero interest in spying on a yard full of drunken classmates who are partying it up at my neighbor's house. Reluctantly, I glance up from the toes I'm painting with a pale pink polish. Coney Island Cotton Candy, to be precise.

When our gazes lock, Alyssa waves me over. She's practically vibrating with excitement. Kind of like a schnauzer.

"Everyone is over there!"

"Not true," I mutter, lacquering my baby toe with an impressively steady hand. "*We're* right here." And that's exactly where I plan to stay.

"Yeah, that's kind of the problem." She steeples her hands together before shaking them at me. "Please?" she begs. "Can't we go over there for a little bit? *Just a little?* That's all I'm asking."

That's all she's asking...ha!

I'm calling bullshit.

Alyssa knows I'd rather chew my arm off than crash one of Beck Hollingsworth's parties. I didn't mention it to her, but Beck shot me a text earlier this afternoon with all the details. If she even suspected an invitation had been issued, she would have dragged my ass across the lawn that separates our properties as soon as the first guest pulled into the drive.

No, thank you.

It's obvious from all the commotion coming from next door that the entire senior class has shown up to celebrate our newly graduated status. If we didn't live on a quiet cul-de-sac tucked away in a gated subdivision, I'd expect the police to make an unannounced visit and shut down the festivities.

Then again, no one wants to mess with Beck's father, Archibald Hollingsworth. He's a high-priced attorney with a fleet of underlings working for him. He's one of those overly tan guys with blindingly white veneers you see on television yapping about if you've been injured, you need to call them—they fight for the little guy! The dude is everywhere. Billboards. Commercials. Newspaper and magazine advertisements.

The local police have tangled with Archibald several times over the years because his son is a magnet for trouble. Let's see, there was the time (or five) when he was picked up for underage drinking. When Beck was fifteen years old, he *borrowed* his parent's brand spanking new Range Rover and did a little off-roading. And the police were involved when he super glued the locks on the high school building doors for senior prank day.

Instead of hauling Beck to the station every time he's picked up, they drop him at his front door and don't bother talking to Archibald about it. Beck is on a first-name basis with a number of guys on the force. A few showed up to his graduation party in June.

It shouldn't come as a surprise that Beck always figures out a way to circumvent the obstacles standing in his path. His parents. School. The law. It's as irritating as it is impressive. Maybe one of these days, he'll use his powers for good instead of evil.

"Come on, Mia!" Alyssa whines, all the while flashing sad puppy-dog eyes at me.

Double whammy.

My bestie knows I have a difficult time resisting puppy-dog eyes.

I wiggle my toes from the bed and grumble, "I can't go anywhere until my nails dry." I'm doing my best to prolong being anywhere near Beckett Hollingsworth. The guy drives me batshit crazy.

And that's putting it mildly.

"Great! So…five minutes?" She swings away before pressing her face against the screen as her voice turns dreamy. "I bet Colton is already there."

Ugh.

Colton Montgomery is Beck's right-hand man, so it's not a wager I'm likely to win.

Against my better advice, Alyssa has been crushing hard on Colton for more than a year. Not only is he popular, but he's a football player. Heavy emphasis on the *player* part. If Alyssa were smart, she'd find a nice guy to fall in lust with, but she has tunnel vision when it comes to the blond-haired, blue-eyed heartbreaker.

Colton has it all going on. Brains, brawn, and more than likely, a one-way ticket to the NFL after college.

The only problem is that he's aware of his own appeal.

His ego is as massive as other parts of him.

Or so I hear.

And not from Alyssa since he refuses to sleep with her. I can't decide if the situation is amusing or sad. The more Colton keeps Alyssa at a firm distance, the more determined she is to have him.

Last football season, Alyssa dragged me to every game. Even the away ones. My greatest fear was that Beck would assume my ass was there to support him. His fan club is already legendary without adding me to the ranks.

When it comes to the ladies, Beckett makes Colton look like an innocent babe. He goes through girls like most people go through underwear. Speaking of panties, the girls at our high school are always happy—hell, I'd go so far as to say thrilled—to drop theirs for him.

It's ridiculous.

He's a chronic user and abuser.

There should be a warning label slapped across his forehead.

Beware. Toxic to the female species.

But you know what?

That wouldn't stop these bubble-headed chicks from spreading their legs wide for him. I've stopped trying to figure out the appeal. All right, I'm well aware of what the attraction is. As much as I've tried to pretend I'm immune to his charms, I'm not. I just do a damn good job of burying them deep down where they never see the light of day. If I didn't, Beck would annihilate me in a heartbeat, and I have zero desire to end up a casualty on his hit list.

Given the choice, I'd rather flip through Netflix and find a movie to watch rather than be dragged over to Beck's bash.

Doesn't sitting around in pajamas and stuffing our faces with pizza sound way better than watching a bunch of our classmates get sloppy drunk, engage in way too much PDA, and puke all over the place before alcohol poisoning sets in?

I won't bother posing the question to Alyssa. There is no way she'll willingly opt for sitting home instead of stalking her crush.

Would you like to guess what Colton will be doing while I wipe the drool from Alyssa's chin?

You guessed it. He'll be flirting with every vagina he thinks he has a chance of penetrating.

Honestly, it's one of the most masochistic things Alyssa could do. I have no idea why she insists on putting herself through this kind of agony. Apparently, my job as her best friend is to support her decision to inflict untold amounts of mental anguish on to herself. I'd slap her upside the head if I thought it would knock sense into her.

My prediction for the evening goes a little something like this— Alyssa will have a few drinks, moon over Colton, before dissolving into a puddle of tears while that manwhore makes out with other girls in front of her face. Then I'll drag her home, and she'll end up knuckle-deep in a gallon of triple-chocolate ice cream.

But that's what friends are for, right?

Don't worry, I've already made my peace with it.

"Fine," I grumble with a scowl, hoping she understands the depth of my reluctance. "But let it be known that I won't be staying for more than an hour. So, you better make good use of your time, girl."

She swings around to face me, bouncing on the tips of her toes as she claps her hands together with excitement. "Yay!" As soon as she gets the affirmative, she beelines for my closet, which is half the size of my room.

I have the kind of closet most girls my age can only dream about. Shoes, purses, clothes, and jewelry. It's all there and organized.

"Cue the montage music while I find something schmexy to wear!" she squeals.

"What you have on is fine." I roll my eyes and yell, "It was good enough for me, wasn't it?"

From within the depths of my closet comes a snort.

For the next ten minutes, I'm treated to an impromptu fashion show. At the rate Alyssa is going, we won't make it to the party any time soon.

Take your time, girlfriend. I'm totally good with that.

A dozen outfit changes later, Alyssa settles on a black knit tank and white skirt that showcases her sun-kissed legs to their best advantage. Alyssa has been taking dance classes since she was three years old. She's toned with long, lean muscles.

"Damn girl, you look hot." Not that her crush will appreciate the effort. Alyssa needs to move on. I'm thinking a twelve-step program would help kick the Colton Montgomery habit.

"I would gladly live in your closet if you'd let me." She grins before doing a little twirl. "It's my happy place."

A reluctant smile quirks my lips.

My mother is a card-carrying shopaholic and has the Amex Black Card bills to prove it. She buys clothes like our house burned to the ground and nothing could be salvaged. Even with racks of space, my wardrobe is bursting at the seams. Three-quarters of the stuff has never seen the light of day. Alyssa is lucky we're roughly the same size so she can borrow whatever she wants.

Now that she's dressed and ready to mingle, her eyes narrow as she takes a hard look at me. Wordlessly, she spins around and races back inside the closet only to resurface a handful of minutes later.

"Here you go," she says, tossing two garments at the foot of my bed.

I glance at the shimmery gold tank and dark-wash jean skirt that resembles a folded-up napkin. The skirt is cute as hell, but I would strongly advise against going commando while wearing it unless you're looking to flash everyone your goodies.

Since that's not my usual style, the price tag is still dangling from the pocket. I have no idea what my mother was thinking when she picked it up.

Unsure why she's throwing clothes at me, I point to the small pile. "What's that about?"

"You need to change." She gives me a look that says—*duh* before clapping her hands together. "Chop-chop."

Changing my clothes was not part of the plan. I'm fine with going in my pajamas. It's not like I'm looking for a hookup. Or anything else, for that matter.

I shake my head and fold my arms across my chest. "No, thank you."

Her gaze rakes over me as she points to my T-shirt. "Is that a coffee stain on your boob?"

With a frown, I glance at my chest and inspect the dark spot marring the fabric of my right breast. My guess is that she's right. Caramel Macchiato, to be specific. "Possibly."

Her lips flatten. "I refuse to go anywhere with you looking like *that*."

"Great!" I stretch out before stacking my hands behind my head. "What kind of movie night does it feel like to you? Romcom? Horror? Psychological thriller? Angsty tearjerker?" A benevolent smile curves my lips. "You can choose."

Alyssa stomps her foot on the carpeted floor. "Mia!" she wails at a decibel that could shatter eardrums. A few neighborhood dogs howl in response. *"You promised!"*

Promised?

No, I don't think so.

I scrunch my nose and tap a finger against my lips. "I don't believe I ever *promised* to do anything. *Reluctantly agreed?* Yes. *Browbeaten into capitulating?* Definitely. But *promised?* Not in this lifetime."

When she straightens to her full height, I groan, knowing exactly what's about to happen. "*Mia Evelyn Stanbury*! Do I need to remind you who was there when—"

Argh.

This is the portion of the evening where Alyssa trots out every damn thing she's ever done for me until I relent. And she'll start with Harper Hastings. The girl who bullied me relentlessly in seventh grade because Xander Rossi asked me to the movies instead of her. After months of Harper's mean-spirited attacks, Alyssa waited for the girl after school. My bestie let it be known that if Harper didn't cease and desist, she'd spread the good word that the other girl was a known bra stuffer. It must have been true, since Harper immediately backed off, and I never heard a peep from her again.

"*Yes, yes, Harper Hastings*," I mutter, not appreciating the direction this conversation has swerved in.

Alyssa folds her arms across her chest as a smug smile twists her lips upward. "Harper Hastings is only the beginning, my friend." She arches a brow. "Need I continue?"

Silently we glare before I fold like a cheap house of cards. "Fine, I'll change." I straighten before scooping up the skirt and top and shaking them at her. "It's only because I love you and you're my best friend that I'm even willing to step foot next door."

An angelic smile spreads across her pretty face before she blows me a kiss. "Love you, too. Now kindly move your assets."

"An hour," I remind. "That's all you get."

Looking unconcerned, she waves a hand. "No worries, that's more than enough time to work my magic."

What she means to say is that it's more than enough time for Colton to ignore her, all the while hooking up with another girl. Part of me almost wishes he would sleep with Alyssa. Maybe then the rose-colored glasses would come off, and she would realize what a douche the guy is.

In one fluid motion, the stained T-shirt is stripped from my body and replaced with the gold tank. Then I slide off the comfy shorts I've been lounging in and yank on the tiny rectangle of material that doubles as a skirt.

I step in front of my floor-to-ceiling mirror that's propped against the wall and stare at my reflection before attempting to tug the skirt further down my thighs, but it's useless. There's not a spare inch of material to be found.

What the hell had my mother been thinking when she picked this up? Was she mistakenly shopping in the toddler section?

I turn around and bend over, touching my toes before peering over my shoulder and glancing in the mirror. It's just as I suspected. My thong is on full display. Actually, it doesn't even look like I'm wearing underwear since the material is wedged between the crack of my ass like dental floss.

Lovely.

Not to mention uncomfortable.

"Is there a second option to consider?" My gaze slides to Alyssa's in the mirror. "One where my ass isn't hanging out?"

"'Fraid not. I'm seriously loving the whole—is she or isn't she wearing panties guessing game you've got going on." She winks. "Play your cards right, and maybe you'll get lucky tonight."

I narrow my eyes as my lips thin. "Believe it or not, I'm perfectly content being unlucky."

"That, my dear, is only because you don't realize what you've been missing."

"Heartache, STIs, and the possibility of an unplanned pregnancy?" I flutter my lashes and smile. "You are so right."

Ignoring my comment, she tosses a pair of gold sandals at me before sliding her feet into black leather ones that strap up her legs, giving her that whole Grecian goddess vibe. She looks amazing. But then again, when doesn't she? Alyssa has long blond hair and dark blue eyes. Her skin has a natural sun-kissed glow that darkens under the summer sun.

It almost offends me that Colton refuses to fuck my friend.

What the hell is wrong with him?

"Ready to go?" she asks, checking her reflection in the mirror one last time.

I slip the sandals on before rising to my full height. "As I'll ever be."

Five minutes later, we've traversed the lawn and are walking around the side of the Hollingsworth mansion. All sixteen thousand square feet of it. Needless to say, Archibald has turned ambulance-chasing into a lucrative art form.

With every step we take, the sound of drunken laughter and the pulsing beat of music grows louder, assaulting our ears. As soon as the party comes into view, I wonder why I let Alyssa talk me into this.

It's complete chaos.

As much as Alyssa would like to convince you otherwise, I'm not a complete dud. I like to party as much as the next girl. But Beck enjoys taking his antics to the next level. He's not content to have a low-key get-together where people sit around and chill. This party is moments away from becoming one of those teen movies where all hell breaks loose, and the host wakes up naked the next morning in a dumpster five states away with a goat.

Over to the left, a few people are holding a guy upside down while he performs a keg stand.

Chants of—*chug, chug, chug* permeate the air.

It wouldn't surprise me if one of these drunken idiots is found floating face down in the pool come morning.

It begs the question of why Beck's parents would leave him alone without supervision. He might be eighteen-years-old and technically an adult, but he needs an adultier adult to keep him in check. Someone who can put the kibosh on his hijinks.

Good luck with that. His older brother, Ari, is out of the country for the summer.

Archibald and Caroline, his parents, must have realized this was inevitable. Every time they go out of town, Beck throws a huge bash. Depending on the amount of damage, he gets grounded anywhere from a few days to a couple of weeks. The threat of consequences— hell, actual consequences being enforced—are in no way a deterrent.

Believe it or not, before our parents left town for a long weekend in New York, Archie asked me to keep an eye on their son. His actual words were—*make sure no one dies.*

As if I exert that much control over Beck?

Yeah, right. Beck doesn't listen to anyone, let alone me.

Exactly what am I supposed to do?

Tattletale?

Facetime his parents so they can get a first-hand glimpse of the ensuing pandemonium?

As much pleasure as that would give me, it's not going to happen. I might be a lot of things (a rule follower and a goody-goody, if you listen to Beck) but there are lines that can't be crossed, and snitching is one of them.

This will be one more antic Beck gets away with. I suppose that's the beauty of being Beckett Hollingsworth. He doesn't give a shit about anything other than football.

The Neanderthal sport is his life.

By the time Beck was a freshman in high school, he'd already drawn the attention of Big Ten college coaches. They couldn't wait to get him on their roster. If he could have gone straight to the NFL after graduation, he would have. But that's not a possibility. Players aren't eligible to enter the draft until after their sophomore year of college. Beck's father has taken it one step further by insisting he wait until senior year because—and I quote—*no damn son of mine is going to be a college dropout.*

Beck will be proof positive that C's really do earn degrees.

As my gaze drifts over the thick crowd of glassy-eyed stares, it collides with bright green ones. A little zip of electricity sizzles its way through my veins as our gazes fasten. The muscles in my belly tense with awareness. Once I realize what's happening, I tamp down the reaction. My life has been filled with a thousand little moments like this one. Moments I like to pretend never transpired.

For all I know, it's gastritis from the sushi I picked up at the gas station last night.

Anything's possible, right?

Instead of glancing away, I hold his stare and scowl. What I've learned is that it's better to brazen out these situations than turn tail and run. Beck's perfect cupid's bow of a mouth lifts into a knowing grin before he crooks his finger.

A gurgle of laughter bubbles up in my throat.

I don't think so, buddy.

I'm not like the bubbleheads he usually toys with. I have a working brain, and I enjoy using it to make good decisions that won't come back to bite me in the ass. Unlike Beck, I have a healthy amount of self-preservation.

I press my lips into a tight line before emphatically shaking my head.

A wolfish grin spills across his face, giving him a boyishly handsome appearance. With dark tousled hair, sharp cheekbones that scream his Russian heritage, and thick eyebrows, he's a danger to females everywhere. I won't mention the chiseled body that looks like it was carved from stone. Broad shoulders and a tapered waist complete the package.

It's almost a relief when a bikini-clad girl steps between us, severing the connection. Now that his sharp gaze is no longer pinning me in place, I'm able to exhale all the air from my lungs.

Alyssa grabs my hand. "There he is," she whisper-yells excitedly over the babble of voices and music. "Oh my God, he's so freaking dreamy."

I regard the crowd of newly minted high school graduates before finding Colton.

Sure, I'll admit it. He's as hot as Beck. Instead of short dark hair, he's golden blond. It's buzzed on the sides and left long on top, so he's constantly pushing it away from bright blue eyes. He's tall and brawny. If I hadn't gone to school with him since elementary, I'd suspect he flunked a few grades. Even his muscles have muscles.

Girls are already circling around him, vying for his attention. The guy is like a rock star picking out groupies to sleep with at the end of the night.

"He's okay," I mutter, wanting to downplay his attractiveness.

"You're so full of shit, your eyes are turning brown. He's way better than *okay,* and you know it."

"Ewww." I scrunch my nose. "That's gross."

"Focus!" She snaps her fingers in front of my face.

I make one last-ditch effort to sway her. "You can do better than Colton. He knows exactly how hot he is and takes full advantage of it every chance he gets. Find someone like," I stand on my tiptoes and pick through the mass of bodies before zeroing in on the perfect guy for Alyssa, "Landon Mathews. Not only is he good-looking, he's a sweetheart."

Alyssa's expression turns thoughtful as she assesses the tall guy with inky-black hair and unusual blue-green eyes. He's standing around with a bunch of football players, laughing at something one of them said.

"He's definitely yummy," she admits.

For one glorious moment, my spirits soar. Maybe she'll drop this whole Colton Montgomery nonsense and go after someone more attainable. Landon is a great guy. He's as hot as his friends, but he's not a total asshat. Unfortunately, he doesn't get nearly the same amount of hype that Colton or Beck do since he's been labeled a good guy.

I mean, who wants to date a nice guy when you can have one who treats you like total crap?

Said no one ever.

Except...there seems to be way more truth to that statement than most females are comfortable acknowledging. Whether they realize it or not, these girls have been conditioned to crave unattainable jerks.

It's disturbing on so many levels.

"Added bonus," I continue, "he knows you're alive!"

"Um, excuse me, Colton knows I'm alive," she grumbles.

"Are you certain about that?"

She bites her lip as we glance at the guy in question who is—surprise-surprise—surrounded by a bevy of scantily clad girls competing for his interest.

Uh-oh.

Alyssa's got that look in her eye. The one that tells me not to bother trying to talk her out of her plans.

She confirms it by saying, "Wish me luck, I'm going in."

It was worth a try.

"Good luck."

One of Alyssa's best qualities is that she's not a quitter. That girl can be as tenacious and persistent as a terrier. And sometimes, just as yappy.

In this instance, it's a negative.

When she's a few steps away, I cup my fingers around my mouth and yell, "Maybe you should take off the panties so you can flash him your puss. That way he'll know you're a sure thing."

She whips around with a grin. "Excellent idea!"

My jaw drops when she shimmies out of her underwear and tosses it in my direction.

"Christ, girl! I was joking! That was sarcasm!" I glance at the wadded-up material I now clench in my hand. "What am I supposed to do with this?"

She shrugs. "Keep it as a souvenir?"

Gross.

"I don't think so." I stalk to a garbage can and pitch it. When I turn around, Alyssa is pushing her way through the crowd, moving steadily closer to Colton and his harem.

If nothing else, this should be entertaining. It takes a moment to realize that I'm alone at a party I didn't want to attend in the first place. I slip my phone from my back pocket and glance at it.

Fifty minutes and counting.

This is shaping up to be the longest hour of my life. Maybe I should head inside and grab a drink. By the number of drunken idiots I'm surrounded by, my guess is that the booze is flowing freely. I maneuver my way through the crowd and into the kitchen before taking in the scene.

If Beck's mom saw all these people sitting their asses on her polished-to-a-high-shine marble countertop, she would probably have a conniption. She's kind of a germ-o-phobe. There's a half-naked girl stretched out on the island with a lime clenched in her teeth as one of the football players slurps tequila from her belly button.

I'm no aficionado on hygiene, but that definitely doesn't seem sanitary.

A few people greet me as I make my way to the keg and take my place in line. I'm in the middle of chatting with a girl from my French class when she turns an unflattering shade of green and bolts to the nearest bathroom with her hands slapped over her mouth. All thoughts of a refill are abandoned as she pushes her way to the back hall. I really hope she makes it in time. Caroline will be furious if she finds out someone has thrown up on her marble floors.

Once I have a frothy cup of beer in hand, I head to the patio to check on Alyssa's progress.

Am I a terrible friend for hoping she's already been shot down and has thrown in the towel for the night?

Probably, but I can deal with that.

Instead of finding a dejected Alyssa crying in the corner, I'm amazed to discover that she's clawed her way to the front of the pack. Who knows, she may actually have a shot of getting picked from the crowd.

This could be a real game-changer for her.

Guess that means I'm stuck here. I look around the patio, searching for a place to park my ass. The Hollingsworth property is about an acre in size, which is the same as ours. The space around the pool is gated with a black-iron fence and tall arborvitae that spear into the dark night sky. Toward the back of the gate is an unoccupied lounge chair with my name on it. I'll hang out there for forty minutes before dragging Alyssa's panty-less ass back to my house.

Before I can take three steps, a deep voice cuts through the raucous noise of the party.

"Well, well, well. Look who decided to make a cameo appearance tonight."

I swing around, knowing exactly who I'll find.

Beck.

As difficult as it is, I try not to notice how delicious he looks in plaid board shorts that hang low on his hips, showing off the cut lines of his abdomen before disappearing beneath the waistband. The chiseled strength of his arms and chest are enough to bring most girls to their proverbial knees.

The operative word in that sentence being *most.*

I, however, am not one of those idiotic girls.

"Coming here tonight wasn't my idea. I was dragged under duress."

"Yeah, I figured you would have better things to do than hang around with a bunch of wasted assholes."

He's got me there.

"You know me too well." When my throat grows dry, I lift the red Solo cup to my lips. Before I can take a sip, he snatches the drink from my fingers and brings it to his mouth. I watch his throat constrict as he drains the contents.

"Rude much?" My fists go to my hips. "What did you do that for?"

He shrugs. Even though it's a slight movement, his muscles ripple, and attraction bursts to life in my core. "You shouldn't be drinking."

"Excuse me?" My eyes pop wide as laughter tumbles from my mouth. "Are you being serious right now?" I wave a hand toward the drunken mob that surrounds us. It's not even eleven, and already people are passed out on loungers. "Look around, dude, everyone is shitfaced." Hopefully, there are a few designated drivers among this group, or Uber will make a hell of a lot of money tonight.

As soon as Beck smirks, I know his answer is specifically designed to piss me off.

"That might be so, but everyone knows you're a good girl. And good girls don't drink. I wouldn't want the society to revoke your membership. You've worked so damn hard for it."

My eyes narrow to slits. The attraction that had flared to life so quickly is extinguished by his teasing.

I hate when he calls me that. And he knows it, which is precisely why he continues to do it. Beck loves nothing better than to crawl under my skin. He's like a rash I can't quite get rid of, no matter how many steroids I use.

It's irritating.

"I'm not a good girl," I growl before stabbing a finger at his ridiculously hard chest. "And *you* are not my keeper. I can drink if I want to." In a haughty voice, I remind, "I'm the one who was requested to babysit *your* ass. Not the other way around."

He crowds into my personal space. Instead of retreating, I stand my ground. I refuse to let him intimidate me.

"Babysitter, you say? Hmmm...I could definitely use one of those tonight." His fingers trace a path down the center of my chest, lingering in the valley between my breasts. "Should we take this elsewhere, and you can demonstrate everything your service entails?"

His nearness does funny things to me and clouds my better judgment. Instead of pushing him away, I'm tempted to pull him closer.

My body wavers before sanity crashes down on me, and I bat his hand away. "Go to hell."

"See?" He laughs as if I've proven his point. "A good girl through and through."

"I'm not as good as you think." The words shoot out of my mouth before I can rein them back in. To be clear, they are a total lie. I *am* as good as he thinks. Probably better. I have to be.

"Is that so?" He steps closer until the tips of my breasts brush against his bare chest. "Sweetheart, I'd love nothing better than to test that theory, but we both know you'll always be Mia Stanbury, little miss perfect."

And he'll always be Beckett Hollingsworth. The guy with little-to-no impulse control who can't walk down the school hallway without finding trouble. The same one who can't be left alone in his own house for a night without inviting a hundred of his closest friends over for an impromptu party.

We are opposites in every sense of the word.

"Shut up, Beck." I've never met anyone who has the power to turn me on and piss me off at the same time. If he ever cranked up the charm, I'd be toast. He's capable of melting the panties right off a girl with one well-aimed look. I've seen it happen with my own eyes. I refuse to be one of those ridiculous females. I won't be used and tossed aside like a dirty Kleenex.

I don't realize that I've become trapped in my own thoughts until his fingers settle under my chin, lifting it so I'm forced to meet his bright gaze. "What's the matter? Truth hurt?"

"There's nothing you can say that will hurt me." If only that were true.

His face looms closer until it fills my vision, blotting out the party. My world shrinks around us until it only encompasses Beck. My breath gets clogged in my lungs and burns like a fire before spreading to the rest of my body. Any moment I'm going to self-combust.

What am I doing?

I should pull away, but I'm powerless to do anything other than stare into his eyes and fall under his spell.

"Beck, baby!" a loud female voice booms over the rowdiness of the party, "over here!"

Even when she continues to bleat like a sheep, our gazes remain locked for several long heartbeats, and I almost wonder if he'll ignore her. But she's persistent and continues to repeat his name until he severs the connection between us and swings around.

As soon as I'm released, the air rushes from my lungs, and my body sags with relief. Or maybe it's disappointment. I tamp down the emotions so I can't inspect them too closely.

What would have happened if we hadn't been interrupted?

Nothing good.

This is *exactly* why I avoid Beck at all costs. Even though we're constantly sniping at each other, there's an undercurrent of attraction that hums beneath the surface. No other guy has ever provoked these kinds of emotions in me. I want to slap him almost as much as I want to kiss him.

Sanity returns with a rush as I focus on the statuesque blonde twenty feet away. Ava Simmons is wearing a teeny tiny bikini that leaves little to the imagination. Once she has Beck's full attention, she reaches around and unties the strings that hold the tiny triangles in place. The material floats to the cement at her feet. She lets him—and everyone else in the vicinity—ogle her perky breasts before running and jumping into the pool.

People cheer, and more girls ditch their tops, following Ava into the water.

A grin slides across Beck's face as he glances at me. A challenging light enters his eyes as he jerks his dark head toward the pool. Water sloshes over the edge of the azure-colored tile as more bodies dive in.

Oh, hell no.

My heart pounds as I throw my hands up in a *what can you do* gesture. "Sorry, didn't bring a suit."

His grin turns predatory. "Doesn't look like you need one."

Yeah...not going to happen.

"As fun as that seems, I'll pass," I wave an arm toward the pool, "but don't let that stop you from mingling with your guests. Ava's waiting." Topless. From the corner of my eye, I see her breasts bobbing like inflatable safety devices.

When his focus is drawn to the people splashing around, I follow suit. It's so much easier to stare elsewhere than hold the intensity of his gaze. Even when that option includes watching a bunch of topless girls I've known since elementary school. I don't check out the guys loitering in the area, but I'm sure most are sporting wood. Honestly, if it weren't for Alyssa, I would get the hell out of here before it turns into a raging orgy.

Beck steps closer, and my gaze snaps to his. "Sure I can't persuade you to go for a swim?"

"Nope." I shake my head.

"That's too bad. This would have gone a long way to prove that you're not the good girl I've always pegged you to be."

Before I can summon up a pithy retort, he runs and dives headfirst into the water. I catch a glimpse of plaid as he disappears beneath the surface.

A mixture of relief and disappointment bubble up inside me until I'm nearly choking on them. It's the latter emotion I'm having a hard time accepting.

With a huffed-out breath, I stalk to one of the many loungers that surround the pool and settle on top of a plush cushion. I glance around for Alyssa, hoping she's given up on Colton so we can head home. It's not too late for the evening to be salvaged with pizza and a movie. Instead, I find her in the pool.

Topless.

Sucking face with Colton.

Great.

As much as I want to take off, I can't leave her here alone. God only knows what will happen if I do.

With a groan, I squeeze my eyes tight and prepare myself for a long night.

Chapter Two

MIA

Landon Mathews, the guy I was attempting to lure Alyssa with, settles on the lounger next to me. We had calculus together last semester and often compared notes. Even though Landon is a football player, I don't hold it against him. He's proven himself to be a good guy. And, in my experience, those are far and few in between.

"Hey, Mia." He hands me a brand-new Solo cup overflowing with beer. "You look like you could use a little pick me up."

I could use a lot more than that, but this will do.

"Thanks." Our fingers brush as I take the cup from him. Unlike when I touch Beck, no spark of attraction ignites in my blood. It's yet another reminder that you can't help who you're drawn to. Not wanting to dwell on that disturbing thought, I lift the glass to my lips and take a swig.

"I wasn't expecting to see you here," he comments.

Does everyone think I'm a killjoy?

It would seem my image needs a little rebranding.

I jerk my head toward the house next door. "We're neighbors."

"Oh yeah, that's right." He nods. "I forgot. Still...this doesn't seem like your type of scene."

I snort and glance at the pool. "Orgies generally aren't, but Alyssa wanted to see a certain someone."

He chuckles, following the direction of my stare to the water and the half-naked bodies filling it. He flicks a humor-filled gaze at me. "Looks like she found him. My guess is that you're going to be here for the long haul."

That's exactly what I was thinking. There is no damn way I'll be able to pry Alyssa out of Colton's arms. And my orgy-o-meter has reached its limit. I need Alyssa to wrap up this little make-out session so we can get the hell out of here before I'm anymore mentally scarred.

"Ugh, let's hope not." With that, I bring the cup to my lips and frown when I find it empty. I tip it further back and pat the plastic bottom, but not a drop remains.

Landon chuckles and holds out his hand. "Pass it over, and I'll get you a refill."

See what I mean? Total sweetheart.

Five minutes later, he's back with two cups of golden deliciousness. Tonight the alcohol is going down surprisingly easy. The more I drink, the more relaxed I become.

Ever since my older sister Brianna died when I was fourteen in a drunk driving accident, I've walked the straight and narrow. I've done my best to shine in school and on the tennis court, hoping it would be enough to help my parents forget their heartache for even a minute. Unlike Beck, I don't go looking for trouble. I avoid it at all costs.

So, it feels good to loosen up for a change and drop the pretense. Since my parents are away for the weekend with Beck's, I don't have to worry about them finding out that I've been drinking.

For one night, it's kind of nice.

Freeing.

Landon drops onto the lounger next to me, and we talk about our plans for the fall. I'll be attending Wesley University, which is an hour away. A lot of people from high school end up there. Landon decided not to play football and is attending Penn State.

I considered going further away, but decided against it. Part of me is afraid of what will happen if I did. Sometimes it feels like I'm the only thing holding this family together. The guy who hit Brianna didn't just steal her from us, he also stole our happiness. He sent us spinning through the universe on a different course. None of us are the same. I don't think we will be again. Instead of coming together, the three of us splintered apart. They say time heals all wounds.

It's a lie.

I chase those depressing thoughts away by draining my cup.

Alyssa was also accepted at Wesley, so we'll be rooming together next year.

Guess who else will be on campus?

My gaze cuts to Beck. There are at least three girls hanging on him. It's been this way ever since seventh grade when he shot up six inches and packed on twenty pounds of muscle.

No matter what I do, I can't seem to get away from him.

Beck was recruited by almost every college in the Big Ten Conference. I had secretly hoped he would go far away so I could finally get over this stupid infatuation, but he shot that to hell when he committed to Wesley. The most I can hope for is that we don't run into each other too often. It's a big campus with tons of people.

When I realize that I'm dwelling on Beck, I lift my glass, surprised to find it's been topped off.

My head swims, feeling pleasantly fuzzy.

Exactly how many of these have I knocked back?

I try to do a rough mental calculation that seems as complicated as calculus.

Two? Three? Four? All I know is the more I drink, the better this beer tastes.

When one of my favorite songs gets cranked up, I jump to my feet and pull Landon with me. Apparently, it's everyone's favorite song as well because the entire party throws their hands in the air and writhes to the beat. When it's over, I collapse on my lounger and giggle hysterically.

"Ready for another?" Landon rises, ready to do my bidding. He really is a nice guy. It's too bad he and Alyssa never got together. They would have been perfect for one another. Instead, she only has eyes for Colton.

Speaking of Colton, guess who else committed to Wesley?

You guessed it...Colton Montgomery.

Alyssa has sworn up and down that her decision has nothing to do with a certain blond-haired Adonis.

I hope that's the case. It would be really stupid of her to plan a future around a guy who has never bothered to give her the time of day until this party. Not that I want to be a Debbie Downer, but who knows how long his interest will last. A couple of hours, at the most.

Alyssa is a talented dancer. Her dream is to get a fine arts degree in dance and open her own studio. She was accepted at several prestigious schools and turned them all down to attend Wesley.

"No," a gruff voice cuts in before I can wrap my lips around a response, "she's already had more than enough."

I glance up, surprised to find Beck towering over my lounger. His hair is damp from his dip in the pool. My mouth turns cottony as I stare at his bare chest.

He needs to put a shirt on so I can think straight.

"Actually," I slur, taking offense to him making decisions for me, "I *will* have another." At least, I hope that's what comes out.

Beck scowls before shifting his hardened gaze to his teammate. "What the hell, dude? Why did you let her have so much? She's offi-cially cut off."

Excuse me?

Who does this guy think he is?

Beck is the king of bad decisions. And he has the audacity to tell me—*me, for God's sake, who hasn't gotten so much as a tardy in her life*—that I can't have another drink? I'm not even driving home.

He didn't nickname me *good girl* and *little miss perfect* for nothing. I'm eighteen-years-old. If I want to cut loose for once in my life and have a few drinks, I'm more than capable of making that decision for myself. I don't need Beck swooping in and telling me what I can and can't do.

That thought alone is enough to piss me off.

"You're not the boss of me," I add belligerently with a slight curl to my lip.

Beck doesn't spare me a glance. His focus is trained on Landon. "You've been relieved of your duties. I've got it from here."

"Chill out, dude. She's fine. We're just talking. No need to bust a nut."

What's Beck's problem? Landon is right. We weren't doing anything wrong. Beck is angry, and I don't understand why. Normally my neighbor and part-time nemesis is laid-back and chill. Nothing riles him up. So, this behavior is definitely out of character.

Beck's lips flatten as the steely look in his eyes intensifies. "Take off, I'll deal with Mia."

Deal with Mia?

Since when am I someone who needs to be *dealt with*?

They glare at each other for a long, tense moment. The muscles in my belly quiver with unease as my gaze darts from one boy to the other.

What's going on here?

It feels like I'm missing a key piece of information.

The intensity dissipates when Landon takes a step in retreat before turning to me with a forced smile. "It was good talking to you, Mia. I'll see you around before I leave for Penn."

"Yeah, sure." I'm still trying to puzzle out what's going on, but my drunk brain is having a hard time reading between the lines. That's usually something I excel at since interpreting what's going on with my parents has become a survival skill.

Landon jerks his head into a tight nod before joining the crowd of rowdy partiers and disappearing from sight. I stare after him, confused by his abrupt departure.

Wait a minute—what did Beck say a few minutes ago?

"Relieved of his duties?" My gaze cuts to the six-foot guy at my side. "Did you ask Landon to *babysit* me?"

Instead of answering, he tilts his head and studies me.

When I raise my brows, he says, "That depends."

"On what?"

"If you're going to be pissed off with the answer."

Even in my inebriated state, I understand what that means.

"I don't need a babysitter," I grumble, slowly rising to my feet. I'm offended he would think otherwise. Using my arms for balance, I carefully straighten to my full height. "Let me remind you that Archie and Caroline asked me to keep an eye on *you*." I jab a finger at his chest. "Not the other way around."

When I stagger to the side, Beck leaps forward and grabs hold of my arms so I don't crash into the lounger I've been parked on.

"It's doubtful they would have done that if they could see you now."

I wave a hand and blow a raspberry with my lips. "I'm fine."

"You're hardly fine. Landon shouldn't have let you drink so much." Beck hauls me closer until his warm breath can feather across my lips, and my core clenches in response. "Have you ever been drunk?"

Nope. Usually I'm the designated driver, but that wasn't necessary tonight.

"Of course, I have. All the time."

"Is that so," he laughs, the muscles in his face relaxing. "You have a secret life I don't know about?"

It doesn't escape me that Beck is still holding me. And that I like the feel of his hands a little too much. I should push out of his arms except…I don't want to.

"That's for me to know and *you* never to find out," I singsong.

Amusement settles over his face. Now *this* is the Beck I know and try to keep my distance from.

"That's strange. I've never seen you at any of the parties and from my count, you've only had four drinks, and you're already drunk off your ass."

"I wouldn't say I'm drunk off my ass," I mumble as my head spins.

He releases my arms and gives my shoulder a little shove. I stumble back a step before righting myself.

Instead of arguing about my inebriated state, I focus on what he admitted. "How do you know how many drinks I've had?"

"I've been keeping track."

"Why? Are you keeping tabs on everyone's consumption?" There have to be at least a hundred people here. Probably more.

A sly grin simmers around the edges of his lips. "Nope. Just you, Stanbury."

His words send an arrow of warmth flooding through me, and my heartbeat picks up its tempo. Refusing to dissolve into a puddle of goo at his feet, I say, "Well, that's not creepy at all."

Unbothered by my pronouncement, he shrugs. "That's me, the creepy stalker from next door."

Neither of us mentions that every chick at this party would give their left tit for Beck to show interest in them. I'm probably the only girl who goes to great lengths to avoid his attention.

Although that doesn't seem to be doing me any good at the moment.

"I don't need a keeper," I tell him. "Certainly not you."

"That's funny. I was thinking the opposite."

I hold up my cup, needing to put some distance between us. "If you'll excuse me, I'm going to partake in another refreshment."

He nips the cup from my fingers before I can take a step away from him. "I was serious, Mia. You've had enough. You're done for the night."

Done for the night?

What is he going to do? Kick me out?

I cross my arms over my chest and shift my weight. "I'm not leaving without Alyssa." I glance around for my friend. But that's a mistake since the pool is filled with naked people who are busy getting it on.

"Alyssa's a big girl. She can take care of herself."

If only that were true.

"Come on, let's go." His fingers wrap around my wrist, and a little pop of awareness shoots through me when he pulls me to his hard body.

Oh my God! He's serious about kicking me out!

"Excuse me?" I try to push my way out of his embrace, but it's like fighting with a steel beam. He's all hard lines and powerful strength. On the football field, he's a force to be reckoned with. "Are you actually going to throw me out of here?"

"Who said anything about tossing you out?" He laughs and shakes his head. "I'm taking you upstairs so you can sleep it off."

Well, that's a relief.

But still…

I dig my heels in, refusing to budge. "No, I can't go until I find Alyssa."

He points to a couple making out beneath the diving board. "She's right there." He pauses before adding, "She's occupied at the moment."

My gaze darts around the pool until I find my best friend. Beck is right about her being busy. Colton has her backed up against the edge of the pool. Alyssa looks like she's attempting to suction the breath right out of his lungs.

The tank top she borrowed earlier has gone missing.

My gaze skitters away. I'm not into voyeurism. Although some of these people are. There are plenty of them standing around, watching. Let's hope that no one is videoing the moment for posterity.

"It's unlikely Alyssa will leave anytime soon."

"Probably not," I mutter.

What am I supposed to do? Taking off feels wrong. But sitting around and watching people get it on feels downright pervy. I suck my bottom lip into my mouth and chew it as I contemplate my options.

"Fine," I say, "I'm going home." I take a step away from Beck, attempting to distance myself. The scent of his aftershave mingles with the chlorine in the pool. It shouldn't be an intoxicating combination.

"Sorry, Stanbury, you're staying here. The last thing I need is for you to choke on your own vomit."

Give me a break. That's not going to happen.

My fists go to my hips. "What does it matter if I sleep alone here or in my bed?"

His voice turns silky. "Who said anything about you sleeping solo?"

When my mouth tumbles open, a slow grin spreads across his face.

"Are you crazy?" I shake my head a little too vigorously, and the party spins. "Forget it! I'm not sleeping with you!"

"That's the thing, you don't have a choice in the matter. The decision has already been made."

Who does this guy think he is?

I open my mouth to blast him into next week when he says, "We can do this the hard way or the easy way. It's your choice."

What does that even mean?

Instead of answering, I jerk my arm, trying to break free. "Let go! I'm leaving, and there's nothing you can do to stop me!"

"The hard way it is."

In one swift motion, he yanks me to him, crouches down, and wraps his arms around my thighs before hoisting me over his shoulder like a sack of potatoes. I don't realize his intentions until my midsection lands against him, momentarily knocking the air from my lungs, and stunning me into silence. I blink and find the party turned upside down. It doesn't do good things for all the alcohol sloshing around in my belly.

The crowd roars and my cheeks flame as the blood rushes to my head. Cool air hits the back of my thighs and I groan, remembering my choice in underwear. When I continue to struggle, a wide palm lands across my backside.

"Ow!"

"Stop fighting me. Maybe you haven't noticed, but everyone is admiring your ass." There's a pause as he turns us around before moving toward the French doors that lead inside the house. "What the hell are you doing wearing a skirt this short?" Before I can formulate a response, he grumbles, "And with a fucking thong? I love it, but no one else should be checking out your ass."

"Here's a solution," I growl, "put me down."

"Not gonna happen."

His hand slides from one exposed cheek to the crack of my ass before he splays his fingers wide to cover as much skin as possible from the gawking crowd. I squirm at the feel of his palm resting against my naked flesh. *Especially there*. I'm not sure which option is more preferable. That people ogle my ass or that Beck continues touching me so intimately. The print of his palm feels as if it has been singed into my flesh.

When I continue to wiggle, his fingers bite into my cheeks. "Stay still." His voice turns low and grumbly. It does funny things to my insides, and a reluctant thrill spirals through me.

Beck weaves through the thick crowd. Every once in a while, he'll stop and chat as if carrying a girl over his shoulder is perfectly normal behavior. "Everyone needs to be cleared out in an hour," he says. "Got it?"

"Consider it done," a deep voice responds.

Before I'm able to get my bearings, we're on the move again. From my upside-down position, I watch the kitchen disappear as he walks through the first floor of the house. My hair swings around my face like a dark curtain, making it impossible to see. I should probably be thankful. I've never been so mortified in my life. If I'm lucky, no one will realize I'm the girl Beck has thrown over his shoulder and is carrying up to his room like a prize he won in a card game.

People clap and cheer as he climbs the staircase to the second floor. My name reverberates through the crowd like a wave. Whispers and giggles assault my ears, making the tips burn with humiliation.

"Can you put me down?" I growl, fed up with his manhandling. Thank God I won't see most of these people again. That's the only thought getting me through this moment.

Beck slaps my ass none too gently, and the sound of flesh striking flesh echoes off the cavernous walls of the hallway.

"Ow!" I yelp.

"Now that sounded like it hurt." Amusement simmers in his voice.

"What the hell was that for?" I demand. The sting of his smack resonates through my backside. No one has ever struck my ass before. Not my parents when I was younger, and certainly not anyone I've gone out with.

The audacity of this guy!

"No reason, just felt like it."

Grrrr.

I grit my teeth as he turns to the left and walks down the hallway. I played here enough times as a kid to know he's taking me to his room. Beck and Ari's bedrooms are on one side of the spacious second floor while their parents' suite is located on the other. He could probably get murdered, and his parents wouldn't hear a thing.

Not that I'm in any position to bargain, but it's worth a shot. "I'll agree to stay the night," I hiss, "if I can have my own room."

"No can do, sweetheart. You'll be bunking with me."

Aggravated by his uncompromising response, I pummel my fists against the wide expanse of his back. "You're crazy if you think I'm going to sleep with you!"

"Don't worry, you're not about to get that lucky," he chuckles. "Maybe if you beg prettily, I'll change my mind."

Ha!

As if...

I ignore the comment. We both know that won't be happening.

Ever.

I wouldn't beg Beck to spit in my mouth if I were dying of thirst in the desert, and he was my only chance for survival.

"You have four guestrooms, put me in one of those for the night. If there's a problem, you'll be the first to know."

"Wish I could, but all the rooms are taken. A few friends might crash. Better safe than sorry. Am I right?"

Damnit.

Beck isn't concerned about my wellbeing. This is another way for him to get under my skin. I'm on to his games. He's probably doing it since his parents asked me to keep an eye on him. Is that my fault? Should I be punished because *he's* an irresponsible child?

Nope. I don't think so.

I never should have allowed Alyssa to talk me into attending this party. It was a mistake. No good deed goes unpunished. This is what I get for trying to be a good friend.

Beck stops in front of a closed-door before reaching for the handle and shoving it open. It only takes two steps before we're crossing over the threshold, and he's slamming the door shut, locking me inside like a prisoner.

With him.

Once inside the spacious bedroom, he hunkers down. I breathe a sigh of relief when his hand disappears from my backside. Cool air hits my newly warmed flesh, making me even more aware of the way he had been touching me. His large hands wrap around my hips as I slide against his body until my sandaled feet are planted on the floor. Then he releases me and rises to his full height.

All the nasty names on the tip of my tongue dissolve. It's as if we're frozen in place, unsure what to do now that he's brought me here.

When he inhales, I do the same. When he releases his breath, I follow suit.

What's happening?

More importantly, how do I make it stop?

How do I shake off the heavy feelings of attraction unfurling inside me?

Over the years, I've become a master at burying the emotions Beck rouses in me. With one look, they've broken free and are simmering at the surface. And that's dangerous. I don't want Beck to suspect how I truly feel about him.

Can you imagine what he would do with that kind of information?

I flinch at the thought.

Beck is careless with people's feelings. Especially the fairer sex. I've witnessed firsthand the trail of tears and broken hearts he leaves behind in his wake.

As if realizing we've become stuck in a moment, he blinks and takes a hasty step in retreat. It's enough to break the spell that has fallen over me. A million questions flood through my brain, but not a single one leaves my mouth. It's a relief when he turns away and relinquishes my gaze. I shake my head to clear it as he pulls open the third drawer of his dresser. I'm treated to an impressive view of his bareback. All those tightly honed muscles that stretch and shift with every movement.

God, but he's beautiful. Sometimes I wonder if I'll ever find another guy as sexy as I do Beck. I really hope so. The thought of being stuck on him forever is depressing.

He grabs a piece of clothing before slamming the drawer shut and swinging around to face me.

"Mia?" His voice sounds deeper, more roughed up than seconds ago. Even though I fight against it, my core clenches in response.

It takes a moment to break free of the trance that has fallen over me. I gulp, wishing there was a way to escape the situation. In two swift steps, Beck is back to invading my space. He towers over me, standing so close that the tips of my breasts brush against his shirtless chest.

"You need to stop staring at me like that," he growls.

"Like what?" I whisper, trying to play dumb.

His face hovers so closely that his warm, minty breath ghosts over my lips. All I want is to close my eyes and lean into him. To take a deep lungful of air and savor it.

How is it possible to want someone and yet hate them at the same time? It doesn't make sense.

"Like you might be interested in hanging up your good girl title."

A wave of arousal crashes over me, making my head swim.

Is that how I'm staring at him?

Like I want him to touch me in ways I've only dreamed about in the privacy of my room?

Guilty.

Here's a little secret I'm loath to admit even to myself—I find Beck ridiculously attractive. For as long as I can remember, his energy and sense of humor have fascinated me. I'm drawn to the way he doesn't give a damn. My fingers itch to tunnel through his dark wavy hair. My lips ache to settle over his. And my body trembles with the need for his large hands to coast over it.

But...

And this is a ginormous *but,* I would never—under any circum-stance—admit that to him.

No matter how tempted I might be.

No matter how much he turns me on.

When Beck is this close, it's almost impossible to remind myself that he doesn't have the attention span to stick with anything other than football for the long haul. He flits from one girl to the next before moving on.

A potent blend of regret and relief rush through me when he steps away and presses something soft into my hands. I tear my gaze from his and stare at the wadded-up shirt.

He jerks his head toward the bathroom attached to his room. "Go change."

"Change?" I repeat. I must be more drunk than I suspected because for some reason, I can't get my brain to function properly.

"Yeah," his voice turns sharp, "but leave on the thong."

My eyes pop wide as his words echo throughout my head.

"As long as there's something covering you," he continues, "it won't be a problem."

What the hell have I gotten myself into?

A fresh burst of panic rolls through me as my gaze darts to the bedroom door. *If I run fast, I could probably make it out of here.*

It's not like he would physically stop me from leaving...right?

"Don't even think about it, Stanbury. You sleeping here is a done deal."

I huff out a breath, irritated that he can read my mind so easily.

Left without options that don't involve him laying his hands on me, I stalk to the bathroom and slam the door before sliding the lock into place. From the other side of the door, his amused chuckle assaults my ears. With shaking fingers, I turn on the tap until water flows into the sink before collapsing against the marble countertop.

Now that I'm alone, I try to settle everything racing madly around inside me before splashing a handful of cold water on my face. Then I strip off the tank top, skirt, and sandals. With my bra and thong still in place, I meet my reflection in the mirror. If I were smart, I would leave the bra on, but I can't sleep with wire cups. They'll dig into my skin.

Unwilling to overthink the decision, I unhook the back and allow the straps to slide down my arms before dropping the bra to the tile floor. Then I pull Beck's T-shirt over my head. I hate myself for giving in to the urge to bring the cottony fabric to my nose before inhaling a breath. My belly quivers as Beck's masculine scent wraps around me.

When I step into the room, I find Beck stretched out on the king-size bed that dominates the space. Gone are the board shorts. In their place is a pair of form-fitting black boxer-briefs that hug his impressive thighs and...

Yeah.

I quickly avert my eyes.

Sweet baby Jesus.

No high school guy should be this perfectly sculpted.

It's just plain wrong.

Beck's gaze cuts to mine, freezing me on the spot. My breath catches, and my heart stutters under the sharp intensity of his stare. Unsure how to proceed, I hover near the bathroom door. His hands are lazily stacked behind his head as they rest against the pillow. When I don't budge from the threshold, he sits up and swings his legs over the side of the bed before rising to his feet and stretching out his hand.

"Come here."

Holy shit. Is this really happening?

It feels like a dream. Maybe a nightmare. Or someplace in between.

My mind flips through the past two hours as I try to figure out how I've ended up in Beck's bed for the night. It doesn't make sense.

My motto has always been *avoid, avoid, avoid.*

This is the complete opposite.

Unconsciously, I close the distance between us. I blink to awareness when Beck's fingers tighten around mine. With a tug, I stumble forward into his embrace.

His other hand wraps around my waist. "You good?"

Even though I jerk my head into a nod, I have no idea if it's the truth. This is unchartered territory. Maybe if he would stop touching me, my mind would clear enough to think rationally. But his grip doesn't loosen. Another unwanted bolt of arousal shoots through me before settling in my lower belly.

When it seems like I'll explode from the thick tension that has gathered between us, his fingers fall away and he turns, yanking back the covers.

I stare, unsure what to do. Am I supposed to slide into his bed as if this is normal?

Just another Saturday night spent with Beck?

When I hesitate, he says, "Nothing will happen that you don't want."

That's exactly what I'm afraid of.

All I can think about are his hands on my body.

Against my better judgment, I climb onto the mattress. It's as soft as a cloud. My movements falter when he groans, his hand sliding over my bare backside. Everything in me tenses as I scamper to the far side of the bed. That little caress leaves my body vibrating.

The mattress dips as Beck settles on top of it and we both stretch out, our heads resting against the thousand-count Egyptian-covered pillows. It takes a bit of adjustment before I'm able to find a comfortable position on my side, turned away from Beck. Even though I try to ignore him, I'm ridiculously aware of his six-foot frame next to me.

A few silent moments tick by as I force myself to relax. One by one, my tense muscles lose their rigidity. I stare at the far wall before trying to close my eyes. Okay. This isn't so bad. Beck will stay on his side, and I'll remain on mine. It's a king-size bed and there's plenty of space for both of us. In fact, there's plenty of room for three or four people. I'm sure Beck has tested that theory out for himself. My guess is that he's no stranger to threesomes.

Why that thought irritates me, I have no idea. But I banish it from my head before I can inspect it too closely.

As soon as the sun peeks over the horizon tomorrow morning, I'm out of here. Or maybe I'll wait for Beck to fall asleep and sneak home. Is he really going to care at that point? It's not like he can hold me hostage in his bedroom indefinitely.

The moment I find a comfy spot and melt into the mattress, Beck wraps an arm around my ribs. I yelp as he drags me toward him until my backside is aligned with his front.

Holy hell.

I stiffen like a board as his arm drapes around my body and holds me so every part of him is pressed intimately against me.

And I do mean *every* part.

One of his hands slips beneath the hem of my T-shirt and settles against my lower abdomen. My breath becomes clogged in my throat until it feels like I'm going to pass out from lack of oxygen. The warmth of his palm singes the skin beneath it. It's all I can focus on.

"Relax," he rumbles against my ear.

Is he joking?

How am I supposed to do that?

"You know," I say, voice shaking like a leaf, "I'm fine. I could—"

"You're staying here. End of story."

I press my lips together until they feel bloodless. As much as I want to argue, I know it won't do me any good. Beck isn't going to release me until he's damn good and ready. So, I'm stuck. Pressed against him. I blow out a breath and try to do as he instructed.

The noise of the party fades as my eyelids droop. I listen for Beck's steady inhalations as my muscles gradually unlock.

I refuse to stay here.

There's no way I'll fall asleep.

He can't keep me against my will. A little longer and I can slip out of his embrace.

I stay perfectly still, listening as his breathing becomes deep and rhythmic. For some reason, it calms me from the inside out.

All I need to do is wait.

Then I can...

Drift off to sleep, wrapped up in Beck's embrace.

Chapter Three

MIA

Undiluted sunlight slants across my face, lighting the back of my eyelids and making it impossible to stay submerged in my cocoon. With a groan, I turn away from the brilliance and promptly come in contact with something solid and unyielding.

That's strange.

I'm still drifting in that in-between place where I'm struggling to wake but can't quite break through to the surface. My fingers stroke over something warm as my brain processes what I'm touching. Tentatively, my exploration continues until my fingers graze over a flat male nipple.

What the hell?

My eyes pop open only to find a big body next to me. A muscled arm is thrown over his face, preventing me from discovering the mystery man's identity.

A choked sound escapes from my lips.

Not in a million years did I ever suspect I'd wake up next to a random dude.

I wrack my brain, trying to remember what happened last night, but it's a blur of images. It takes a moment for them to coalesce until, one by one, they flash through my head like a slow-motion picture show.

Hanging with Alyssa at my house.

Beck's party.

Sitting on a lounger and talking with Landon.

Landon.

Is that who I ended up in bed with?

For some reason, I don't think so.

The rest of the night tumbles through my fuzzy brain at an alarming pace. Landon was not only kind enough to keep me company, but also in refills.

Jeez. Exactly how much did I drink?

That must be the reason I feel like I've been hit over the head with a sledgehammer.

And then Beck, of all people, cut me off. Considering the state I'm waking up in, he should have done it sooner. Although I'll refrain from telling him that.

An image of Beck tossing me over his shoulder, carrying me through the party, and up to his room flickers through my head.

Wait a minute...were people actually *cheering*?

Oh, the horror of it all.

Unwilling to face the reality of the situation, I squeeze my eyes tightly shut and attempt to block out this whole unpleasant episode.

"Morning, sleeping beauty," comes a gruff voice chock-full of amusement.

Damn.

Damn.

Damn.

I recognize that voice all too well. It haunts my nightmares. And a few of my dreams.

He's the one I ended up in bed with?

I groan in embarrassment.

"What's wrong, Stanbury? Didn't sleep well? If anyone should be complaining, it's me. You kept me up all night with your snoring."

My eyes fly open only to find him hovering inches above me. A devilish smile spills across his face. He's loving every moment of my self-inflicted torment. As much as I don't want to notice how ridiculously hot he is, it would be impossible not to. Air rushes from my lungs as those unwelcome thoughts invade my brain.

It takes effort to focus on the conversation now playing out. "I don't snore."

"Sure you do, just like a chainsaw."

Heat slams into my cheeks. "I do not!"

He lowers his face until our mouths are almost touching. "Yeah, you do. But I didn't mind because I enjoyed holding you in my arms."

The breath leaks from my lungs.

That much I remember.

His arms were banded around me all night. And I'd slept...okay. Better than that, if I'm being honest with myself.

Arrrgh.

This is exactly why I don't drink. Bad choices are inevitably made when alcohol consumption is involved. It's much too easy to make a fool out of yourself and sleep with—

Oh, God...did we have sex?

No.

No.

No.

Frantically I search my brain, trying to remember if anything physical happened. Silence rains down on us, and my heart constricts before pounding into overdrive. I moisten my lips before pushing out the words. "Did we..."

"Don't worry, little miss perfect, your virtue is firmly intact."

There's a definite smirk in his voice.

I shift my focus to him, searching his eyes carefully.

Why would he say that?

He has no idea I'm a virgin.

I clear my throat and attempt to remain calm. Beck is the last person I want knowing my personal business. The teasing would be merciless. I'd never hear the end of it. "Why would you say that?"

"Educated guess." His eyes crinkle at the corners. "Am I wrong?"

Every muscle in my body fills with tension.

How do I answer that without giving away the truth?

A slow grin moves across his face, making him more handsome than he already is. An arrow of lust explodes in my core.

His hair is artfully disheveled. I'm tempted to reach out and run my fingers through the strands. Instead, I tighten them and resist the urge. It's so unfair. No one should look this good at the butt crack of dawn. The guy could grace the cover of a men's magazine. While I, on the other hand, probably have that whole—just-stuck-my-finger-in-an-electrical-socket look going for me.

"Your silence is answer enough."

I grit my teeth. The only other choice I have is to lie, and I'm a terrible liar.

"Plus, you let the cat out of the bag last night."

I bolt up. My eyes widen until they feel like they might roll right out of my head. *What?*

I wrack my brain again, carefully combing over our conversations. But things are still muddled.

"Liar," I accuse. There is no way I would share something so intimate with Beck. Even if I'd been completely shitfaced, I wouldn't have confessed that to him. But still, doubt lurks in the back of my brain.

"Whether I'm lying is a moot point." He chuckles, leaning closer until his warm breath can drift over my lips. "You had to think about it, which tells me you are, indeed, pure as the driven snow." He tilts his head as his eyes dance with humor. "See how easy it was to get the truth out of you?"

Grrrrr.

"You are such an asshole!" Even though I press my palms against his chest and push with every ounce of my strength, Beck doesn't budge an inch. *"Get. Off. Me!"*

"Being a virgin isn't something you should be embarrassed about."

Oh my God! Stop talking about it before I self-combust!

"I'm not embarrassed," I grit out.

"Then why is your face turning bright red?"

"Because I'm embarrassed, all right? There! I said it!" I snap. *"Are you happy now?"*

"Kind of."

"You're impossible!"

He shrugs. "Not really."

"It's like your mission in life is to make me feel stupid." I knew he would use this information against me, and that's exactly what he's doing. Thank God we're no longer in high school. He would probably shout it from the rooftops, and I would be the butt of everyone's jokes.

His playful manner falls away as seriousness fills his eyes. "That's the last thing I'd ever want to do."

Ha! Liar.

In one swift motion, he wraps his arms around me and rolls me over until I'm stretched out on top of him. My breath catches at the feel of his hard body beneath mine.

Holy moly.

We're so close that I'm able to see the golden flecks that dance in his irises. "I know better than anyone what it's like when people make you feel stupid," he whispers, "and I would never do that to you."

The sincere expression on his face makes this feel like the first honest moment we've ever shared. As if all the bullshit has fallen away, and I'm catching a rare glimpse of the real Beckett Hollingsworth. The notion is as disconcerting as it is dizzying.

His hands cradle my cheeks tenderly. "You're one of the most intelligent people I know, Mia. If I made you feel like you weren't for even a second, I'm sorry. That was never my intention."

A strange intimacy grows between us.

"Your virginity is nothing to be ashamed of." His voice drops lower, becoming deeper. "I like that you're still a virgin."

His words create a warmth that slowly spreads throughout my body.

Even though I'm afraid to voice the question, I'm more afraid of never discovering the answer. "Why?"

His focus drops to my mouth. In response, my tongue darts out to smudge my lips. A groan rumbles up from deep in his chest.

I gasp when his cock twitches against me. Beck remains perfectly still, his hands cupping my face. His eyes darken to a deeper shade.

"I don't know," he admits. "Maybe I want to be the first one to touch you."

My brain explodes, and the world around me ceases to exist.

"Do you want that, Mia?" He rolls his hips, and his thick erection slides against me. Sensation explodes in my core before reverberating throughout my body in the most delicious way.

A moan slips free from my lips, filling the silent room.

"Fuck," he whispers before repeating the movement.

I bite down on my lip to keep the sound trapped inside.

"Don't do that," he mutters thickly, "I want to hear you."

He thrusts against me again, stroking my heat with his length. Only this time, the head of his cock butts up against my entrance. It's gently that he prods the opening. The combined material of his boxers and my thong keep him from sliding in deeper.

My eyes roll back inside my head as waves of pleasure wash over me. He's only stroked me a few times, but already my lower lips are slick with arousal. I'm so greedy for more.

"Does that feel good?"

I whimper in response, unable to form coherent words, as he moves rhythmically against me. The friction we're creating is the most amazing sensation I've ever felt. My thong is soaked. It doesn't escape me that all Beck has to do is stretch the material to the side, and he could slide inside me.

What would it feel like to have Beck buried deep in my body? I've fantasized about it too many times to count. I've touched myself to thoughts of him, but it never felt like this.

My core tightens as he picks up his pace. I arch, needing more contact as another whimper slides from my lips.

"I want you so much," he murmurs.

I gasp as Beck rolls us over, his body stretched out on mine. His gaze burns as he yanks his boxers down so his cock can spring free before pulling my thong to the side. My eyes roll up inside my head when his thick length comes in contact with my slick flesh.

"Do you like that?"

The smooth head of his erection nudges my entrance. He holds himself rigid, only an inch penetrating my heat. But it feels so damn good. I widen my thighs, wanting more.

We've barely done anything and already there is so much pleasure rushing through my system. It's almost too much for the confines of my body. I want to drown in it and never come up for air again. No one has ever touched me like this. There have been a few boyfriends over the years, but nothing that ever progressed to this level.

"We can't keep doing this without a condom," he grits between clenched teeth. "I don't want anything to happen."

His movements still as he hovers above me with the tip of his hard length buried inside my body. The urge to thrust my hips upward and press closer pounds through me.

"Okay."

"Okay?" he repeats as if he doesn't understand.

"Get a condom," I say, arching my back, trying to get him to slide deeper. When he pulls out, I growl with frustration.

"Are you sure?"

"*Yes!*" In this moment, I'm certain of what I want. And what I want more than anything is Beck inside me, filling me, making me feel things I never dreamed possible.

In one swift motion, he rolls away from me and toward his nightstand. He yanks open the slender drawer and grabs something from inside.

His gaze settles on mine as he holds a thin packet in his hand. "You're absolutely sure?"

My core pulses uncomfortably with awareness. I don't think I've ever felt this achy in my life. "Positive."

He bites his lower lip as indecision flickers across his face.

"Beck, I want this." I shimmy out of my thong before tossing it to the floor.

A groan escapes from his lips when he stares at my pussy. There are no more questions as he tears the boxers from his body before ripping open the package. My focus drops to his cock.

Holy cow.

His erection is long and thick. I'm no aficionado on dick size, but he seems impressively built.

"Take off your shirt," he says, sheathing himself with latex. "I don't want anything between us."

My belly hollows out as I tug the T-shirt over my head. It joins the thong on the floor.

Unsure what to do, I lie still as his gaze lingers over my naked length. We've known each other our entire lives. It seems strange that we're about to have sex. But there's no one else I could imagine doing this with. It's always been Beck. Whether I've wanted to acknowledge those feelings or not. So, in a way, what we're doing feels right.

"Having second thoughts?"

I shake my head.

"Okay." His body loses some of its rigidity. It's almost as if he's afraid I'll change my mind. "Spread your legs."

When I widen my thighs, he carefully maneuvers himself between them, stroking his hands from my belly to my breasts.

"You're so fucking perfect."

As he palms the soft weight, I arch into his hands and press myself closer. My eyelids feather shut as he squeezes them. And then he's back to stroking over my body again. Touching every part of me. He stops at my inner thighs and attempts to pull them further apart.

When I resist, his gaze settles on mine. "I want to see you."

A protest sits perched on my lips. I've never been on display like this. As I open my mouth to voice my concerns, he lowers himself and swipes the flat of his tongue across my slit. The stroke is long and languid.

A whimper explodes from my lips as he repeats the movement. The velvety softness of his tongue circles my clit, and sensation gathers, building like a storm inside me until it becomes almost too much to bear, and I groan out my release. He strokes me the entire time, wringing every drop from my body.

After my orgasm dissipates, Beck crawls up the length of me. Heat fills his eyes as a smug smile lifts his lips. I'm too dazed to care. As far as I'm concerned, the guy has every right to be arrogant about his skills.

I'm jostled from those thoughts when he places his cock against my entrance and rocks his hips back and forth. With each thrust, he slides inside my body. I groan as pleasure spirals inside me again, but then he continues to move, and a twinge of pain overshadows everything else.

"Are you all right?" He pauses. "Should I stop?"

I shake my head. Stopping is the furthest thing from my mind.

Maybe I didn't plan this, but I want to experience this moment with Beck.

"It's going to hurt," he whispers.

Beck has been so gentle. I never imagined he could be this way. It only makes me fall harder for him.

I suck in a breath and nod as I mentally prepare myself for what will come next.

He flexes his hips, and his hard length slides further inside me. I wince as pain blooms, becoming more of a burning sensation. He leans down and takes my lips with his own before carefully thrusting against me. When it feels like he can't slide any deeper, he angles himself differently and moves further inside my body.

A whimper escapes, and he swallows it down. Our tongues tangle as he holds himself perfectly still, balancing on his elbows so the full weight of his body doesn't pin me to the mattress. It takes a few moments for the sharp bite of pain to recede.

I blow out a steady breath, and he gently withdraws from my abraded body.

That can't be all there is, right?

There has to be more.

Just when I wonder if he'll pull out all the way, he slides back inside, burying himself to the hilt.

I gasp at the flash of pain as my insides stretch around his girth. It's not entirely unpleasant.

"Are you okay?" He holds himself above me. "I don't want to hurt you, Mia."

"I'm all right. Don't stop." All the previous pleasure swirling madly around inside me is long gone. My insides sting with the intrusion. His cock buried inside my body feels like a foreign entity.

He pulls out again before gliding back inside.

Once.

Twice.

By the third time, the sting has subsided, and a tiny ripple of desire sparks to life in my core.

His thrusts are gentle and rhythmic. Pleasure continues to flourish deep inside me until I'm gyrating my hips, trying to match his movements.

He closes his eyes as his breathing picks up speed, becoming more labored. His tempo becomes faster as I'm pushed to the edge again. When his body stiffens, he throws his head back and groans out his release. As his thrusts become deeper, it sets off my own reaction, and a firework of sensation explodes in my core. A flood of warmth fills me as he chants my name over and over before collapsing on top of me in a heap.

I wrap my arms around Beck and pull him closer. His harsh breathing fills my ears as I stare at the ceiling with dazed amazement.

With a huff, he lifts himself up and balances on his elbows. He stares at me with eyelids at half-mast. Pleasure swirls through his eyes. "Are you okay?"

My lips lift into a tentative smile. "I'm fine."

"Did I hurt you?"

I shrug. "It wasn't too bad."

His lips curve as he presses them to mine. "I tried to be gentle."

I give in to the nagging urge to tunnel my fingers through his mussed hair. I've never felt closer to another human being, and it feels so good.

No. Better than good.

Amazing.

There's a connection between us, one that bonds us in the most intimate way possible. It's something I've never shared with anyone else, and that makes it infinitely special. I want to soak it up and marvel at the unexpectedness of it all.

Carefully, Beck pulls out of my body and flips onto his back. The loss of his warmth and closeness is staggering. It brings unwanted questions hurtling to the surface.

Was this nothing more than a hookup?

Or did it mean something?

I open my mouth to ask when a deep voice cuts through the silence of the bedroom.

"Goddamn it, Beckett Archibald Hollingsworth!"

Every single thought swirling through my head disappears as my eyes widen. I screech at the top of my lungs and scramble under the comforter, yanking it to my chin.

What the hell?

Instead of freaking out, Beck doesn't move a muscle. More surprising than that, he looks unfazed. As if his father hasn't walked in on us. He throws a well-muscled arm over his eyes and huffs out an exasperated breath.

With his body on full display, my gaze drops to his condom-covered cock. Now that his erection has deflated, it's nowhere near the size it was earlier. If I weren't dying of mortification, I'd be tempted to investigate the situation.

"Goddamn it, Beckett Archibald Hollingsworth!"

Annoyance bleeds from every syllable.

I yelp again and glance around the room in confusion. Beck's father is nowhere to be seen, but there's no mistaking that booming voice. I've heard those very words fly out of his mouth dozens of times. That's Archie's usual reaction when Beck has done something boneheaded and gotten himself into trouble. Which he does often.

"What *is* that?" I croak.

"My phone," Beck grumbles before rolling over and swiping the thin silver rectangle from the nightstand. He taps the screen. "Hey, Dad."

Archibald's voice bursts over the line, but I can't quite make out the conversation.

Beck runs a hand through his hair. Instead of taming the locks, the movement only ruffles them more. I'm so tempted to reach out and straighten it into submission.

"Yeah, just a couple of people." A smirk curves his lips as he winks at me. "Perfectly chill."

Ha!

His dad and I snort at the same time. I might not be able to hear every word being spoken, but that sound comes across loud and clear.

Amusement flashes in Beck's eyes. "It'll be cleaned up by the time you get home. No worries."

They exchange a few more words before Beck hits the disconnect button and tosses the phone onto the nightstand.

The comforter is still pressed against my breasts. "Are you in trouble?"

"Nah." He doesn't look the least bit concerned as he collapses against the pillows. "It's all good."

My attention becomes snagged by his body. Skimming over perfect pectorals and six-pack abdominals to the muscular V and then lower to his—

"You keep looking at me like that, and you'll wind up flat on your back again."

I gasp. The arrogant smirk is back in full force.

He rolls toward me until his lips can ghost over mine. "And I would love nothing better than to bury myself in you again, but that's probably not a good idea." His hand drifts under the covers until he can cup my heat. He squeezes his fingers, and a trill of pleasure reverberates through my core. "I'm sure you're sore." There's a pause, and I realize this moment will go one of two ways. "Right?"

"Yes," I answer truthfully.

"That's what I thought." He releases me and rolls off the bed before sauntering to the bathroom.

I watch him, unable to stop myself from checking out his ass.

Lord in heaven, he is gorgeous.

As Beck crosses the threshold, he throws a glance over his shoulder. "I like the way you look naked in my bed, all flushed from sex. I could get used to it."

Thankfully, he doesn't wait for a response. Other than a pounding heart and the bubble of pleasure growing inside me, I don't have one.

And that's dangerous.

Beck is dangerous.

Now that he's no longer affecting my hormones, doubt and cynicism creep in at the edges. I'm reluctant to throw caution to the wind and believe this is anything more than sex.

Good sex.

Great sex, even.

But sex, nonetheless.

With him in the bathroom and all these heavy thoughts crashing down on me, I toss back the comforter and grab his T-shirt from the floor before slipping it over my head and down my body. I search for my thong before yanking it in place. Now that I'm clothed, I feel more in control of myself and the situation.

A few minutes later, Beck strolls out of the bathroom.

Naked.

He closes the distance between us until one hand can slide into my hair. Gently, he pulls my face closer before pressing his lips to mine.

"Thank you," he whispers against my mouth.

"For what?"

"For giving me your virginity."

Heat fills my cheeks as I glance away.

"Hey."

Reluctantly, I meet his gaze.

"It meant a lot to me." He pauses, his voice dropping. "You know this is more than sex, right?"

I shrug.

Is it?

His mouth seeks out mine again. When his tongue sweeps across the seam of my lips, I open, and he deepens the kiss. It's like being dragged to the bottom of the ocean. I lose all sense of time and space. I'm unsure where I begin, and he ends. Beck overwhelms me in every possible way. When he pulls away, I'm dazed and more confused than ever. His breath feathers against my lips, and I want to stand here and breathe him in forever.

"Mmm," he growls, "your mouth is so fucking sweet." He presses another kiss against my swollen lips. "Just like the rest of you."

A whimper escapes from me. All the doubts crowding inside my head disappear with his nearness.

"Goddamn, I want to be inside you again." He nips my lower lip playfully. "But we can't."

My breath hitches as he turns his back on me and walks to the dresser on the other side of the room. His muscles shift with every step. It's mesmerizing. Everything about him is hard and chiseled. I know he spends a lot of time in the gym. I've heard my parents talk about his dedication to the sport and how much money his parents spend on private coaching and agility trainers.

"I need to clean up before my parents get home, or my dad will have my ass," he says.

It takes effort to blink out of the mental fog that has settled over me and focus on his words. Sheesh. I have sex one time, and now my brain is a pile of mush?

Keep it together, girl.

"I should probably get dressed." With that, I hightail it to the bathroom. I need a moment to collect myself. Maybe more than one.

Once shuttered inside the room, I lean against the door and squeeze my eyes tightly closed. Every part of me feels like it's vibrating. When my heartbeat settles, I open my eyes and search for my clothes. I find my bra, tank, and skirt neatly folded on the counter. Unlike my bathroom at home, his is devoid of tubes and bottles of products cluttering the space.

I don't remember folding up my clothing. If memory serves, I left them in a heap on the floor. The thought of Beck picking up my garments and taking the time to straighten them before setting the pile on the counter sends a shiver scampering down my spine. Why would he bother? Unwilling to linger on those thoughts, I yank Beck's comfy T-shirt off and replace it with my bra and shimmery gold tank. Then I tug the skirt up my thighs.

I glance at the mirror, assessing the damage. The reflection that greets me is just as I suspected.

Total mess. I look like I've been put through the wringer. Even though I know it won't do any good, I rake my fingers through my hair, attempting to smooth it down. After a moment, I give up.

When I leave the bathroom, Beck is dressed in khaki shorts and a black Ramones T-shirt. My pulse skitters as I take him in. I need to pull myself together and stop making such a big deal out of what occurred. People hookup all the time. I don't want to read too much into the situation.

His attention shifts to me. "What are you thinking?"

Unwilling to share my innermost thoughts, I shake my head. "Nothing."

"That's doubtful." With three long-legged strides, he swallows up the distance between us. "If I know anything about you, it's that your brain is always working."

He's right, but I'm still not sharing anything with him.

When I remain silent, he reaches out and strokes the side of my face. I'm tempted to lean into his touch, but I stop myself at the last moment. The attraction surging through me is so much more than what it once was. It's like the floodgates have been opened, and there's no closing them.

"You didn't answer the question," he comments.

And I'm not going to. Somehow, he's already burrowed his way inside my head. I need a bit of distance to wrangle these feelings back under control where they belong.

"All right, I see how it is." He flicks the tip of my nose with his finger. "Ready to head downstairs and check out the damage?"

Relief floods through me when he changes the subject instead of pressing for more. "Yeah."

The amount of regret and loss that flickers through me when he steps away is disconcerting. I've always suspected it would be like this with Beck. It's the reason I've given him a wide berth.

With his back turned to me, I press my hand against my lower abdomen as if that alone will still the butterflies that have winged their way to life inside me. Then I follow him out of the bedroom and into the long stretch of hallway.

Professional family photographs dating back to when Beck and his older brother, Ari, were toddlers dot the light gray walls. By the time we reach the curving staircase, I have a handle on myself. I pause and survey the spacious entryway and a slice of the living room.

My brows rise as I take in the party's aftermath.

Oh, boy.

"You coming?"

I blink and realize Beck is waiting at the bottom of the staircase.

"Yeah," I mutter, racing down to join him.

The foyer of the Hollingsworth mansion is elegant and stately. There is a sea of black-and-white checkered marble tile and a chandelier suspended from the ceiling that probably costs as much as a high-end car. White Doric columns break up the space between the foyer and the living room.

What seems out of place are the beer bottles and red cups crowded on the antique credenza. One cup has been tipped over. The wood where the liquid has settled is discolored and cloudy. Caroline will flip out when she discovers the damage. Every piece of furniture in this house has been carefully curated by European craftsmen.

I inspect the living room and find the mess to be just as extensive. More beer bottles and red cups litter the coffee table and floor. A wadded-up shirt, a pair of flip-flops, and a bra have been abandoned by their owners. Couch cushions are strewn about. What the hell were people doing? Building a pillow fort?

I shake my head and blow out a breath.

"Huh," Beck murmurs, rubbing his shadowed jaw, "I thought the damage would be worse."

"Really?" I glance at him. "This seems pretty bad. It will take hours to clean up."

"This is nothing," he replies dismissively.

The idea of allowing a bunch of random people from school to destroy my parent's house is unfathomable.

"Should we check out the kitchen?" he asks, interrupting those thoughts.

"Do we have a choice in the matter?"

"Nope. It's like pulling off a Band-Aid. We need to do it quickly so it's not as painful."

I groan as we step into the two-story kitchen. I've been here enough times to know that under normal circumstances, this place is spotless. It's so clean you could eat off the floor. That's no longer the case. In fact, I'd rather vomit in my mouth than eat anything off the floor.

If I'd thought the living room was trashed, this is ten times worse. Even Beck, who is usually unflappable, skids to a halt.

"Well, shit." His hand goes to the back of his neck as he surveys the damage.

"My thoughts exactly," I say with a snort.

Bottles of booze, bags of chips, empty pizza boxes, plates of half-eaten food are strewn about the room and take up every bit of counter space. Even the long expanse of island is covered with debris.

"What time are the parentals arriving home?" I ask.

He slides his hand through his hair, mussing it more than it already is. "A couple of hours."

"Alrighty then." I clap my hands together. "We better get to work." I have no idea if we'll be able to get this place cleaned up in time, but anything is better than them walking into this shitshow. We haven't even assessed the damage outside.

When Beck fails to respond, I turn to him. "Where are the garbage bags?"

"I appreciate your offer to help, but you don't have to. You're not the one who made the mess, you shouldn't have to clean it up." His lips quirk into a smile. "Don't stress. I'll take care of it."

It's a tempting offer. The idea of going home and crawling into bed for a couple of hours is enticing.

But...if I leave Beck to his own devices, there's no way he'll get done in time.

"It's fine," I murmur, mentally committing myself to three or four hours of cleanup, "I'll stay and help."

Emotion flickers in his eyes. "Are you sure you feel all right?"

Heat slams into my cheeks. Every shift of my thighs reminds me of what we were doing thirty minutes ago. "I'm fine."

He jerks his head into a nod. "Okay, thanks."

Breaking eye contact, I glance around. "I guess we should get started."

"Whatever you say, boss." Beck heads to the pantry and grabs a box of garbage bags and gloves. Without a word between us, I slip the latex over my hands and take a couple of white bags with me to the living room. Beck handles the kitchen as I tackle the other spaces. After all the bottles and random items have been disposed of, I make a sweep of the first floor. At least one good decision on his part was to lock the matching offices.

By the time I've finished straightening up, I've filled three garbage bags with remnants from the party. I've found everything from underwear to baseball caps. Satisfied with the cleanup, I return to the kitchen and find that Beck has cleared all the surfaces and has loaded the dishwasher. I grab the vacuum and run it through the first floor as Beck sweeps the hardwoods in the kitchen.

When I glance at the clock on the microwave, I'm surprised to find that almost two hours have slipped by. I survey the kitchen and two-story family room with a critical eye. "It looks pretty good in here."

Beck leans against the broom. "Teamwork makes the dream work."

"It's entirely possible your parents won't realize you invited the entire senior class over last night."

"They'll know. I'm sure Dad has already watched the security footage."

"Oh." I shoot him a frown. "Why would you have a party if you knew you'd get caught?" That makes no sense.

His lips lift into a lazy grin. "Mostly because I don't give a shit."

And there you have it. Beck's motto in life.

When I remain silent, he adds, "I'll get in trouble regardless, so might as well do exactly what I want and have a good time doing it."

That's one of the many differences between us. The idea of doing something I would get in trouble for is a foreign concept.

"I don't get you," I say.

Not the least bit offended, a slow grin spreads across his face. "It's not possible for you to make a move without carefully weighing all the consequences, is it?"

"It's called being responsible. Why are you trying to make it sound so bad?"

"Because spontaneity can be a beautiful thing." His eyes ignite with heat. "Don't you think so?"

An answering desire kindles to life inside me. "There's a difference between impulsiveness and spontaneity."

"True." He steps closer.

My breath catches when he reaches out and twirls a lock of hair around his index finger before staring at the dark strands as if fascinated by them.

"Don't you ever get tired of being so damn good?" He pauses. "Aren't you ever tempted to break out of the little box your parents have put you in?"

Nerves scuttle through me, and goose flesh rises in its wake. "No one has put me in a box. They give me the freedom to do what I want. Unlike you, I make better choices."

"You don't think I make good decisions?" His fingers continue to grip my hair as he invades my personal space.

"Look around you," I whisper, wanting to break the sexual tension building between us. "The answer is evident."

"Hmmm, you might be right." His lips lift into a wry grin before twisting with a hint of bitterness. "You've been branded the good girl, and I'll always be the bad boy. Right, Mia?"

The question arrows painfully to the heart of me. I'm not *good,* and he's not *bad.* We're just different. Both of our families have money, and we have all the trappings of wealth at our disposal, but our viewpoints and experiences are vastly unique.

Before I can collect my scattered thoughts and summon a response, a loud noise breaks the silence. Air rushes from my lungs as Beck releases my hair and peers through the French doors.

The moment his gaze flickers away, relief rushes through me, and my knees weaken. I glance at the large inflatable swan floating in the middle of the pool. A soft breeze pushes it lazily across the water. I squint and realize that a guy is sprawled on top of it. Arms and legs dangle over the rounded edges. His mouth hangs open as a snore rents the air again. He makes a few grumbling noises as he turns onto his side. The float wobbles, sending ripples throughout the calm water.

I glance at Beck. He shakes his head as if this is beyond even him. We step through the door and walk to the edge of the pool. Placing his thumb and forefinger together, he brings them to his lips. I flinch when the sharp whistle pierces the silence.

When that does nothing to rouse the jackass floating in the pool, Beck yells, "Hey! Wake the fuck up, man!"

There's not even a twitch from the guy. His total unconsciousness is almost impressive.

Beck grumbles under his breath before stalking to the pool house. He grabs a long metal pole with a net attached to the end and brings it to the edge of the water before jabbing the float.

"Time to rise and shine," he mutters.

It takes another five minutes and a handful of none-too-gentle blows for the guy to rouse from his Sleeping Beauty-like slumber. With his hair sticking up in all directions, he gradually pulls himself to an upright position before rubbing his face and staring at us with eyelids at half-mast.

He plows a hand through his mussed hair and yawns. "Hey, what's up?"

Beck hikes a brow. "It's eleven o'clock in the morning. Party's over."

The guy blinks and glances around as if only now noticing his surroundings. "Ummm...how did I get here?"

Beck shrugs. "Your guess is as good as mine."

"Sorry about that, man. Must have passed out." He scratches his head and glances at the float. "In the pool."

"No problem," Beck mutters before extending the net and towing the guy to the tiled edge.

Once he's been assisted from the blow-up swan, he takes off around the side of the house and disappears from sight.

I shift my weight and stare after him. "Any idea who that was?"

"Nope." With one side of his mouth lifted, Beck shakes his head. "Never seen him before."

We both chuckle before looking around us. The patio is more trashed than inside the house. Beer cans and red plastic cups litter the cement surrounding the pool. One of the loungers is flipped on its side. Cushions and clothes are scattered around the yard. It's enough to make me wonder what people left the party wearing because it wasn't T-shirts and shorts.

Or shoes.

How do you leave without shoes?

It's a mystery.

I shake my head and huff out a sigh of resignation. "This is only a suggestion, but maybe you should consider dialing down the parties from now on."

"I'll take it under advisement."

Beck uses the net to scoop up a couple of beer cans that bob in the water, and I pick up the cups and trash littering the cement and lawn. He runs the pool vacuum and adds a few chemicals to the water. Four trash bags later, and the backyard looks as good as the inside of the house.

I survey the area. "It appears we've accomplished the impossible."

"Yup, looks pretty damn good." He glances at me, and surprisingly, there's no smirk in sight. "Thanks for all your help. I couldn't have done it without you."

"Consider it my good deed for the year. Although, next time, you're on your own."

"Noted." The word is barely out of his mouth before he's yanking off his T-shirt and tossing it to a chaise lounge. "Interested in a quick dip?"

I glance from him to the freshly cleaned pool as the crystal-clear water sparkles in the bright sunlight. It's not even noon, and already it's eighty-five degrees. It's shaping up to be a gorgeous day. A swim in the pool after three hours of cleaning would feel oh-so-good.

But after everything that's transpired between us, is it necessarily a good idea?

Probably not.

I told myself I'd help Beck clean up and then go home where I can clear my thoughts and get a little perspective. Spending all this time alone with him is making me want things that aren't in my best interest.

Sensing the refusal perched on the tip of my tongue, Beck tilts his head before cajoling, "Come on, Stanbury. We've spent the last couple of hours cleaning, and our parents won't be home for at least another hour." He pauses before adding, "You might not realize this, but you don't have to be perfect all the time."

"I'm not trying to be," I mutter. It's difficult to admit, even to myself, but he wasn't wrong earlier when he claimed I'd been put in a little box. Except my parents aren't the ones who put me there. I did. I haven't been able to figure out another way to hold my family together. I'm afraid that if I cause trouble or make waves, it'll be the straw that breaks the camel's back, and we'll splinter even further apart. I can't allow that to happen.

"Are you sure about that?" With the sun beating down on Beck's bare chest, he looks like a god. "You're so fucking perfect that it's difficult to stomach."

His words are like a slap in my face.

I am not perfect. I'm just not careless in the decisions I make. My goal in life isn't to cause as much havoc as I can. Since when is that a crime?

When I remain locked in place, he drags his khakis down until the material is puddled at his feet. Grey boxer-briefs cling to his lean hips and thighs. Years of working out and playing football have honed his body into a work of art.

"Sometimes all I want to do is mess you up. Even if it's for a moment."

His words knock the air from my lungs, making it impossible to breathe.

A wicked grin dances across his face before he dives into the water. I track his movements as he arrows through the clear liquid, surfacing about twenty-feet from the edge of the pool. When he whips his dark hair away from his face, droplets of water scatter around him in the bright sunlight.

Staring at him makes my heart hurt.

"What's it going to be?" He treads water in the deep end near the diving board. "The water feels amazing. Don't you want to find out for yourself?"

What I should do is go home, but my feet are frozen in place.

Fooling around with Beck is stupid. And if there's one thing I don't do, it's stupid. My moment of weakness from earlier this morning is messing with my head.

Go home, my brain instructs.

I'm startled out of those thoughts when beads of water land on my bare arms and dot the gold tank I'm wearing.

Beck grins. "Come on, Stanbury. Get your ass in the water."

Before I realize what I'm doing, the top is over my head, and I'm standing in front of Beck in my bra. Heat leaps into his eyes, and my belly trembles in response. I slide the denim skirt over my hips and down my thighs. Once it lays crumpled at my feet, I step out of it and force myself to walk toward the water.

What I'm doing is so unlike me, and I can't help but feel that I'm digging a deeper hole to crawl out of. Even though I know spending more time with Beck is a bad idea, that's exactly what I want to do.

Once I reach the edge, my toes curl around the azure-colored ceramic tiles before I dive into the water. Beck is right, the pool is refreshing. The coolness slides over my heated flesh as I glide through the liquid before surfacing. I wipe the water from my face and glance around, but Beck isn't where I last saw him. I startle when hands wrap around my waist from behind and yank me backward.

"You're so fucking sexy that it kills me to look at you," he growls against my ear.

A thousand shivers scamper down my spine.

Before I can summon a response, he hoists me from the water and tosses me through the air as if I weigh nothing at all. A scream rises in my throat as I slip beneath the surface. When my toes touch the bottom, I bend my knees and push off against the tiles, fleeing in the opposite direction. I don't get far before Beck grabs me, tugging me into his arms again.

I hate to admit how much I enjoy being with him.

Don't get used to it.

For the next thirty minutes, we goof around. Every time Beck gets his hands on me, he tosses me in the air. As soon as he lets go, I slide beneath the water and try to escape. It never takes long for him to catch me again. Our hands stroke over slippery wet skin as we kiss before breaking apart and doing it all over again. There's only so much I can take before my breathing becomes labored. Even though I'm in good shape from a decade of competitive tennis, I'm exhausted. We've raced from one end of the pool to the other countless times. We can't keep our hands off each other, and I don't even want to try. For the first time in my life, I don't stop to weigh the pros and cons. I go with it.

After a while, we grab a yellow inflatable raft big enough for the both of us before hoisting ourselves on top of it. The raft wobbles as we collapse in a heap and allow the hot sun to bake our wet flesh. The sides of our bodies press together, arms and legs touching as the water lulls us into a contented state of being.

Electricity zips through me as Beck's fingers tangle with my own.

This shouldn't feel nearly as good as it does.

If I were thinking clearly, I'd hightail it home. I'd forget all about the feelings Beck rouses inside me and put some much-needed distance between us. But I'm reluctant to do that. I like the way my hand fits in his larger one and the way his body feels pressed against mine. There's a rightness that shouldn't be there, and I'm loath to do anything that will bring reality crashing down on our heads.

My breathing evens out as my body melts into the warm plastic of the raft. After a string of quiet moments, Beck rolls toward me. The float trembles with his movements. He props himself up with an elbow, and warmth fills me as his gaze rakes over my nearly naked body.

The heat of his stare lingers on my breasts, which spill from the cups of my bra. I glance down and realize that the pale pink material has turned sheer.

He leans over and captures one tightened peak between his lips. The moment he touches me, my breath becomes clogged in my throat. A moan slides from my lips as my fingers tangle in his damp hair, drawing him closer. Once he releases the stiff little peak, he pulls the material aside until my nipple is exposed. Then his lips are back, sucking the bud deep into his mouth. It's as if there is an invisible string connecting my breast to my core. Every tug of his lips sends shock waves of pleasure reverberating through me.

He scoots closer, giving the same attention to my other breast. Except this time, he pulls the material down before drawing the tightened bud into his mouth. Sensation ricochets through my body until it reaches my toes. My eyes feather shut as I arch my back, needing to close the distance between us.

His fingers caress the valley between my breasts before sliding lower to my navel. He circles the indentation a few times before one hand slips beneath the elastic band of my thong. Back and forth, his fingers arc from one hip bone to the other. My body trembles beneath his touch. Every movement drives my senses into delirium and scatters my thoughts.

"You're so fucking beautiful, Mia."

It's almost a relief when his fingers drift lower until they're able to trace the seam of my lips. An ache builds in my core and I widen my legs, wanting to give him more access. Not once do his fingers dip inside my body. They circle around my entrance, gliding over the soaked flesh before sliding upward to circle my pulsing clit. The moment he touches that throbbing bundle of nerves, a moan escapes.

His mouth fastens onto mine. I open so our tongues can tangle as his fingers feather over my flesh, forcing me to the brink. When I can't stand another moment of this sweet torture, he lifts his face from mine and presses his thumb on my clit, sending a surge of shivers through my body. His fingers continue to move until every bit of pleasure has been wrung from me, and I'm nothing more than an exhausted heap on the raft.

I crack my eyes open when Beck slips his hand free from my thong before lifting his fingers to his mouth and sucking them clean.

"So damn delicious," he murmurs, watching me the entire time.

He leans closer and captures my lips. The taste of my arousal explodes on my tongue, sending yet another ripple of pleasure through me.

Who knew something like that could be such a turn-on?

He pulls away enough to say, "Maybe I should have led with this earlier, but I'd like to take you out."

"Out?" I echo dumbly as if unable to string those words together to figure out the meaning. "Like on a date?"

Amusement dances in his eyes as his lips bow into a smile. "Exactly like a date."

My brain is telling me to walk away, but my heart is leaping for joy. I tamp down my excitement before it can become infectious.

The higher you fly, the harder you fall, I remind myself.

"You don't have to do this," I force myself to say.

The humor filling his face turns serious. "I know, but I want to."

Walk away and don't look back, girl.

You know it's the smart thing to do.

Beck Hollingsworth isn't someone you can depend on. He's proven that time and time again. He'll flake, and I'll be left holding the bag in my hands.

He lowers his face until everything around me is blotted out, and he's all I can focus on. His warm breath drifts over my lips. "Let me take you out and prove I'm serious about this. *About us*."

Every ounce of good sense flees. "Okay."

"Good." His mouth brushes over my top lip before doing the same to my bottom. Then he sucks my lower lip into his mouth before giving it a gentle tug with his teeth and releasing it with a pop. Need bursts to life in my core. Apparently, it doesn't matter if I just came. I want him all over again.

He pulls away enough to say, "Open."

I do as he instructs, and his tongue delves inside my mouth to tangle with my own. One hand slips around my head to cradle my skull with his palm. The kiss unfolds lazily until I lose all sense of time. The only thing I'm aware of is the feel of Beck's lips coasting over mine, drawing me deeper into this caress until I'm drugged with the taste of him.

From the far recesses of my brain, a noise penetrates the thick fog that cocoons me. It's only when Beck jerks away that reality crashes down upon my head. He swears harshly under his breath as I try to find my bearings.

"It might be a good idea if your friend took off, don't you think?"

Oh, God.

Archibald.

And this time, it's not the ringer on Beck's phone.

Heat scalds my cheeks as I realize that he just witnessed me making out with his son. In my underwear. The humiliation is almost enough to swallow me whole. Why haven't I burst into flames yet? That would be preferable to brazening out this situation.

Beck rolls off the raft and into the water, leaving me exposed and vulnerable. Even though the sun strokes over my warmed flesh, a chill slithers down my spine. I sit up and band my arms around my knees to cover as much of my body as possible.

"Don't move," Beck mutters, "until I get your shirt."

"Okay." I stare at my folded legs until Archibald's loafers come into view.

"*Mia?*" Shock reverberates throughout Archie's voice. "Is that *you?*"

Please kill me now before this situation becomes any more excruciating.

I wince, unable to meet his eyes before lifting my hand and giving him a half-hearted wave. "Hi, Mr. Hollingsworth." Barely can I squeak out the greeting.

Beck's father stuffs his hands into the pockets of his khakis and rocks back on his heels as his narrowed gaze bounces between us. "What are you doing here?"

"We were swimming." *Amongst other things.* Even though I don't tack that on, I have the feeling he knows *exactly* what we were up to.

"I wasn't aware you two were friends." His voice becomes stilted. "I'd assumed you traveled in different circles."

"We've always been friends," Beck shoots back, glancing at me with a slight frown. "Right?"

Yesterday the answer would have been an unequivocal *no*, but I can't bring myself to say that. "Yes."

"Hmmm." Archibald's lips bow into a frown. The heaviness of his gaze is enough to make me squirm.

Once we reach the edge of the pool, Beck hauls himself out. It would be impossible not to notice the way his muscles flex and bunch as water rolls off his sun-kissed flesh. He grabs my tank from the cement and tosses it to me. I snatch it from the air and thrust my arms through the thin straps before yanking the flimsy material over my body. It doesn't cover much, but it shields my bra and thong from sight.

Sort of.

As soon as I'm covered, Beck extends his hand for me to grab hold of before hoisting me from the raft. The moment my feet touch the concrete, he releases me. I stumble before finding my balance.

I peek at Archibald and tug the back of my tank, so it covers more of my ass.

A thunderous expression settles on Archie's face as he bites out, "I'm going inside." His attention shifts to his son. "See me in the office after Mia leaves."

Beck jerks his head into a tight nod. Once his father disappears through the French doors, I force the air from my lungs, not realizing it had become trapped.

"I would seriously like to die right now," I whisper, afraid of being overheard.

"Yeah, sorry about that." He shoves a hand through his hair. "I thought we had more time."

Nausea stirs in the pit of my belly as I consider how mortifying it would have been if Beck's parents had arrived home ten minutes earlier. Archibald and Caroline are like family. How could I ever look either of them in the eyes if they saw me getting off?

Unsure where to go from here, I search Beck's expression for clues as to what he's thinking. All the lightheartedness has been sucked from the atmosphere. There's a pervasive feeling of tension that has settled over us like a heavy blanket.

Beck scoops up my skirt and tosses it to me. "You should probably head out."

He's right, but I'm reluctant to leave. If I walk away, this will end up being nothing more than a dream. And I'm scared of that happening.

"Okay." I yank the skirt up my thighs and over my hips until it settles at my waist.

Awkwardness descends. There is so much I want to say, but I have no idea how to express my thoughts. Instead of taking that leap and putting myself out there, I turn away. With every step, doubt and fear rain down on me.

"Mia?"

I swing around, unsure what I'll find.

"I meant what I said about wanting to take you out."

A burst of giddiness chases away the misgivings that creep in at the edges.

Uncertainty flickers in his eyes. "You want that too, right?"

"I do." More than I'm willing to admit because as much as I want to believe in Beck, I need him to prove me wrong.

"Talk soon?"

"Yeah."

A hint of a smile curves his lips and touches his eyes, softening the hardness filling them.

When he remains silent, I raise my hand in a wave and return home. My head spins as I relive everything that has transpired in the last twelve hours.

I'm no longer a virgin.

Beck and I are going on a date.

Alyssa will shit her pants when I tell her what happened.

It's enough to bring a gurgle of laughter to my lips.

Chapter Four

BECK

Once Mia disappears from sight, everything inside me uncoils. Reluctantly, I glance toward the house, well aware I'm about to get my ass chewed out for the impromptu party. Although I can't bring myself to regret it. If I hadn't thrown the bash, I wouldn't have hooked up with Mia.

Fuck, I shouldn't even call it that. What happened between us is way more than a fuck and flee situation. I've had plenty of those in the past, and they've never meant a damn thing.

This feels nothing like that.

It blows me away that she allowed me to take her virginity. Even the thought of being buried deep inside her body is enough to have my cock rising to attention. Instead of giving in to the urge to follow Mia, I yank on my khakis and T-shirt.

Guess it's time to face the firing squad. Best to get it over with and move on with my day.

Silence greets me as I walk through the first floor. This place is monstrous. I have no idea why we need all this space except that Dad likes to showcase our wealth since it's a direct translation to his professional accomplishments. Over the last twenty years, he's built a successful law practice from the ground up. Now he has four partners and fifty associates. His plan is to expand and open a couple of practices in major cities across the United States.

That's where my brother comes in.

Archibald the second—or Ari as everyone calls him—will be starting his senior year of college at Wesley. If everything goes according to plan, he'll attend Stanford Law School like the old man. Ari has a four-point GPA and scored a one-seventy on the LSAT, so getting accepted shouldn't be a problem. He's one smart motherfucker. My parents couldn't be prouder.

Me, on the other hand?

Not so much.

I know Dad had hoped I would follow in his illustrious footsteps, but that's not going to happen. Unlike my older brother, I had a tougher time in school. Concentration has never been my friend. It's not that the work was too hard, just boring. My mind wanders. I get antsy. When I was in elementary school, I'd stare out the window while the teacher droned on. All I could focus on was getting outside and throwing the football around with my friends. I lived for recess.

It wasn't until second grade, after a shit-ton of calls and notes from the teacher and principal, that I was taken to a psychologist, tested, diagnosed with ADHD, and promptly put on medication. It helped to settle my ass down, but school has always been torture. I force myself to do it since it's the only way I'll make it to the NFL.

It's no secret that my father is disappointed in how I've turned out and the issues I struggle with. Has he come out and said it?

No, but there have been enough sly comments and little digs over the years to let me know how he truly feels. Maybe he thinks I'm an idiot, too stupid to pick up on what he's laying down. Just because I have trouble focusing, doesn't mean I'm a dipshit.

My father prizes intelligence over athletic ability. He might boast to anyone who will listen that his son is a talented enough football player to be scouted by the pros, but that's still second best in his book.

Ari is the heir, and I'm the spare.

I didn't ask to have ADHD. It's been a pain in my ass, but I deal with it the best I can.

What other choice is there?

The medication helps, but it's not a cure-all. Football is the only thing that holds my attention. When I have that ball in my hand, and I'm searching the field for an open receiver, my mind slows down, and I'm able to think clearly. Or maybe it speeds up, and I can see all the possibilities. It only takes a split second to process my surroundings. My brain cuts through all the guys, and I find a receiver who can complete a pass and take it down the field, eating up the yards with his cleats.

God, but I fucking love it.

It's my reason for living.

The only other thing that's come close to holding my attention is Mia. Up until this point, she's kept me at a firm distance. I don't blame her for it. Mia is gorgeous, smart, athletic, and focused on her future. She wants to be a lawyer.

We're complete opposites in every way.

I'll never be good enough for that girl.

As soon as that thought creeps into my head, I push it away.

For whatever reason, the stars have aligned, and I have the two things I want most in this world. Football and Mia. I don't want anything to fuck it up.

The moment I cross over the threshold into Dad's office, he glances from the computer screen and points to the leather armchair parked in front of his antique mahogany desk. I slip onto the chair and wait for him to read me the riot act.

Should I have invited so many people over last night?

Probably not.

My bad. Won't happen again.

When I open my mouth to apologize, he cuts me off.

"What the hell was Mia doing here?"

I raise my brows, thrown off by the question.

This is what he wants to talk about?

"We were swimming." When he glares, I shift on my seat and tack on, "It's hot out."

He snorts in disbelief. "What I walked in on was more than," he uses his fingers to make air quotes, "*swimming*." There's a pause. "*She was practically naked.*"

"She was wearing her bra and underwear," I mumble, embarrassed to be discussing the situation with my father. "She didn't bother to go home and change. Don't make a big deal out of it."

My parents have never questioned my relationships. Dad has even slapped my back a time or two and told me to make sure I wrap it up tight. The last thing I need is to get some chick pregnant at this stage of the game. And he's right.

This fall, I'll be attending Wesley. As long as I can prove myself in training camp this summer, the starting quarterback position is mine for the taking. That's unheard of for a freshman, and I damn well know it. What I need to do is work my ass off so these guys can see I'm the key to a winning season.

I've tried to convince the old man that entering the draft after my sophomore year would be better, but he's not having it. The deal is that I wait until my senior year and earn my diploma. As long as I don't get injured, there's no reason everything shouldn't pan out the way it's supposed to. The plan is to major in communications so I can lay the foundation for a broadcasting career at ESPN after I retire. Without playing ball, that communications degree won't be worth the paper it's printed on. Dad likes to remind me of that every chance he gets.

"What was she doing here in the first place?" he growls, drawing my attention back to the conversation.

"Helping me clean up after the party last night." Hell, I would much rather discuss *that* situation. Even thinking about what he walked in on has the tips of my ears burning. If it had been any other girl, I wouldn't have given a shit. I would have patted her on the ass and sent her on her merry way. But I can't do that with Mia. I should have been more careful.

"It better not be anything more than that," he snaps, shaking his head.

I straighten on the chair. There's something about his tone that rubs me the wrong way. "Why does it matter so much?"

"You know why it matters." His booming voice echoes off the

wood-paneled walls before he strains forward, resting his forearms on the polished wood. "I don't want you fucking around with that girl."

"We weren't *fucking* around."

"It sure as hell looked like you were." He stabs a finger at me. "Whatever plans you might have hatched in that brain of yours, get them out right now!"

What the hell?

Are we seriously having this conversation?

"I don't understand what the problem is."

Dad leans back on his chair and stares at the ceiling before muttering under his breath, "Do I really need to spell everything out for you?"

His words feel like a backhanded smack. My jaw locks as heat floods my cheeks. "Yeah, it would be helpful if you did."

With an exasperated sigh, he glowers at me like I'm ten kinds of stupid. It only serves to piss me off more. "Mia's a nice girl. *A good girl.* The last thing I need is for you to mess with her head and hurt her."

"Why would I do that?" A pit the size of Rhode Island settles at the bottom of my gut.

A knowing smile tilts the corners of his lips. "Come on, Beck," his voice trails off as he shrugs. "You're not the most focused guy in the world. Especially where the ladies are concerned. You've spent the last couple of years screwing your way through this town, and other than me telling you to be careful, I haven't said a damn word about it."

"Mia is different," I say through stiff lips.

"Of course, she is." There's a pause. "Which is exactly why she's not for you."

Even though I shouldn't be surprised by the comment, I am. This entire conversation has blown me away.

"And why is that?" I grit between clenched teeth, forcing him to admit the truth.

The silence between us stretches until it becomes almost painful.

"Mia deserves a guy who has his head on straight, and that's not you. She needs someone like your brother." He waves a hand airily as if he hasn't just crushed my spirit. "Someone solid."

So...now I'm not solid?

My ADHD makes me a wild card? Someone unworthy?

His comments stun me into silence. For once in my life, I have no idea how to respond.

Dad must realize he's overstepped because he clears his throat and attempts to backtrack. "Look, Beckett, I love you. You know that, right?"

Laughter bubbles up in my throat.

Really?

After everything he said?

That's how we're going to wrap up this conversation?

With a—*hey, buddy...you're an idiot, but you're* our *idiot.*

My parents think I'm a fuckup who will never amount to diddly squat. And I sure as hell am not worthy of a girl like Mia.

"I'm grateful you have so much athletic talent, or I don't know what the hell you would do with your life."

Thank fuck I'm sitting for that backhanded compliment.

Unable to listen to another word of his bullshit, I pop to my feet. "Are we done here?" I stare at the space above his shoulder, not wanting to make eye contact.

Fuck that guy.

"Yeah, we're done," he sighs.

"Great." Five strides, and I'm at the door. I need to get out of here before I lose my shit.

"Beck..."

My step falters, and my shoulders stiffen, but I don't turn around. "Yeah?"

"Stay away from Mia. I don't need any problems with her parents. And that's exactly what I'll get if you go sniffing around her."

When I fail to respond, his voice sharpens. "Did you hear me?"

"Loud and clear."

And then I'm gone, disappearing through the hallway and taking the stairs two at a time before turning down the hall and slamming the door to my room. I need a joint so I can zone out and forget about the garbage my father just spewed.

For a day that started out so well, it sure turned to shit in the blink of an eye.

I swipe my phone from the nightstand beside the bed and read the last text from Alyssa. I fully expected her to announce that after all these years, she had her dirty little way with Colton, but that doesn't appear to be the case. Apparently, their little make-out session in the pool didn't go any further than that.

I haven't mentioned what happened with Beck. It feels too intimate to share through text message. For the time being, I want to keep the news to myself. It's been hours, and I'm still in a state of shock.

I'm no longer a virgin.

That seems crazy.

Alyssa will go off the deep end when I tell her.

As I'm replying to Alyssa's text, something pings against the bedroom window. I startle, and my head whips up. A shiver of unease slithers down my spine. I stare in that direction, ears pricked for the slightest noise, but there's nothing.

Thirty seconds later, and there's another plink against the glass.

Someone or something has to be out there.

I rise from the bed, and tiptoe my way across the carpeted floor before squinting into the darkness. When a ghostly face materializes out of nowhere, I scream at the top of my lungs and stumble back a few steps.

Large palms press against the glass as the face looms closer.

I slap a hand across my mouth as my heart threatens to explode from my chest.

What the ever-loving hell?

Slowly, the features take shape.

Wait a minute…

I rush toward the window, remove the screen, and unlatch the lock before shoving it open. *"Have you lost your freaking mind? What are you doing out there?"*

The last time Beck climbed the tree to my bedroom was the summer before sixth grade. Once middle school hit, we drifted apart. Everyone realized what a football phenom Beck was, and his popularity skyrocketed while mine stayed the same.

Not waiting for an invitation, Beck tumbles through the open window, landing on the other side before popping to his feet and slamming it shut behind him. My normally spacious room shrinks around his muscular form, making it feel tight and oppressive. As if there's barely room to breathe.

Is it strange that I was just thinking about him and now he's here?

If I'm being honest, Beck has consumed all of my thoughts today. Everything we did this morning has been playing through my head on a constant loop. Every shift of my body reminds me of the soreness between my thighs.

I've always been so good about shutting down thoughts of him.

But now?

Beck has taken up residence in my brain, and there's nothing I can do to evict him.

My gaze drops from his eyes to his lips. Arousal bursts like a firework in my core. It takes all of my self-control not to throw myself at him.

I've officially become a Beck Hollingsworth groupie.

I'm not sure how to feel about that.

"Mia," he whispers. His voice comes out sounding strangled, and it strums something deep inside.

Excitement pounds through my veins. It shouldn't surprise me that Beck is the only one capable of making me feel this way. Even when I tried to pretend the chemistry between us was a figment of my imagination, I knew the truth.

"Yeah?" My mouth turns cottony, and I'm barely able to push the word out.

"You need to stop looking at me like that."

"Like what?" Heat flames my cheeks because I know *exactly* what he's alluding to. But I can't seem to help it. I'm desperate to lay my hands on Beck. I want him inside me again, filling me to the brim.

He forces his gaze away before plowing a hand through his hair. His movements are full of agitation, and his face is set in grim lines. Only now does it occur to me that something is off with his behavior. This morning he was at ease and relaxed. That's not the case anymore. Even though we're only a few feet from one another, it feels as if there is a gaping chasm between us.

Unease dances down my spine as the excitement swirling around inside me is snuffed out. I shift my weight nervously. I want everything to feel like it did this morning, but I'm not sure how to get us back to that.

"Did you get in trouble for the party?" Maybe his parents grounded him. Archibald wasn't pleased to find us in the pool.

"No."

He shakes his head, and relief bursts inside me like an over-inflated balloon. Before I realize it, the distance disappears, and I'm pushing my fingers through his dark hair. I marvel at how soft the strands are.

"What's wrong?" Cautiously I search his shuttered gaze for answers that don't seem forthcoming.

His teeth sink into his lower lip. "Nothing, but we need to talk."

Nothing good ever came from those words.

"About what?" My hands fall to my sides as if they're made of lead.

When he remains silent, I step away. It's impossible to think when we're standing so close. "What do we need to talk about?"

An uncomfortable silence stretches between us.

"Beck?" Nerves dance across my skin.

"We can't go out," he blurts.

His words are like rapid gunfire and feel just as painful.

"What?" My heart drops to the bottom of my toes.

"I'm sorry, Mia." He glances away. It's like he can't hold my stare for more than a few seconds. "As much as I want to take you out, I can't."

Disappointment blooms in my chest until I almost choke on it.

Why am I surprised?

Deep down, I knew this would happen. And still, I allowed myself to be swept away by his bullshit. I straighten to my full height and cross my arms over my chest. Refusing to beg him for answers, I press my lips together until they feel numb.

"Mia? Are you all right?"

"I'm fine." That's a lie, but I'll be damned if I give him the satisfaction of knowing how much he hurt me.

Beck plows a hand through his hair. "We both have a lot going on. I leave for training camp next week, and after that, I won't be home much. I need to focus on football. I can't allow any outside distractions to get in the way. You understand, right?"

Did he just call me a distraction?

I blink back the wetness that stings my eyes, refusing to allow the tears to fall.

"There's no need to explain. I got it loud and clear. You used me, and I was stupid enough to fall for your lies." I press a shaking hand to my chest. "My bad. Won't happen again."

His eyes flare as he shakes his head. "No, it wasn't like that..."

Laughter explodes from my lips.

Who is he trying to kid?

I fell for his smooth talk—hook, line, and sinker. In all honesty, I deserve everything I got. Lesson learned the hard way.

"You can stop with the BS, Beck." My voice hardens.

When he reaches out, attempting to stroke the curve of my cheek, I bat his hand away and retreat, needing to put as much distance between us as possible.

"Mia, please," he whispers, "you have to know that I'm sorry. It's not what I want."

The sad thing is that I almost believe him.

That he's able to break my heart all the while trying to convince me how sorry he is only proves that I'm no better than all the foolish girls who trail after him. This is exactly why Beck Hollingsworth is dangerous to the female species. Even when he's cutting your heart out, you want more.

Not bothering to respond, I stab a finger toward the window. If he thinks I'll cry and beg him to reconsider, he has another thing coming. "Get out."

When he opens his mouth, looking like he might argue, I cut him off. "*I said get out!*"

Anguish flashes in his green eyes as his shoulders collapse, and he jerks his head into a nod. He wavers for a moment before retreating to the window. Silently, he pushes it open before turning back to me. "I'm sorry for letting everything get out of hand this morning. It's my fault for hurting you."

I snort.

Beck can take his apology and shove it up his ass.

A wave of nausea crashes over me. I've never felt so used or dirty. Even though I took a shower earlier this afternoon, the need to take another and scrub every memory of him from my skin pounds through me.

I'm an idiot for believing I was anything more than a one-night fuck. Or that Beck was mature enough to have a real relationship. All he did was prove that he's exactly what I suspected he was.

An asshole who will use and abuse you before throwing you away.

Guess the joke is on me for believing I was too smart to fall for his lines.

Chapter Six

MIA

Sophomore year of college...

Alyssa grabs my hand and drags me through the doors of the football house. For obvious reasons, it's the last place I want to be on a Saturday night. The Wesley Warriors crushed Tennessee this afternoon, and everyone is out celebrating.

"Can't we go somewhere else?" I yell, so she's able to hear me over the thumping beat of the music that reverberates off the walls. It's so loud that it feels like my brain is rattling against my skull. When she fails to respond, I add, "In case you haven't noticed, there are a ton of other parties."

We traipsed past a dozen of them to get here.

"No," she shouts, bursting my bubble. "I told Colton we would meet up at nine."

Yup, you heard that correctly.

Colton and Alyssa are officially a *thing*.

It's still relatively early in their relationship, so who knows if it will last.

Alyssa is thrilled.

And me?

Shocked speechless would be an adequate description.

But I have to give the girl props where they're deserved. She was bound and determined to bag her man, and against the odds, she made it happen.

As you can imagine, she's become something of a legend on campus, having attained the unattainable.

She's known as the Yoda of Wesley.

The jock whisperer.

Girls come from near and far to seek out her sage advice. It's amusing to watch her dole out her wisdom magnanimously like a queen.

I glance around, noticing that most of the students are football players or friends thereof. Making up half of the population are the jersey chasers. Those girls are prepared to cling to the first meaty bicep they can attach themselves to.

Without trying to be obvious, I search the surrounding vicinity for one face in particular. My muscles loosen when he remains elusive. Ever since we had sex after graduation, I've done my best to keep my distance from Beck.

The first couple of months on campus were nerve-wracking. Once I realized I wouldn't run into him around every corner, I could relax and have fun. Since our families always celebrate Thanksgiving and Christmas together, I was concerned we would finally come face-to-face, but he was conspicuously absent from the holiday parties. It's been more than a year without contact.

Other than to serve as a warning not to mess with athletes, I like to pretend it never happened. It's my dirty little secret to keep. I feel guilty about not telling Alyssa, but I don't need her pushing me toward Beck. And that's exactly what she would do. Especially now that she's with Colton.

That girl is always trying to drag me to the parties where her new boyfriend hangs out. And since Colton and Beck are roommates, I know there's a good chance Beck will be there. Until this point, I've been creative with my excuses.

Homework.

Volunteering at the tutor lab.

A meeting for the many clubs and associations I've joined on campus.

Headache.

You name it, it's in my arsenal of alibis.

Unfortunately, she wasn't buying any of them tonight. I even tried to convince her it was shark week, and she told me, in no uncertain terms, to pop a couple of Advil and woman up.

So here I am.

Thus far, Beck has been a no-show. I'm hoping my luck will hold, and it stays that way for the next couple of hours.

It takes effort and a fair amount of prodding to push our way into the kitchen where the makeshift bar is located. Every kind of conceivable booze is available, along with a few homemade varieties of moonshine.

Word to the wise—you have to be careful with those, they'll knock you flat on your ass. One-hundred-and-eighty proof Everclear is no joke.

We grab two cups of beer from the baby-face freshman football player who has been forced to man the keg before steamrolling our way through the backdoor. With so many bodies packed in the house, it's warm and stuffy.

Alyssa's head is on a constant swivel as she searches for her new beau. She's happier than I've seen her in a long time. I really hope, for her sake, everything works out with Colton. The last thing I want is for her to get hurt. He's never been one for labels or permanent situations. I'm not sure how she convinced him to pull the trigger.

"Maybe he's not here," I say hopefully.

The look she shoots me is chock-full of exasperation. "He has to be. It's his party."

Which means it's Beck's party, too.

When Alyssa grinds to a halt, I slam into her from behind. Barely do I avoid spilling my beer down the back of her shirt. I peer around her shoulder, trying to see what's going on. My gaze sweeps over the area until it lands on Alyssa's golden-haired boyfriend and the bevy of girls that surround him. There are at least six vying for his attention. I glance at my bestie to see how she's taking it. As much as Alyssa likes to pretend that she's secure in their relationship, she's not. And who can blame her?

"Why do they have to act so thirsty?" Her nose scrunches like she caught a whiff of something nasty. "It's embarrassing."

This is the downside to dating a football player—or any athlete on campus—there are always a ton of females trying to lay claim to what's yours. I have no desire to put up with that.

I lay my hand on Alyssa's arm before giving it a gentle squeeze. "You all right?"

"I'm fine." She rolls her shoulders in an attempt to lock down her jealousy before it rears its ugly head. Glancing at me, she hoists a fake smile. Alyssa would never mention it, but I know the constant groupie attention bothers her. "Colt would never cheat."

I can't tell if she's trying to convince herself of that or me. It's not like I want to be a hater, but I'll do what I have to in order to protect my friend.

"Lys—"

"Don't say it."

I press my lips together and remain silent.

What I will admit about the situation is that Colton has surprised me. I never expected him to settle down. And he's been good to her. That being said, I'll remain on high alert until he proves to me that he can be trusted with her heart. Colton has never been the poster boy for monogamy. More like the opposite.

"He's not the guy he used to be," she murmurs. "He's changed. If you spent more time with him, you would see that."

No, thank you.

When one girl reaches out and trails her fingers over the bulging muscles of Colton's arm, Alyssa clenches her teeth and pokers up like someone just rammed a two-by-four up her ass. "Looks like I need to put a few bitches in their place."

Before I can respond, she stomps away, cutting a path straight to the golden football god. She's like a heat-seeking missile. Let's hope she doesn't explode upon impact. It only takes a few minutes before those thirsty females are scattering in all directions.

A smile tilts my lips.

Alyssa is a force to be reckoned with.

Colton is damn lucky she didn't give up on him. I hope he recognizes that and acts accordingly.

And then there was one. Realizing that I've been left to my own devices, I tip my nearly full glass to my lips and take a swig. Then I pull out my phone from my pocket and fire off a quick text before stuffing it back where I found it. With a huff, I spin on my heels and promptly slam into a wall of muscle.

When I stumble back, strong fingers wrap around my upper arms to anchor me in place. I don't have to look up to realize who I've crashed into. The way his fingers burn my flesh is answer enough. A zip of adrenaline shoots through me when my gaze locks on familiar green eyes.

As soon as the attraction flares to life inside me, I stomp it out. You would think the way he dumped me after we had sex would be enough to kill any tender feelings I'd once held for him, but apparently, that's not the case.

"I didn't expect to see you here." There's a pause as he searches my eyes in the darkness. "It's been a while."

Fifteen months to be correct, but who's counting?

I step away so he has no choice but to release me from his hold before jerking my thumb over my shoulder. "Alyssa dragged me here to see Colton."

He glances toward the newly minted couple. "Yeah, they appear to be going strong. Good for them."

I almost snicker. *Really? Good for them?* Ha! "For the time being." I can't resist adding, "I'm sure it won't last."

"Wow," he murmurs, raising his hand to scratch his jaw, "that's harsh."

I shrug. I prefer to think of it as being more pragmatic than anything else.

"It's the truth."

Sadness settles over his features. "Mia, do you think we could go somewhere and—"

"Talk?" I lift the glass to my lips and drain the remainder. I need a moment to tamp down all the emotion trying to break free inside me. I'll be damned if I allow him to undo all my progress.

When I'm once again under control, I shake my head. "Sorry, that didn't work out so well last time. Let's do ourselves a favor and leave the past where it belongs. Sound good to you?"

"Yeah, sure." His broad shoulders collapse. "If that's what you want."

"It is."

An uncomfortable silence falls over us. When it turns unbearable, Beck clears his throat. "Are you still planning on going to law school?"

Is this what it's come to? Inane chitchat about our majors like a couple of strangers who met at a lame party? Someone needs to pull the plug on this conversation before it can jackhammer to a new level of painfulness.

"Yup, still pre-law."

"Ari just started at Stanford. He seems to like it."

"Yeah, I know. I spoke to him this summer about taking the LSAT. We've made plans to get together over Thanksgiving break. He's going to give me some pointers for taking the test. He also invited me to check out the campus since Stanford is on my shortlist."

Beck's eyes darken before scouring mine. "You're going to California to visit him?"

"To check out the law school," I correct. It has nothing to do with Ari and everything to do with Stanford. Ari is like the big brother I never had. We got close this summer when we interned at his father's law firm.

"That's great." His voice turns flat. "You guys are a perfect pair."

Huh?

"What does that mean?" I ask.

Wait a minute...does Beck think I'm interested in his brother?

Not that I owe him an explanation, but the words tumble out of my mouth before I can stop them. "I'm interested in Stanford, not your brother."

"You sure about that?" Bitterness twists his lips. "Ari's a great guy."

That's probably the one thing Beck and I can agree on.

"Not that it's any of your business, but Ari is nothing more than a friend." I snap my mouth closed, irritated with myself for telling him that. After more than a year of separation, it's demoralizing to realize that my attraction to Beck is as strong as it was in high school.

"Good." He steps closer, and the distance between us shrinks. "We need to talk, Mia. There are things I need to explain."

Out of nowhere, a muscular arm slides around my shoulders and tugs me close.

"Hey, babe. I've been looking everywhere for you." Arron Reinhold, the guy I've been casually seeing, kisses the side of my face. "Where have you been?"

"Right here, talking with Beck." Even though Arron has never struck me as the jealous type, I add, "We went to high school together."

"That's cool." Arron smiles at Beck before giving him a chin lift in greeting. "Great game this afternoon."

"Thanks." Beck shifts his weight as his narrowed gaze bounces between us.

Needing to escape this situation before it becomes anymore stifling, I shake my empty glass. "Looks like I could use a refill."

Arron nips the red plastic cup from my hand. "Sure thing, babe. I'll grab it for you. Be back in a minute."

I open my mouth to protest, but he's already disappearing through the crowd. Unsure what to do now that my plan has been foiled, I glance at Beck from the corner of my eye.

An amused smile tugs at the edges of his lips as his muscles relax. "He seems like a nice guy."

"He is," I grunt.

"How long have you two been together?"

"I don't know." I shrug and mutter, "A few weeks, maybe." My relationship with Arron is the last thing I want to discuss.

"So, it's not serious?" Beck picks up a stray lock of my hair and twirls it around his index finger.

"It's serious enough." I bat his hand away as my heartbeat picks up its tempo.

He steps closer. His voice lowers, and even though the music is obnoxiously loud, I hear every word, every breath that leaves his lips. The chaos surrounding us melts into nothingness.

"What if I wanted another chance?"

Air leaks from my lungs until breathing becomes a foreign concept.

Why is he doing this to me?

Because I'm with someone else?

I force my voice to stay level. I won't give away my inner turmoil. "I'd say that you were shit out of luck."

With his gaze pinned to mine, he moves closer, invading my personal space. The familiar scent of his cologne wraps around me and clouds my better judgment. When I find myself swaying toward him, I blink back to awareness and yank myself away from the precipice.

"I fucked up, Mia. What happened between us...it's not how I wanted it to go."

It doesn't matter.

None of his excuses matter.

"I can't do this with you," I whisper as panic surges through me.

"I hurt you, and I'm sorry. I never intended for it to happen."

But it did.

And now it's too late.

I don't realize I've uttered the words until he says, "It doesn't have to be."

This time, he wraps his fingers around my biceps and drags me closer.

Our faces are inches apart. "Give me a chance to make it up to you."

As I stare into his eyes, I'm reluctantly sucked into his orbit. How does he do it? How does he make me forget to take care of my heart?

"Mia?" A voice cuts into my thoughts and brings me crashing back to earth with a painful thud. "Here you go."

Beck's hands fall away. I blink, focusing my attention on Arron, who holds my newly filled cup of beer.

It takes effort to shake off the web that Beck has woven around me before hoisting my smile. My fingers tremble as I take the Solo cup. "Thanks."

Arron's narrowed gaze slides from me to Beck and then back again, where it stays pinned. His tone changes, turning gruff. "Everything all right here?"

"Yup," I say a little too quickly. "It's fine."

Arron slips an arm around my waist and tugs me close so I'm no longer standing next to Beck. Thick tension blankets the air. Beck's jaw tightens as he glares at the guy at my side. The last thing I want is for a fight to break out, although I have no idea why it would.

As if reading my thoughts, Arron clears his throat. "There's a game of beer pong going on. Any interest in taking on the winners?"

I'd be up for anything that involves getting away from Beck.

"Sure, that sounds fun." I lean into him, and the concerned expression he'd been wearing dissolves. "Let's go."

Arron drops a quick kiss on my lips before glancing at Beck. The friendliness in his eyes disappears. "Take care, Hollingsworth."

"Will do," Beck grunts.

As Arron steers me through the thick crowd, a mixture of relief and disappointment flood through me, and I can't resist stealing one last look over my shoulder. A shiver scampers down my spine when I find Beck watching me.

I glance at Arron as we weave our way through the crowd and feel... *Nothing.*

Frustration blooms inside me.

I like Arron. He's a nice guy, and we have a ton in common.

Only now do I realize how hard I've been working to talk myself into this relationship. I had convinced myself that he was someone I could get serious with, but after my run-in with Beck, and the feelings that continue to simmer beneath the surface, I understand there's nothing between us but friendship.

What bothers me most is that I might never get over Beck.

I can't imagine spending the rest of my life pining after someone I can't have. And yet, that's a very real possibility.

Summer before junior year of college...

I throw on a bikini before pulling a cover-up over my head. For the last few days, the temperatures have been soaring in the nineties. It's sweltering out, and I'm tired of being cooped up in the air conditioning. If I don't get out of this house, I'll go batshit crazy.

Since the Hollingsworth family is away on a two-week European vacation, I'm going over to take a dip. Caroline is always telling me to feel free and stop by any time I want. Since I'm usually operating in avoidance mode, I never do. But Beck has been conspicuously absent this summer, so I assume he's on vacay with his parents. Or maybe at football camp. I have no idea.

I try not to think about him.

With Dad at a business dinner and Mom playing Bunco with a group of neighborhood friends, I'm a lone, lonely, loner for the night. The house is quiet as a tomb. Sometimes it feels like it's always been like this, but that's not the case. Before Brianna died, light, happiness, and laughter had filled our home. No matter how much I want to change it, there doesn't seem to be anything I can do. Mom and Dad drift through their lives on autopilot. Dad works at least eighty hours a week, and Mom fills her time with retail therapy.

I didn't realize how lonely of an existence it had become until I went away to college and lived in the dorms. It took a while to get used to the constant commotion. Now, when I return home for breaks, I'm reminded of the loss all over again.

I shove those depressing thoughts from my head and grab a towel from the bathroom before heading next door. The moment I step outside, the hot air hits me like a wave. Even at nine o'clock at night, it feels like a sauna with the temperatures hovering in the upper eighties.

Unable to wait, I hasten my step. It's not until I walk through the black-iron gate that surrounds the Hollingsworth pool that my step falters, and I realize the critical error that has been made.

Beck isn't at school or on vacation with his parents.

He's here.

Swimming.

Silently I watch as he pushes off the far end of the pool, arrowing gracefully through the water. My mouth dries as I track his movements. I hate the attraction that leaps to life inside me whenever I catch sight of him. It's like a living, breathing entity. I've tried so hard to stomp it out, to deny its existence, but it refuses to be eradicated.

Luckily, Beck hasn't caught sight of me. There's still time to backtrack before he's ever the wiser. Beck surfaces at the midway point of the pool before rising to his feet. As he straightens, he shakes the water from his dark hair. It scatters around him, and the muscles in my belly contract as a burst of arousal explodes in my core.

Every time.

It's like this every damn time I see him.

I hate it.

Even more, I hate that he's the only one capable of making me feel this way.

His eyelids lift as his attention fastens on me. It's like he knew I was watching him.

Which is impossible...

But that's exactly how it feels.

A slow smirk curves his lips. It's like a punch to my gut.

"I was wondering if I'd ever see you again." There's a pause. "Seems like you've been avoiding me."

He doesn't realize how right he is.

Or maybe he does.

The way his gaze rakes over my body is like a physical caress. One that leaves me restless and fidgeting beneath the heaviness of it. Even though I'm wearing a cover-up that reaches mid-thigh, Beck has the rare ability to make me feel like I'm standing before him naked. It's disconcerting and serves as a reminder as to how dangerous this guy can be.

Toxic, really.

I won't try to fool myself into believing that Beck isn't my Kryptonite. I spent years trying to do that. There's no point.

"You're looking good, Mia."

His deep tone sends a fresh wave of nerves cascading over my bare flesh.

When I fail to respond, he continues. "How's your summer going?"

"It's good." My gaze stays locked on him. It's like I can't look away.

Why does he have to be so damn hot?

Twenty-one-year-old Beck blows eighteen-year-old Beck clear out of the water. It's like they're not even the same guy. Everything about him is bigger, broader, more finely sculpted. It's doubtful I could wrap both hands around one bicep.

"Have you been playing a lot of tennis?"

I'm definitely starting to salivate.

Did he ask me a question?

It takes a moment for my mind to play mental catch-up. I clear my throat as my eyes skitter away. "A bit."

When he chuckles, my attention returns to him. The sound strums something inside me.

His teeth flash in the darkness. "Dad tells me you've been interning at the office."

My head bobs in relief at the innocuous conversation. "Yup, I've been working full-time."

"I'm sure that's been keeping you out of trouble."

I snort as my muscles lose their rigidity. "I've never been known for my antics like some people."

A slow-moving grin overtakes his face. An answering ribbon of attraction curls in the pit of my belly. Nope. Not even gonna go there. This seems like the perfect time to take off.

I point to the gate. "I'm going to—"

"Leave?" He pops a brow. "So soon? Didn't you come here to swim?"

I shake my head.

"Really? Aren't you wearing a suit?" There's a pause. "And isn't that a towel in your hand?"

I glance at the fluffy material I'm holding and frown.

Damnit. Caught red-handed.

"That's all right." I swat my hand and take a tentative step toward freedom. "You're obviously enjoying some alone time, and I wouldn't want to disturb that."

Beck stretches his arms out in front of him. His muscles ripple with the arcing movement as his fingertips skim the surface of the water. "There's enough room for both of us, don't you think?"

Unfortunately, the pool is big enough for the Olympic swim team. So, yeah...there is.

He knows I don't want to be alone with him. Can't he let me slink away without calling me out on it?

"No worries," I wave a hand, "another time."

"Damn girl," he laughs, eyes crinkling at the corners, "do I frighten you that much?"

Abso-fucking-lutely.

"Don't be ridiculous!" I bristle and straighten to my full height. "Why would you say that?"

Challenge sparks to life in his eyes. "Because you avoid me like I've got a contagious disease."

"For all I know, you do."

"Nope. Totally clean." He gives me a wink. "I always wrap it up tight."

Ugh. "Gross."

"So prove it."

"Excuse me?"

"Prove that you're not afraid to be alone with me," he continues.

I force out a laugh even though my mouth has turned cottony. "I don't have to prove anything to you."

"You're right." He nods. "Then prove it to yourself."

I gnaw my lower lip. If I'm not careful, it'll be a bloody mess in a matter of minutes. I glance at the gate, tempted to walk away without another word.

"Come on, Stanbury," Beck cajoles, his voice turning silky. Too many panties to count have fallen around ankles from just such a tone. "You came here to swim, so do it. I wasn't planning to stay much longer. Then you'll have the pool to yourself. Isn't that why you came over? To cool off?"

Yes, it is. But Beck wasn't part of the deal.

I stare wistfully at the water from the cement patio. It looks so inviting. It's crystal clear and sparkling. Already beads of sweat are rolling down my back, and I just stepped outside. I've been looking forward to this all day.

It's not like I owe Beck an explanation.

And I certainly don't have anything to prove to him.

But...

Maybe he's right about needing to prove it to myself. If I can swim with him and nothing happens, then I can stop going to such great lengths to avoid him. Avoiding Beck at home and on campus is exhausting. It takes a ton of energy to constantly be on guard.

By his own admittance, he isn't planning to stick around for very long. There's no reason we can't swim together for ten or fifteen minutes without me ending up wrapped around him and sucking face.

So what am I concerned about?

"Fine." The word slips from my mouth before I can stop it.

When his lips bow up at the corners, I have to tamp down the nerves that flutter around in my belly like a million butterflies.

Why do I feel like I've fallen into a well-laid trap?

Like a deer in headlights, I stand frozen, waiting for Beck to get back to swimming laps, but he doesn't move. Instead, he continues to watch me. I lower my gaze, needing to break eye contact. Even though

I'm not looking at him, the heat of his stare crawls over my covered body.

It takes a moment to gather my courage and shed the cover-up shielding me from view. With his attention focused solely on me, it feels like I'm putting on a striptease which couldn't be further from the truth. Nerves skitter along my spine as my fingers grasp the hem. With a shaky breath, I yank it over my head in one fluid motion before tossing it to the plush lounger. It takes eight steps to reach the edge of the pool and dive headfirst into the water.

As soon as I'm submerged in the cool liquid, all the anxiety swirling through me vanishes. This feels just as amazing as I imagined it would. It's a refreshing slice of heaven. My body hums with pleasure. If I had allowed Beck to chase me away, I wouldn't be enjoying this now.

All I have to do is keep my distance.

How difficult can that be?

As I resurface, Beck's attention stays focused on me. A satisfied expression fills his face. No matter how much I try to pretend otherwise, I'm ridiculously aware of him on every level.

Every shift of muscle.

Every flick of his green eyes.

I'm all too cognizant of the attraction that buzzes between us.

Pretending to ignore him, I swim a few laps. As far as I'm concerned, he's not there.

That's what I tell myself, anyway.

"How's Arron doing?"

I glance at him with confusion. "Who?"

"I guess that answers the question, now doesn't it?" One side of his mouth hitches in amusement. "The last time we ran into each other, you were with some guy named Arron."

Oh, right.

"Yeah," I mutter. "We're not together." Two weeks after that party, I told Arron that I thought we were better off as friends. He didn't agree, and I haven't spoken to him since.

"That's too bad." He doesn't sound the least bit sorry. "What about now? Is there someone special in your life?"

These questions are becoming much too personal.

"I thought we were going to swim," I blurt, unease weaving its way through my voice.

"We can't swim and talk at the same time?"

Actually, I would very much prefer we didn't. It's difficult to ignore him when he won't stop yapping at me.

"I'm trying to figure out what kind of competition I'm up against," he says.

"Excuse me?" I whip around, disconcerted to find him a few feet away. When the hell did he get so close?

Ignoring my question, he asks one of his own. "Do you remember the last time we were in the pool together?"

All too well.

I've done my best to forget about that morning, but it's been singed into my memory. Even thinking about the way he touched me under the blazing sun sends a thick shaft of desire spiraling through me.

I press my lips together and shake my head.

"Liar," he accuses.

"No, I'm not."

"Well, I remember how good it felt when I—"

"Beck!" I snap. "You know what? This isn't working. Maybe I should go home."

He raises his hands in a gesture of surrender. "All right, all right. Sheesh. I was just making conversation."

"Well, don't."

"Fine. We'll talk about something else."

"We don't have to talk at all," I shoot back.

"Oh, come on, where's the fun in that?" Humor simmers in his voice. "We have so much catching up to do."

I scrunch my face. "Do we?"

"Sure." There's a pause. "So, where's your sidekick?"

The further I propel myself away from him, the more tension seeps from my body. "Alyssa left for England last week. She's spending the year there."

"Huh." Surprise fills his eyes. "Colton never mentioned it."

There's a reason for that.

Colton and Alyssa called it quits after six months. Alyssa never came out and specifically said it, but I suspect Colton broke up with her because he wasn't ready to be tied down to one specific girl. Alyssa might not realize it yet, but she's better off without him. I hate that he broke her heart, but hopefully, the year away will do her some good, and she'll get her groove back. I'm not used to seeing my bestie down in the dumps. She moped around for a while and then applied for the study abroad program. Alyssa has been my best friend since middle school. This will be my first time flying solo without her. The plan is for me to visit during Christmas break, but that's five months away.

"How's she doing?" he asks.

As I tread water, my muscles loosen. "She's fine." I don't want Beck to report back to Colton that she's not living her best life.

I don't bother reciprocating the question. Colton is the one who pulled the plug on their relationship. I'm sure he's doing just fine—drowning in groupie pussy.

After a few moments of silence, he asks, "Are you interested in playing a game?"

I shoot him a cautious look. "What do you have in mind?"

His arms cut through the water as he swims closer. "How about truth or dare?"

Truth or dare?

The tension that had sprung to life inside me dies a quick death. "Seriously?"

Isn't that a kid's game?

I've played a few times with Alyssa and a couple of friends. Truth mainly consists of revealing deep-dark secrets about your latest crush. Dares might be twerking in front of a passing car or calling the above-mentioned boy.

It's juvenile stuff.

Why would Beck be interested in playing that?

What's next?

A rousing game of Marco Polo?

When I don't offer a response, he arches a brow. "Are you down with it?"

A kernel of unease blooms in the pit of my belly, which is ridiculous. What's the worst that can happen?

It's probably best not to answer that.

Sidestepping the question, I shoot back with, "Isn't it time for you to leave?"

His mouth curves into a full-blown smile. The effect is devastating. It does funny things to my belly. "If I didn't know better, I'd think you were trying to get rid of me."

That's *exactly* what I'm attempting to do.

Instead of admitting the truth, I shrug and tamp down my growing discomfort. "Wouldn't want you to be late for whatever plans you have tonight."

He swims so close, I'm able to pick out the tiny flecks of gold that dance in his green eyes.

"For you, I've got all the time in the world."

The way his gaze pins me in place makes me realize that engaging in this game is a mistake, but it feels too late to back out now. The moment I saw him in the pool, I should have quietly retreated instead of allowing myself to get baited into joining him for a swim.

"You can start," he says casually, as if there aren't any ulterior motives at play.

And maybe there aren't.

Maybe I'm paranoid.

It's a game, I remind myself.

No biggie.

The sooner I get this over with, the quicker he'll get bored and take off. I need to stay focused on that.

"Truth or dare?" Tiny ripples lap at my shoulders as a warm breeze wafts over my exposed skin.

"Truth."

I search my brain for an interesting question, but nothing comes to mind. "What's your favorite thing to do?"

He pretends to yawn, looking completely bored. "That's easy."

If he says sex, I'm out of here.

"Football."

Everything inside me relaxes. That answer isn't exactly a shocker.

Ever since Beck could walk, he's been tossing around a football with his brother. He started out with flag football before moving on to Pop Warner youth leagues. By the time he hit middle school, Beck was a star on the football field with a cannon for an arm. In ninth grade, he skipped playing freshman or JV and went straight to varsity as the first-string quarterback. In college, he's broken state records in total career passing yards, passing touchdowns, and total pass completions.

I blink back to the present when he asks, "Is that it?"

I jerk my head into a nod.

"All right, guess it's my turn," he says lazily, eyes turning flinty. "Truth or dare?"

That's a no-brainer. If I choose a dare, Beck will come up with something to humiliate me with. I know how his mind works, and I refuse to fall for any of his sly trickery.

"Truth."

I expect a surface-level question like the one I asked, but that's not what I get.

"How many guys have you slept with?"

My heart stutters before beating into overdrive. *"What?"*

He enunciates the words as if I'm hard of hearing. *"How. Many. Guys. Have. You. Slept. With?"*

"I'm not going to answer that!" I sputter. "It's none of your damn business!"

"You have to." He shrugs as if this isn't a stupid game he talked me into playing. "I've already answered your question, now it's your turn to answer mine. Fair is fair."

Heat floods my face. "I didn't ask something so personal."

"You could have asked me anything you wanted, and I would have answered truthfully. But you didn't, and that was your choice."

I scowl, hoping he'll laugh and tell me to forget it.

"Tick tock, Mia. Answer the question." His voice drops. "Are you worried I'll tell people all your secrets?" He shakes his head. "I won't. Anything you share stays between us."

That's not the point. I don't give a rip if he cries it from the rooftops. What I don't want him to find out is that—

"Answer the question," he prods. "It's not that difficult."

I press my lips together.

"Mia—"

"One!" I groan as humiliation floods through me. *You're the only person I've slept with. Okay? Just you.*

Ugh!

His eyes darken to a deeper shade of green as he treads water. "What happened with Arron?"

I glance away and jerk my shoulders, unwilling to reveal the real reason our relationship fizzled out. "I don't know. Got busy with school."

He cocks his head. "And there's been no one else since?"

"You asked your one question," I snap, face flaming with embarrassment. "You won't get anything more from me."

"Fair enough, your turn."

Wait a minute...that's it? He's actually going to drop the topic of my limited sexual experience?

I'm as shocked as I am relieved.

"Can we end this stupid game?" I ask with a glare.

He shakes his head. "Not yet, we just started."

I huff out an exasperated breath and grunt out the question. "Truth or dare?"

"Dare."

I glance around the yard. "All right, I dare you to do a backward flip off the diving board."

Added bonus—it'll get him away from me, so I have some much-needed breathing room to collect my scattered thoughts.

Beck is a lot to take in.

He glances at the blue springboard before flicking his attention to me. "That's your dare? You want me to flip off the board?"

"Yup, that's it." Goosebumps prickle along my arms as I grow uneasy under the steady intensity of his stare. "After this, I'm going home." Where I can avoid Beck for the rest of my life. Clearly, this idea has backfired. I'm no closer to getting over him than I was in high school.

"You can quit after your next turn," he informs me with a smirk.

Grrrrr.

"Fine." I stab a finger at the board. "Do your flip so we can get this stupid game over with."

"You got it, sweetheart." His powerful arms cut through the water as he swims toward the side of the pool. When he reaches the ceramic tile edge, Beck hoists himself out of the water. His muscles ripple, and my mouth dries.

No one should be this devastatingly handsome.

It defies the laws of nature.

For now, I'll silently enjoy the show and pretend heat isn't pulsing to life in my core. Rivulets of water run down his back before continuing to his naked ass.

What the—

"Where are your shorts?" I croak.

He throws a devilish look over his shoulder before a wide grin breaks out across his face. Mischief dances in his eyes. When his feet land on the concrete, he straightens to his full height.

Oh.

My.

God!

He's naked!

Full-on naked!

It's not like I haven't seen the goods before, but that was two years ago. I've tried so damn hard to eradicate the image from my brain.

"In the house." He tosses out the comment nonchalantly, as if it's no big deal I've been swimming around naked with him for the last half an hour.

How did I not realize it sooner?

Maybe because I was trying to avoid looking at him altogether?

My tongue darts out to moisten my lips. They feel as dry as the Sahara.

"Don't be shy, Stanbury, take a good look." There is so much heat filling his voice that it could burn me alive. "I don't mind at all."

It takes effort to avert my focus. "Just do the dare."

I need to get this over with before something happens between us. Something I'll inevitably regret.

"Don't rush me, woman." He raises his hands, palms out. "I'm moving." There's not a bashful bone in this guy's body as he saunters to the diving board before climbing up the stairs.

Once on the board, he pauses as his hands grip the metal railing before strutting to the end that juts out over the water. Beck softens his knees before taking a few preliminary bounces. His cock flops around, and I can't help but laugh. The sound breaks the sexual tension brewing dangerously between us.

A smile cricks the corners of his mouth. "Is there something funny?"

I press my lips together and shake my head. "Nope, not at all."

"All right, if you say so." He bounces, and his dick continues to slap against his lower belly and balls.

I don't think I've ever seen something so ridiculous. I'm all but dying now. My shoulders shake at the image he makes standing on the board in all his glory. Even when he's making a complete jackass out of himself, he's still gorgeous. All six foot three inches of him.

"You ready to be blown away by my mad skills?" he asks, bouncing away gleefully.

I clear the laughter from my voice and remind, "It's a backward flip."

"Oh, yeah." He points at me. "I almost forgot."

"Maybe this isn't such a good idea," I say. "Seems like you could do irreparable damage to some rather sensitive pieces."

An unconcerned expression settles on his face as he shrugs. "It's sweet that you're concerned about my tender bits and pieces."

Hardly.

"A dare's a dare, right?"

"Yeah, I guess." Here's my chance to end this stupid game. "If you want to quit, I'd be fine with that."

A knowing glint enters his eyes as he smiles. "Sorry, sweetheart, you're not getting out of this that easily. I'll have to keep my legs together when I land and hope for the best."

He turns around until I have a perfect view of his ass. I hate to admit it, but Beck has one hell of a gorgeous backside. The urge to squeeze those perfectly shaped cheeks rushes through me, and I have to tamp down the impulse that stirs inside.

With his back to me, he stands at the edge of the board until his heels can hang off the end. He holds his arms straight out in front of him and takes a few initial bounces before bringing them down to his thighs. Beck squats and launches himself off the board. I hold my breath as he tucks into a ball, legs rotating over his head before landing in the water.

I hate to admit that I'm impressed. The guy gets a ten for perfect form.

Once he breaks through to the surface, I ask, "Did your giblets make it out all right?"

"Yup. Kept my legs firmly pressed together." He gives me a wink along with a sly grin. "Just like you've been doing for the last two years."

All of my good humor evaporates as I narrow my eyes.

Now that I know Beck isn't wearing board shorts, I keep at least ten feet of distance between us at all times. When he swims closer, I back away. But still, it feels like I'm being stalked in the pool. And I can't migrate to the shallow end unless I want to get an eyeful of him.

Not that he would mind.

He tilts his head as a smirk simmers on his lips. "You afraid I'm going to give you cooties?"

I shrug and keep a tight rein on my nerves. They're vibrating like crazy. "Anything's possible."

"Ready to take your turn?"

What I'm ready for is to get this over with. If I play my cards right, I'll be out of here in three minutes. Five, tops. And then I'll be able to breathe easier.

I jerk my head into a tight nod.

"Truth or dare?"

Ha!

I'm not falling for that again.

"Dare."

"A dare, huh?" he drawls before pursing his lips. A thoughtful look enters his eyes. "All right, I got one." There's a pause as my anxiety ratchets up a few hundred notches. "Your dare is to kiss me."

My arms and legs freeze, and my body sinks to the bottom of the pool. Right before my head can slip beneath the surface, I kick my feet and propel myself upward.

"*What?*" My voice comes out sounding high-pitched and shrill.

"And you have to wrap your legs around my waist while doing it."

No way!

"But—but...you're *naked*." My voice escalates until it's barely a squeak.

"So?" He raises a brow. "It's nothing you haven't felt or seen before."

"We're not going to talk about *that*," I bite out harshly.

"Why not?"

"Because..." My voice trails off as I search for a way to escape the situation, but there isn't one. I'm stuck. Goddamn it. Why did I agree to play this stupid game in the first place? It might have sounded innocent in the beginning, but it's turned out to be anything but.

When I remain stoically silent, he says in a challenging voice, "You're not going to puss out on me, are you, Stanbury?"

I blink back to the present.

To the naked guy treading water in front of me.

"No."

Surprise flickers across his face. Trust me, he's not the only one shocked by my surrender. I'm feeling a little stunned myself.

Beck might be the only guy I've had sex with, but he's not the only one I've fooled around with. The sad truth is that every time I get close to sealing the deal, all of my Beck-filled memories rush to the surface and ruin everything. Even though I don't want to, I end up comparing the guy I'm with to my hot, next-door neighbor. And they always come up lacking.

It's frustrating. I've tried to convince myself that what I experienced with Beck wasn't nearly as good as what I've built it up to be.

But not even *I* believe that.

Maybe this is my chance to prove that Beck isn't as amazing as I remember. One mediocre kiss with too much saliva is all it would take to move on and stop dwelling on him.

Beck grins before he raises his hand and curls one finger in a *come here* gesture.

Am I really going to do this?

I suck in a shaky breath before carefully exhaling it from my lungs and forcing myself to close the distance between us. When I'm only a foot away, I pause, unsure how to proceed. Tension and excitement spiral through me. My hands flutter tentatively to his shoulders before my nails bite into his flesh.

His eyes darken with desire.

What am I supposed to do now?

My movements falter, and I stare pleadingly, willing him to take control of the situation. This is more difficult than I imagined it would be.

"Come on, Stanbury," he murmurs, "you've come this far. Don't stop now."

I press closer until our bodies can brush against one another beneath the water.

Inside, I'm freaking out.

This isn't a big deal.

You're wearing bikini bottoms.

Any other girl would be wrapped around him like a python, devouring him whole.

All you have to do is pretend you're one of those girls.

Averting my gaze, I widen my thighs before wrapping them around his waist.

"Eyes on me," he says gruffly.

My attention snaps to him as I swallow down my nervousness. There's a fire burning in his bright green eyes. It kindles an answering flame deep in my core.

My ankles hook around his waist, bringing me flush against his taut abdominals. Like the rest of him, they're rock solid. I'm tempted to explore the grooved musculature with my fingers, but don't dare. He stares at my mouth as his tongue darts out to lick at his lower lip.

A punch of arousal slams me in the gut.

All right, maybe it hits a little lower.

With a pent-up breath, I wait for Beck to make the next move. Instead, he remains still, eyes focused patiently on me. Seconds tick by, and it becomes obvious that he isn't going to take control of the situation. A fresh wave of anxiety crashes over me. This is my dare, and Beck is going to force me to follow through with it.

Okay. I can do this.

Unsure how to proceed, I tilt my head, bringing my face closer until his breath can drift across my lips before mingling with my own. The intimacy is dizzying. It's like I've been drugged. We stay frozen, breathing each other in and out before I work up the courage to press my lips against his.

Everything about Beck is hard and chiseled. Except for his lips. I forgot how soft—almost plush in their plumpness—they are.

A strange sense of boldness surges through me, and I angle my head, stroking over his top lip before repeating the caress with the bottom. Beck doesn't move a muscle. He gives me the freedom to explore him at my own pace.

A sigh of pleasure leaves my mouth before floating in the air between us. His hands wrap around my backside. Both of his wide palms settle on my cheeks before tugging me closer, pressing me against his body. I tangle my arms around his neck until there is no space between us. My nipples pebble at the feel of his unyielding strength. Heat builds like an impending storm in my core.

He groans when my tongue slips inside his mouth. His grip tightens on me, fingers sinking into flesh. In the beginning, I was desperate for him to take over, but not anymore. There's something empowering about the way Beck allows me to control the situation. We both know that if he wanted, he could have me out of the water and flipped onto my back, panting beneath him.

Instead, he allows the kiss to unfold leisurely.

At my speed.

There is no pressure, only pleasure. So much that I'm almost drunk with it.

Our tongues tangle, sliding against each other. The exquisiteness of the movement is more erotic than I could have dreamed possible. My fingers slide into his hair to hold him in place. Barely am I aware that I'm grinding my pussy against his stomach.

It feels like my body is spinning out of control.

When I pull away, he grumbles, "Not yet."

Relief pounds through me.

Maybe I dragged my feet about following through with this dare, but now that my lips are on his, I want to take full advantage of the situation. If I'd thought kissing him would prove that I'd over-embellished his skills, I was woefully mistaken.

I reposition my head before my mouth settles on his. When he opens, my tongue slips inside, and I lose myself in the feel of him. The way our tongues tangle, becoming one, weaves a dream-filled cocoon around us. The outside world disappears. A moan slips free as I continue to move against him.

The friction feels so damn good. Need gathers in my core. It pulses through my body like that of a steady drumbeat as I remember what it felt like to have Beck's thick erection sliding inside me.

I need so much more than this.

The words are on the tip of my tongue when a sound penetrates the Beck-induced haze that has fallen over me. A whimper of protest erupts from my throat when he pulls away. It takes a moment to regain my bearings.

Why did we stop?

I'm on the verge of exploding. Any moment, I'm going to come right out of my skin. It's the best and worst feeling in the world. I want his mouth back on mine, dragging me under so I don't have to think about the repercussions of my actions.

"Dude, I thought we had plans."

Those six words are like a bucket of cold water being dumped over my head. The fog evaporates, and I'm once again clearheaded as I blink up at Colton. A shit-eating grin lights up his face.

Oh.

My.

God.

Please tell me this isn't happening.

"Hello there, Mia," he chortles. "Can't say I expected to find you here."

Colton knows *exactly* how I feel about Beck. When he and Alyssa were together, he tried numerous times to cajole me into joining the three of them, and I always shot him down. After a while, it became a running joke between us. He would ask, and I would refuse.

The biggest kick in the ass is that I only have myself to blame for my current predicament. All I want to do is slink home with my tail tucked between my legs, but that's not possible since I'm pinned against Beck's body. And he doesn't seem to be in a hurry to let me go.

"Colton," I mutter. Any moment I'm going to burst into flames. To be found like this is beyond humiliating.

He stuffs his hands in the pockets of his shorts and rocks back on his heels. "So, what have you crazy kids been up to?"

Ugh. He is so loving this.

"Wait in the car," Beck snaps, "I'll be out in ten."

Heat fills my cheeks, making them feel like they're on fire. I'm sure they resemble overripe tomatoes by now. It only adds to my upset.

At myself.

For allowing the situation to get out of hand.

What is it about this guy that makes me lose my head?

"You gonna come out with us, Mia?" Before I can respond, Colton continues. "I doubt the chicks we're supposed to hookup with tonight will appreciate that, but oh, well." He shrugs. "Sucks for them."

Chicks we're supposed to hookup with...

I press my palms against the steely strength of Beck's chest and try to push out of his embrace, but I don't get far.

Why am I such an idiot? How many times do I need to get burned by this guy before I finally learn my lesson?

"Dude," Beck snaps, "get the fuck out of here before I beat your ass."

Colton holds up his hands in a gesture of surrender as if he doesn't understand why Beck is pissed off. "Whatever. Don't get your panties in a bunch." As he slips through the iron gate, he calls over his shoulder, "You got ten. Wrap this shit up, and let's go."

Once Colton disappears around the side of the house and we're alone, I slam my fists into Beck's chest. "Let go of me!"

"Mia—"

"No!" I shake my head, unwilling to hear him out. No more excuses. "Just let me go."

"Give me a chance to explain!"

With his arms locked around my body, it's impossible to move.

"Don't bother. It was just a stupid game." Even though I try to keep the hurt and anger locked deep inside, it all comes flooding out in a rush. "You better get moving. You've got *chicks* waiting for you."

I hate the jealousy that drips from my words.

"They're just a couple of random girls we're supposed to meet up with tonight, that's it."

I can't hear anything through the pain that has all but swallowed me whole. "I don't care. Let me go." I feel like such a fool.

"Mia," his voice becomes so low that it sounds as if it's been dredged from the bottom of the ocean, "please."

"Let go!" I pound on his chest with my fists. If only it were possible to do damage. Instead of hurting him, I'm inflicting pain onto myself.

When he refuses, I snake a hand between our bodies until I'm able to wrap my fingers around his balls. His eyes flare as mine narrow. Once I have his undivided attention, I give them a good squeeze.

A hiss of breath escapes from his lips.

As soon as he releases me, I bolt toward the tiled edge and hoist myself from the pool. I glance over my shoulder and find Beck where I left him. He's hunched over with his hands cupping his dick and balls.

"Was that necessary?" he groans.

"Yup." Even though he's in pain, I can't bring myself to regret the damage I've caused. He deserves every bit of agony.

I grab my towel and cover-up, hightailing it from Beck's yard before he can recover.

As I'm about to push through the gate, he calls out, "This isn't over, Mia."

I swing around. "That's where you're wrong because nothing was ever started."

With that last parting shot, I walk away, leaving him to hold his balls.

Hopefully, he'll be too sore to use them tonight.

We'll just consider that a little gift to the chicks he's meeting up with.

Chapter Eight

BECK

For years, I've fantasized about Mia touching my junk. Although, in my mind, it was more of a caress. Maybe there would be a little licking and sucking thrown in for good measure. In no way did I expect her to try popping them.

Fuck me.

My poor balls throb with a strange mixture of need spiked pain. Surprisingly, that last maneuver wasn't enough to kill the desire rampaging through my system. Although it took the edge off. All I have to do is think about Mia's curvy body pressed against mine, and I'm once again rising to the occasion.

My tongue swipes across my lower lip, and a taste that is distinctly Mia explodes in my mouth. I don't want to dwell on how different the outcome would have been if Colton hadn't interrupted us.

Stupid motherfucker.

The moment he realized I had my hands full of the only girl I've ever wanted, he should have turned around and walked away. Fuck the chicks we're meeting up with. Instead, he took joy in pissing her off, and now I'm back to square one. She wouldn't even give me a chance to explain.

Does she really think I have any interest in other girls?

Hell, no. It's always been Mia.

Colton is the one trying to drown himself in pussy, not me. He might not be willing to admit that he fucked up when he cut Alyssa loose, but deep down, he knows he made a mistake. I have no idea why Colton thinks nailing as much ass as he can get his hands on is the solution. The only thing it's going to do is up his chances of contracting an STI.

Right now, I'm all but wishing it on him.

With a sigh, I swim to the side of the pool and hoist myself out. I scoop up my towel, running it over my hair and body before heading inside the house. As I jog up the staircase to the second floor, I force down my growing erection. I'm not sure what's worse. A case of blue balls or bruised ones.

Seems like I was dealt both.

Every time I take a step forward with Mia, something inevitably happens, and I get shoved back four or five steps. It's like playing a game of Chutes and Ladders. Those damn chutes will get you every time.

I jump in the shower and lather up under the warm fall of water. What I should have done was turn it ice cold. My fingers stroke over my cock, and I realize that I'm going to have to rub one out. Otherwise, I'll be stuck in this perpetual state of need, and I'm not willing to put up with that. I close my eyes and remember how good it felt to have Mia's body wrapped in my arms. The way our mouths fused together as she gyrated against me has my dick turning hard as a rock.

So.

Fucking.

Hot.

My fist tightens as I pick up speed. Seven strokes later, I throw my head back and groan out my release as water pours over my body. It feels nothing like when I came inside her, but it'll have to do.

Mia would freak out if she knew that she was my go-to spank bank material. I'm tempted to shoot her a text and let her know, but it would only aggravate her more, and I'm not about to do that. I irritate her enough without even trying.

My phone chimes with an incoming text. I glance at it, knowing that Colton has grown impatient. But that's too damn bad. He can cool his ass in the car after the way he jacked up my night. I would have rather spent it with Mia than sitting around with a couple of girls, watching Colton make moves in his quest to get laid.

Although, let's be honest, he doesn't have to try very hard. Colton is the pied piper of pussy. He can get his dick sucked anytime he wants. There are always girls waiting for his text. They don't care if it's a one-time deal. As long as there's no expectation of something more, he'll keep them around.

Not bothering to respond, I toss the phone on the bed and grab a T-shirt and a pair of jogger shorts. I thrust my fingers through my hair and head out the door. Colton glances up from his phone as I slide onto the front seat of his convertible Beemer.

"Took you long enough," he grumbles. "I was about to take off without you."

"Too bad you didn't do that when you realized I was busy."

"Give me a fucking break," he snorts. "We both know Mia can't stand your damn ass. What were you gonna do? Screw her in the pool? You might not realize it, but I did you a solid. That girl would have hated you even more than she already does."

Fuck. He's right.

If we'd taken it any further, she would have been more pissed off than she already is.

When I don't respond, a grin slides across his face as he cups his hand to his ear. "I'm sorry, what's that?" He pauses for a moment. *"You're welcome, Colton? Thanks for saving me from myself?"*

"I wouldn't go that far," I mutter, slouching on the seat and staring straight ahead.

"Please. I couldn't get Mia to come out with us if there was even a slight chance you would show up." He cocks his head. "Doesn't that tell you something?"

Of course, it does, but I'm not ready to throw in the towel just yet.

Colton has turned into a real surly bastard since the breakup with Alyssa. One of these days, he's going to get a fist in the face.

"Just drive," I snap, unwilling to continue the conversation.

"You know I'm right," he singsongs before starting up the engine and squealing from the driveway. "I hate to be the one to break it to you, but it's never gonna happen with that girl. You need to move the fuck on."

I slouch further onto the buttery-soft leather. He's not telling me anything I don't already know, but that doesn't mean I want to hear it. Especially from him.

"Maybe," I bite out, "you should do yourself a favor and take your own advice for a change."

His jaw tightens as he stares at the ribbon of road in front of him. "Don't think I'm not trying," he mumbles. "Every damn night, I'm trying to get over that girl."

"You fuck so much," I snort, "I'm surprised your dick hasn't shriveled up and fallen off. Remind me to buy you some balm for your birthday."

A hint of a smile lifts his lips, but it doesn't quite reach his eyes. "Don't I know it, brother."

Silence falls over us as Colton turns the Beemer onto the main stretch of road.

He clears his throat and continues to stare straight ahead. "Did Mia mention Lys at all?"

I glance at him and consider sharing the intel I've gathered. Maybe it'll help him realize that she's really gone, and he needs to take his own advice and move on. Colton would never admit it, but he blew up that relationship because he was too chickenshit to have one.

"Guess she's studying abroad in London for the year."

His lips tug down at the corners. "No shit?"

"Yup."

"Huh."

He says nothing more, and I don't bother asking questions. That's the beauty of our relationship. We don't need to sit around, whining about our feelings and crying over the girls who got away.

At the end of the day, what the hell would it change?

Not a damn thing.

August of senior year of college...

I pull my Jeep over to the curb and hit the hazards before jumping out. A burst of hot air hits me as I search the thick crowd of people flowing in and out of the airport.

The moment I see her blond head, I shout at the top of my lungs, "Alyssa!" There is so much noise and people that it takes a few minutes for her to notice me. "Over here!" I wave my arms like a crazy person to grab her attention.

A bright smile lights up her face as she drags a pile of suitcases behind her. Alyssa doesn't understand what the concept of traveling light entails. Actually, for her, this *is* traveling light.

I race toward her, maneuvering around weary passengers. As soon as she's within striking distance, I throw my arms around her, pulling her close and squeezing her tight. For a solid minute, we jump up and down with excitement.

"It's so freaking good to see you!" Unable to contain my giddiness, I hop from one foot to the other.

"It's good to be seen," she laughs, embracing me again. "I missed your face!"

"I missed yours more!" Tears of joy prick my eyes. My parents bought me a plane ticket for my birthday last year, and I flew over to visit during Christmas break. We had an amazing time. I met all her new friends, and we visited museums and Buckingham Palace. We drank pints at the local pub and flirted with cute footballers.

Who knew that soccer players were so sexy?

My trip to England gave me a whole new appreciation for the sport.

I pull away, holding her at arm's length, before giving her a quick once-over. "You look fantastic!" Alyssa has always been tall and muscular from years of dance, but she looks sleeker. In the shorts and T-shirt she's wearing, her muscles appear both longer and leaner.

She grins and does a little twirl on the sidewalk. "Thanks, babe. You're not looking so shabby yourself."

A shrill whistle rents the air, and we both turn toward the cop loitering near a squad car. He points a finger at us. "Breakup the love fest, ladies, and move it along before I write you a ticket."

I give him an apologetic wave before grabbing the largest suitcase and dragging it toward the Jeep. "Holy hell," I grunt, "what do you have in here? A dead body?"

"Surprise!" she laughs, "I brought you one of those cute footballers we met."

"Ha! I wish." Those accents alone were enough to dampen my panties.

Gathering my strength, I hoist the bag into my Jeep. It takes another ten minutes to jam all of her suitcases into the trunk and backseat. It's like an impromptu game of Tetris. By the time we slide onto the front seats, I'm a sweaty mess, and officer friendly is glaring at us.

"Too bad he had a massive stick wedged up his ass, he was kind of cute." Alyssa blows him a kiss as we roll past and merge into traffic.

Once we hit the freeway and are barreling toward campus, I reach over and squeeze her hand. "I know I said it before, but I'm really glad you're back." Junior year wasn't the same without her. "I was kind of afraid you might become an ex-pat."

With a soft sigh, Alyssa leans her head against the cushion. "I had an amazing time in London, and I did consider extending my visa," she rolls her head toward me, "but I wasn't about to leave you here all by yourself. It's senior year, baby! We have to spend it together!"

I flash her a grin, relieved that my bestie is home where she belongs.

Alyssa and I chatter about everything that happened during our time apart. She tells me about all the cool people she met and her dance classes. Once a month, she took amazing weekend trips and traveled all over Europe. The more she chatters, the more envious I become, wishing I'd done something like that, too. It sounds like an incredible experience.

"How did you leave things with Jack?"

Jack is the British guy Alyssa started dating a few months ago. When I visited over Christmas break, they had been just friends. He was definitely smoking hot. And that accent...

Yeah.

Alyssa huffs out a weary breath and closes her eyes. "It wasn't serious. We both knew I'd be leaving in August, so we kept it light."

"Smart. No broken heart to deal with on top of jetlag."

"Definitely not," she snorts. "I refuse to be in that kind of situation again."

The *situation* she's referring to is Colton Montgomery.

Neither of us say anything more on the topic.

I nibble my lower lip as we swing into the apartment parking lot.

Freshman and sophomore year, Alyssa and I shared a dorm room. Wesley has a strict policy about first-and-second-year students living on campus. Junior year, I rented a house with a bunch of girls I met in the dorms. It worked out well and was fun. Although there were always people coming and going, and that got old after a while.

When Alyssa confirmed that she would return for senior year, I found us a two-bedroom apartment a few blocks from campus. It's on the third floor and has a tiny balcony. The building is centrally located, so we can easily walk to a few restaurants and a small grocery store. I moved my stuff in on the first of August and have been living there for a couple of weeks. Alyssa's parents brought over her bedroom set, and we were able to piece together enough furniture to fill the apartment.

Alyssa beams as we pull into a parking space near the front entrance of the building. "I love this place! I'm so pumped you could get us an apartment here!"

"Yeah, it's super convenient. We can walk to campus and the parties..." my voice trails off. There's only one tiny problem, and I'm kind of afraid of how she'll react when she finds out.

So, I put it off.

And then off some more.

And now I've run out of time. I have to come clean before it's too late.

"Um," I clear my throat and turn off the engine, "there's something I need—"

Before I can force out the sentence, Alyssa jumps out of the Jeep and walks around to the back. Reluctantly, I follow, knowing I need to get this over with. Maybe it would be better if I wait until we're inside the apartment. Once she sees how awesome it looks, she'll fall in love with it. Then, hopefully, what I have to tell her won't be such a big deal.

We grab the smaller suitcases and set them on the sidewalk before pulling out the behemoth that feels like it weighs at least two hundred pounds.

Seriously, what's in here?

As we drag her luggage to the lobby door, it swings open, and two guys stroll out.

Alyssa grinds to a halt and grabs my arm. Her nails bite into my flesh. "What the hell is *he* doing here?"

Crap.

I glance at Colton and Beck, who return our stare with interest. "Right. I, ah, meant to tell you about that."

Her eyes narrow to slits as she frowns. "About what?"

"They also live here."

"I really hope you're joking," she says flatly, clearly displeased by the news.

It would be so much easier if I were. By the steam coming out of Alyssa's ears, she's more pissed off than I imagined she would be.

"Sorry, Lys. When I signed the rental agreement, I had no idea they lived here or that we're neighbors."

"What?" she growls.

I wince. Maybe I should have held off on the whole *neighbor's* part.

"Hey, Lys," Colton murmurs, swallowing up the distance between them. If he knew what was good for him, he'd give his ex a wide berth. Alyssa looks like a rabid dog who could attack at any moment.

Instead of biting his head off the way I expect, she pointedly ignores him. "Did you hear that?" With wide eyes, she makes a big production about glancing around as if looking for something. "It almost sounds like a ghost from boyfriends' past."

This isn't good.

After more than a year and countless relationships, I had assumed Alyssa moved on, but her reaction is proving that's not the case. During the year she was away, she gave me a play-by-play on the boy situation in London. She definitely got a taste of what England had to offer in the guy department. Every time I spoke with her, she was talking about someone new.

And then there was Jack.

Not once did she mention Colton. And since she wasn't asking questions or digging for information, I avoided the topic of her ex as well. I knew she wouldn't be pleased about this, but I didn't expect her to go off the deep end.

Big mistake on my part.

Beck glances at me, and I shrug in response.

Not dissuaded by Alyssa's cold demeanor, Colton tries again. "It's really good to see you, Lys." When she continues to avoid eye contact, he pulls her in for a hug.

She bares her teeth and growls before fighting her way out of his arms.

Alyssa dismisses him by turning her attention to Beck. "Hello, Beckett. It's lovely to see you." She flashes a mega-watt smile at him.

"Did Mia happen to mention the welcome home party I'm having this Saturday at Bang Bang? If you're free, definitely stop by."

Beck's lips quirk upward. "Nope, she didn't mention it." I hear the humor simmering in his voice. He knows there is no damn way I would invite him to a party.

I wince when Alyssa gives me a bit of side-eye.

"Hmm. That's strange. She must have *forgotten* to mention the party to you the same way she *forgot* to mention that a certain someone who shall remain nameless is my new neighbor."

I narrow my eyes.

You know what? I was feeling like a shitty friend for not telling her about our living situation, but now?

Not so much.

"Hey, what about me?" Colton interrupts, "Don't I get an invite?" When her glare intensifies, he adds, "How about for old times' sake?"

Alyssa tilts her head and glances around again. "It's so strange the way I keep hearing something."

"Really, Lys?" Colton's voice drops. "You're acting like a child."

Oh, boy.

I sigh.

If Colton wanted her attention, he's got it now.

With a scowl, Alyssa spins toward him. Two steps bring her close enough to drill her finger into his chest. Anger vibrates off her in heavy waves. "*I'm the child?* That's rich! You dumped my ass because you couldn't keep your dick in your pants! Don't you *dare* turn this around on me!" Her voice escalates. People passing by stop and stare. "You and I are *not* friends. We will *never* be friends! I was an idiot for thinking you were anything other than a *manwhore!*"

Even though I'm pissed that Alyssa invited Beck to her welcome home party, I wrap my arm around her shoulders and drag her away from Colton before the situation can spiral any further out of control.

Tears prick her eyes as she blinks back the moisture and glances around, only now realizing that she's drawn an audience. A dull red color floods her cheeks. My guess is that the jetlag has caught up with her.

Not one to shrink away, she meets the inquisitive looks from the surrounding people with a scowl. "Move it along! Show's over, there's nothing to see here."

Maybe I should talk to the building manager and see if there's a way to break our rental agreement. If this episode has proven anything, it's that Alyssa isn't over Colton as much as she led me to believe. And living in this close of contact with her ex won't end well for any of us.

Chapter Ten

BECK

I drop onto the bench after a two-hour practice under the blazing sun. I'm fucking exhausted and want to jump in the shower and wash away all the sweat and turf sticking to me. As I peel off my jersey and throw it in my locker, Colton does the same.

We've been playing football together since we were kids. We know each other's quirks and tells. Half of the time, he knows which play I'm going to run before I do. I never have to seek him out on the field, he's always where I expect him to be. As far as football is concerned, we have some kind of weird mental connection.

Which is exactly why the last couple of practices have been so concerning. No matter what I threw out there today, he wasn't where he was supposed to be. It's not uncommon to have an off day. We all have them. You have to stay focused and work through it. But this has turned into more of a slump and that, we can't have.

Not with the season right around the corner.

I've got plans this year. And they include bringing home a conference championship. Breaking a few more NCAA football records before I leave wouldn't be so bad either. But I can't do any of that without my wide receiver being dialed in.

And he's not. I don't know where his head is, but it's not where it should be.

Colton doesn't bother making eye contact. He's too busy shoving his shit into his locker. His agitation is palpable. He knows there's a problem.

It's been eating at him for a while.

The locker room turns quiet as Coach stalks through with his Wesley Warriors ball cap pulled low over his eyes and a clipboard clenched in his hand. "Montgomery," he barks, "get your ass in my office as soon as you're dressed."

Colton jerks his head into a nod but keeps his lips pressed together.

Coach Taylor glares at the group of half-naked guys and snaps out a few more names. When he's done, he slams the door to his office with so much force that it rattles on its hinges.

Devon Baker, a three-hundred-pound lineman, calls out, "Better bring some lube with you, Montgomery. Doesn't look like he's in the mood to give it to you gently."

Colton glares before giving Baker the finger. There is, unfortunately, truth to the statement.

Our first game against Tennessee is in two weeks. I need Colton to pull his head out of his ass and play like I know he can. I've got enough of my own bullshit going on without worrying about him.

Whatever this is, he needs to get it figured out fast and stop bringing it on to the field. "So—"

"Don't even say it, man." He falls silent, ripping off the rest of his padding as if it's choking the life out of him.

"Say what?" I ask, doing the same.

"That I'm off my game." He gives me a bit of side-eye. "That it's been off for a few weeks."

I shrug and backtrack. Coach is already going to rip him a new one, so maybe, for the time being, I'll keep my trap shut, and we'll see what happens. "Wasn't going to mention it."

"Good." His brows pinch together as he shoots an anxious look toward Coach's office. "For once in his life, Baker is right. I'd better grab some lube. Coach is going to ream my ass."

Nik Taylor is one of the toughest coaches you'll find in Division I football. He runs his program like a tight ship. If he's giving one-hundred percent to his team, he expects his players to do the same. If you're not willing to bleed for the guys standing shoulder to shoulder with you on the field, there's no place for you on this roster. He's the reason both Colton and I committed to Wesley. Practice may be grueling, but we're better players for it. Ever since Coach Taylor took over the program, the Warriors have won their conference along with five national championships. I'm looking to keep the momentum going, not shit the bed during my farewell season.

"Please," I snort, wanting to put him at ease, "Baker is a bonehead. Don't listen to a word he says."

Colton shrugs as concern flickers in his eyes. He's never been one to expose his true feelings. This is the first time I've seen his mask of indifference slip from place.

"Look, man, we all have off days. Don't stress about it."

"Easier said than done," he mumbles.

We fall silent, stripping out of our gear before hitting the showers. Now that Coach is cloistered in his office, the locker room turns rowdy. Everyone has caught their second wind. Guys are talking about the parties happening off-campus. The team has been at Wesley practicing twice a day since the beginning of July. We've spent hundreds of hours going over plays, practicing, working out, and watching game film. With school starting up next week, this will be our final hoorah. Everyone wants to cut loose and party their asses off before we have to buckle down for the season.

I hit the shower, wash up, and grab a towel before heading to my locker. I find Colton on the bench, staring pensively at his hands. I'm not sure if he's deliberately hanging back, waiting for the team to clear out, so they don't hear Coach rip him a new one, or if something else is bothering him.

"Come on, get a move on it," I prod. "I want to get out of here."

"Go on without me." He glances toward the office. "I have the feeling this will take a while."

I pull on a pair of athletic shorts before shoving my feet into slides. "Does this have anything to do with Alyssa?"

"Fuck if I know," Colton sighs, dragging a hand over his face.

I'm surprised when he doesn't shut down that line of questioning. The Colton I grew up with would never let a girl mess with his mojo on the field. But then again, Alyssa is the only girl he's ever dated. In all honesty, it shocked the hell out of me when they got together. Who would have suspected Colton could be monogamous?

Or that he wanted to be.

Just when I was getting used to them as a couple, he cut her loose. The call of the wild turned out to be too much temptation to resist. I had assumed Colton would move on without a problem. But maybe I was wrong about that. I'm not saying I have all the pieces to the puzzle figured out, but here's what I know—he's been messed up for a while now, and it's gotten worse since we ran into Alyssa.

Unsure if I should continue, I say, "You could talk to her."

"Yeah, I tried that." He snorts and flicks his attention to me. "That girl could give Coach a run for his money in the ass reaming department."

One side of my mouth hitches.

"You heard her. She wants nothing to do with me. In fact, she'd rather I not breathe the same air as her." He shakes his head and chuckles under his breath. "If Lys had her way, she'd rather I didn't breathe at all."

He's right.

"Can you blame her?" The way he dumped her was harsh. From what I heard, it involved a text message.

Any trace of humor that had sparked to life in his eyes vanishes as he goes back to staring at his clasped hands. "Nope, not at all."

As I yank my T-shirt over my head, Colton asks, "Are you going to Alyssa's party?"

I shrug and try to play off the question. Not because I haven't given the invitation any consideration. You bet your damn ass I have, but I don't want to rub it in his face. There are some couples who can part ways and remain friends.

Alyssa and Colton are not one of those couples.

When he remains silent, I say, "You could always crash the party."

"Somehow, I don't think that would go over well."

"Have you considered giving her a gift she really wants?" When he raises a brow, I smirk. "Like your balls on a silver platter?"

He wads up his sweaty practice jersey and throws it at my face. I bat it away before it can make contact.

"You're a dick," he laughs.

I grin, relieved the tension has been broken. "Tell me something I don't know."

"Welcome home, bitch," I shout, attempting to be heard over the pulsing beat of techno music as we clink our shots of Fireball together and toss them back. The cinnamon-flavored liquor burns a fiery trail down my throat, killing any bacteria in its path.

"Holy shit, that's terrible!" I sputter, coughing as tears gather in my eyes. "No more shots. I'm tapping out."

She laughs and orders another round.

Alyssa is in her element, chatting with friends who have shown up to celebrate her return to Wesley. For the festivities, she bought a short sparkly silver dress that clings to every curve. Her hair has been curled and left loose so it can float around her bare shoulders. The girl looks seriously hot. And I'm not the only one who thinks so either. There's been a ton of guys sniffing around, and she's been flirting with all of them.

Not that I've been keeping track, but my guess is that she's downed at least half a dozen shots. More impressive than that, she's standing upright and doesn't look the least bit affected. Apparently, dancing wasn't the only thing she worked on in England.

My head is already swimming, and I haven't consumed nearly as much. A few mixers and three shots.

When a song with a great beat comes on, Alyssa squeals and grabs my hand, dragging me to the dance floor. "I freaking love this one!"

We shove our way through the crush of bodies before carving out a tiny space. Our hands go in the air as we lose ourselves in the music. It's not difficult. All I have to do is close my eyes, and everything that has been nagging at me melts away into nothingness. The mounting stress of applying to law school and trying to figure out the next chapter of my life floats away on the beat.

One song bleeds into the next, and we continue to shake our asses, shouting the lyrics in each other's faces. At one point, I grab Alyssa's hand and twirl her around. A smile lights up her face as she laughs hysterically.

Friends come and go as the music continues.

As the DJ plays another song, Alyssa leans in and shouts, "I need to use the bathroom."

"Want me to come with you?"

"Nah." With a shake of her head, she waves me off. "I'll be back in a sec, stay here so I can find you."

In the blink of an eye, she's swallowed up by the crowd, and I'm surrounded by a writhing mass of bodies. The club is dark with strobe lights that flicker. It's difficult to tell what limbs belong to who. Music reverberates off the walls before seeping into my bones. Even though I'm alone, it's all too easy to lose myself in the rhythm.

Alcohol pounds through my system, making me feel alive and free. I want this feeling to last forever. Or, at the very least, until the end of the night.

Male hands wrap around my hips and tug me close. I turn my head and find a guy I recognize from a few of my classes. He's always seemed nice enough.

"Hey, beautiful, want to get out of here?" he slurs.

"No, thanks." I shake my head, hoping Alyssa returns quickly.

"Aww, come on," he growls against my ear, tugging me uncomfortably close. "You're so damn sexy."

"Thanks, but I'm not interested." Why can't these guys take no for an answer? Is it really that difficult of a concept to comprehend?

As I attempt to knock his hands away, they disappear on their own, and a deep voice I recognize all too well says, "You heard her the first time. She's not interested, so do us both a favor and back off."

I spin around, surprised to find Beck standing beside me.

The guy jerks his chin in my direction. "Is she with you?"

"All you need to be concerned about is that she's not with *you*."

The guy's lips flatten as he glares. From the look on his face, it's obvious that he's thinking about starting something with Beck. Which is surprising. Most people take one look at the muscular QB and back away. This idiot must be drunker than I suspected.

The last thing I want is Alyssa's welcome home celebration ending with a brawl.

In an attempt to avoid conflict, I press my body against Beck's. His arm snakes around my shoulders, and he hauls me so close that my breast flattens against the steely strength of his chest. Tingles of awareness shoot through me as my nipple pebbles. When I try to put some distance between us, he pulls me closer.

There's no way he doesn't feel my arousal.

"Whatever," the guy grumbles before disappearing through the crowd.

Now that it's just the two of us, Beck repositions me until I'm crushed against his front. I inhale a breath, and the scent of his woodsy cologne wraps around me.

"I don't like other guys touching you," he growls in my ear before nipping the delicate flesh with his teeth.

His possessiveness sends a sharp thrill through me. As much as I don't want to like what he's saying, I do.

Way too much.

With a groan, my arms slip around his neck to tug him closer.

"You're fucking killing me in that dress, you know that, right?"

Alyssa made sure I was appropriately attired in club-wear. The black dress I'm wearing is short and probably a size too small. It show-cases all of my curves. Normally, I don't have the girls on display, but they're out tonight.

"I didn't wear it for you." That's a big fat lie. I knew there was a chance he would show up after Alyssa issued an invitation. Maybe I wanted him to see what he couldn't have.

Considering that I'm wrapped up in his arms, it would seem like that plan backfired spectacularly.

His fingers bite through the material and into my backside. "Is there another guy I should be concerned about? Someone I need to rip apart with my bare hands for touching you when you look like this?" His voice deepens. "Because I will if I have to."

The muscles in my belly clench at the jealousy filling his voice.

"There's no one else," I admit. It would be easy to pretend that he has reasons to be envious, but there's no point, and I've never been one for games.

His body loosens, and his jaw unlocks. "Good to know."

When he steps away, his warmth disappears, and a sense of loss fills me. Before I can figure out where he's going, he grabs my hand and spins me around until his front is aligned with my back. His fingers brush over my sides before wrapping around my ribcage. It's been so long since his hands have been on me, and I've missed his touch more than I've wanted to admit.

With a groan, my head lolls back until it can rest against the solidness of his chest. Beck lowers his face to my neck so that his warm breath can feather against my skin. My arms loop around his neck as he holds me close.

Why does this have to feel so right?

It would be so much easier if it didn't.

One song blurs into the next, and the throng of people dancing fades until it's just the two of us. Beck holds me so close that I'm not sure where he ends, and I begin. The feel of him wrapped around me is intoxicating. His fingers rest under the swells of my breasts, singeing me through the slinky fabric of my dress. I writhe against him, wanting to feel his hands on me.

"I can't take any more of this," he growls before spinning me around to face him. "I need to touch you."

Not waiting for a response, he grabs my hand and tows me through the crowd.

"Where are we going?" I stumble in my heels, trying to keep pace with him.

"I don't know. Some place where we can be alone."

A thrill of anticipation spirals through me before settling in my core. As turned on as I am, there's a tiny voice in the back of my head that questions whether we should be doing this.

"Are you sure this is a good idea?" I ask.

"It's the best damn idea I've ever had," he throws over his shoulder.

As we move past the long stretch of bar, I catch a glimpse of Alyssa through the crowd. Instead of smiling and laughing like she's been doing all night, her brows are beetled together, and there's a scowl twisting her lips.

"Alyssa," I murmur, pointing to her as Beck hustles me along.

"Leave them alone. They need to get their shit hashed out."

Huh?

That's when I realize she isn't alone. Colton is with her.

No wonder Alyssa looks so pissed off. Before I can decide what to do, the bar area disappears, and we're turning down a narrow hallway and past a set of bathrooms. When we come to a door, Beck reaches out and turns the handle. I think we're both surprised when it swings open. And I'm even more alarmed when he tugs me inside and locks us in the dark space.

Without hitting the lights, it's impossible to tell if we're in a storage closet or an office. Either way, I don't care. I need to get my hands on this girl before I explode.

In my jeans.

"Beck—"

I tug her close and seal my lips over hers. When her palms flatten against my chest, I half-expect her to push me away. Instead, her fingers dig into my shirt. My tongue sweeps over her mouth. When her lips remain sealed, I nip at her lower one. She yelps, and I plunge my tongue inside.

The sound of her whimper reverberates inside my brain.

It's the best fucking sound in the world.

One I want to hear more of.

It doesn't take long for Mia to melt. Her hands slide up my chest before wrapping around my neck and drawing me closer. I'm starving for the taste of her. For years we've been dancing around each other, and I can't take any more of it.

Whether she realizes it or not, things are going to change.

My hands drop from her waist to the roundness of her ass. I widen my fingers before squeezing the softness and pulling her flush so she can feel the thickness of my erection. I'm so fucking hard for her. No one has ever driven me this crazy.

After I've plundered the sweetness of her mouth, my lips blaze a hot trail to her chin. A groan escapes from her when I nibble at the curve of her jawline.

"We shouldn't be doing this," she whispers.

Is she serious?

I can't think of anything else I'd rather be doing. And I'll be damned if I leave this room without getting my fill of her. She may want to deny it, but she melts every time I put my hands on her.

The black dress she's wearing is dangerous. She looks hot as hell. The moment I spotted her on the dance floor, I knew the night would end with her wrapped up in my arms and my hands all over her body.

My fingers trail from the curve of her ass to the hem that barely skims her thighs before I give it a slight tug. "Nice dress."

"It's Alyssa's."

"I figured, but you look amazing in it."

"Thanks," she sighs, bearing more of her neck to me.

Does Mia even realize what she's doing?

It's all the invitation I need to continue. My lips roam over the delicate flesh of her neck before drifting to her collarbone and kissing the smooth skin of her exposed breasts.

Fuck...I want to rip this dress off her body. Images of her stretched out in my bed flash through my head like a slow-motion picture show.

One hand slides beneath her dress, shoving the slinky material over the curve of her bare ass. As my hand explores the supple skin, I realize she's wearing a thong, and it makes the erection I'm sporting even more painful. My finger traces the slender length of fabric from the elastic around her waist to her slit. Even through the thong, I can tell she's completely soaked.

"Beck," she moans.

"I need to touch you, Mia." I pause as my heart races. "Do you want that, too?"

A deafening silence crashes around us, and I wonder if she'll deny me. If that happens, I'll have no other choice but to step away.

"Yes."

The breath rushes from my lungs in a painful burst as she gives me the green light to proceed. When I stroke my fingers over the damp material, she arches her body.

"Please," she murmurs.

My fingers slip beneath the thong to stroke over bare flesh. I caress her silky lower lips, never once dipping them inside. Restlessly she shifts against me. A whimper of protest escapes when I ease my hand away from her.

"Shh." I press my mouth to hers before swallowing her displeasure. I hook my fingers in the band around her waist before dragging it down her hips and thighs until the tiny scrap of material puddles around her ankles. Now that my eyes have adjusted to the darkness, I realize there's a desk shoved in the corner of the small space. I drop to my haunches and snatch the thong from the floor before shoving the lacy scrap in my pocket. As I straighten, I wrap my arms around her so that my hands splay wide on her naked backside before lifting her from the floor. Her legs band around my waist until her core is pressed against me.

Mia groans, her hips gyrating with need.

Fuck...All I want is to feel her naked flesh against mine.

It only takes three steps to swing around and set her on the desk. Once her ass hits the metal top, I drop to my knees. Anticipation floods through me as I push her thighs wide and bury my face against her heat.

There have been too many times I've fantasized about this moment not to take full advantage of it.

I need to feel her.

Taste her as she explodes on my tongue.

Hot licks of arousal rampage through me.

Even in the darkness, her gaze pins mine in place. She is completely at my mercy. There haven't been many times when I could say that. Carefully, I rub the pad of my thumb across her slit, caressing the soft lips of her pussy. With lazy strokes, I circle her heated entrance. Mia bows her body, widening her legs until she is fully exposed to my touch.

I glance up, wanting to see the pleasure unfold across her features. My fingers tease her, coming close to sinking inside before skittering away. She shifts impatiently as her frustration grows. Every couple of strokes, I slide my thumb over her opening before swiping it across her clit. Her body tightens as a breathy moan falls from her lips. It's sweet music to my ears.

"Beck," she whimpers, "please."

"What do you want, baby?"

"More."

"More what?" I know exactly what she's asking for. I'm as eager for it as she is.

Unable to resist tormenting her, I press my finger deep inside her tight sheath before dragging it out again.

"God, yes," she breathes.

When her muscles clench around me, I nearly come in my pants.

So fucking hot.

If I keep this up, I won't last long. But I'm going to have to because this moment isn't about me, it's about the girl I've been chasing all my life. I won't lie, it's a foreign concept to put someone else's pleasure above my own. With other women, it was always about my gratification. I made sure they enjoyed themselves, but I was there for me.

This couldn't be more different.

Mia is different.

All I want to do is give her pleasure. I want to see the satisfaction unfold on her delicate features. I want to feel her muscles contract around me. I want to taste her excitement.

I want it all.

My fingers glide through her arousal before circling the tiny bundle of pulsing nerves. The way her hips move against my hand tells me she's close.

Her growing excitement only increases my own.

Needing to taste her, I lean in and swipe my tongue across the lips of her pussy. The honeyed taste of her explodes on my tongue.

"Beck," she moans, "that feels *so* good."

Damn right, it does.

"I know, baby," I murmur against her heated flesh. "I want you to enjoy this."

"I don't think I've ever enjoyed anything more." Her voice slurs as if she's drunk with pleasure.

My lips quirk as I nibble at her sweetness. I could stay buried against her soaked skin for hours.

Days.

Fucking years.

The word *forever* flickers through my head. I'm not ready to go there quite yet, but I'm not too far from it either. In the back of my mind, it's always been Mia. No other girl has ever come close to making me feel what she does.

Somehow, I need to make her mine.

And this, it's a start.

I hope.

When Mia spreads her thighs impossibly wide, I run the flat of my tongue over her core before circling her clit and spearing it deep inside. When she groans, I do it all over again. We fall into a rhythm as I continue thrusting into her softness.

When her body tightens, and she lifts herself from the desk, I know she's on the verge of splintering apart. I don't change the tempo of my movements. I keep everything the same until she grows frenzied. Until her harsh breathing is the only sound that fills the tiny room.

"Let go," I whisper.

That's all it takes to send her crashing over the edge. She groans out her orgasm, spasming around my tongue. I don't let up as she rides the wave, grinding herself against me.

When her muscles finally loosen, she slumps onto the desk with a contented sigh. Her legs stay splayed open as I withdraw my tongue from her sheath and lick her shuddering softness with long, languid laps.

She's so fucking creamy.

I want to devour it all.

With a satisfied sigh, she stretches out against the metal surface. Her head hangs off the edge. I give her swollen pussy one last kiss before straightening to my full height. The picture she makes sprawled out with her dress bunched around her waist and her body limp from the intensity of her orgasm is enough to send me hurtling over the edge.

Even though it's dark, I burn the image into my brain. She's so perfect, it's almost painful. The only thing that could make this moment better is if she were mine.

I step closer, lowering my body to hers until my lips can settle against her mouth. The head of my throbbing cock lines up to her entrance. When I thrust my hips, she makes a small mewling noise deep in her throat.

I pull back enough to whisper, "I'm giving you fair warning. Your days of running from me are numbered."

Her movements still.

"Do you understand what I'm saying?"

She remains silent as her teeth sink into her lip.

Instead of pushing for an answer, I nip at the plump flesh and tug it from her teeth, sucking the fullness into my mouth before releasing it.

"Are you going to make me chase you?"

"Beck, I—"

I smack a kiss against her lips. That's all I needed to know.

"Challenge accepted."

Chapter Thirteen

MIA

I shovel a spoonful of Honey Nut Cheerios into my mouth as the door to Alyssa's bedroom swings open, and she stumbles out. The sleek, sophisticated girl I picked up from the airport the other day is nowhere in sight. The transformation is almost impressive.

Alyssa's blond hair is sticking up from every angle. It wouldn't surprise me if birds have nested in the disarrayed strands. Eyeliner and mascara are smudged under her eyes, giving her a raccoonish appearance.

The girl is one hot mess, which hopefully means she had an amazing time at her party last night. I wasn't expecting Alyssa to show her face until at least noon. I left the club around two o'clock and promptly passed out on my bed. I have no idea when Alyssa made it back to the apartment.

"Hey," my spoon pauses midair, "how are you feeling?" By the looks of her, I'm pretty sure I know the answer to that question.

"Stop shouting." She winces before grabbing the sides of her head. "Please, I beg of you."

"That good, hmm?" The way she was tossing back shots last night was enough to make me nauseous. I didn't consume nearly the amount she did, and I was feeling it. How else do you explain my lapse in judgment?

Alyssa should probably thank her lucky stars she didn't die of alcohol poisoning.

"Let me guess, you're looking for a little hair of the dog that bit you?" I can't resist teasing her. "I'm sure we have a bottle of tequila around here somewhere. Want me to get it?"

"God, no." Her skin turns an unnatural greenish hue at the mention of alcohol. "I'm never drinking again."

I snicker. Alyssa has never been a big drinker, but she likes to have a good time. I give it a week or two before she's back on the horse again.

Once her color returns, she points to the kitchen. "I need massive amounts of Tylenol and Gatorade.

She staggers into the other room before returning with a humongous bottle of the orange sports drink. Her fingers fumble as she attempts to twist off the cap.

"Why did you let me drink so much," she groans, successfully prying off the top and chugging a quarter of it. Then she presses her fingers against her mouth before releasing a loud belch.

"If memory serves, I told you several times to slow down, but you weren't in the mood to listen. At one point, you called me a buzzkill." When she remains silent, I ask, "Exactly how many shots did you have?"

"I lost count after eight." She shakes her head and waves a hand. "Please, I can't even think about that. It'll make me sick. Never mind, I'm already sick." She points to her room. "I'm going back to bed. Wake me up tomorrow. Or maybe the day after that. Hopefully, I'll have bounced back by then."

Alyssa walks a couple of steps before swinging around to face me. With her free hand, she grabs her head as if she's trying to hold it in place. "Wait a minute." She raises a hand and massages her temple. "Were you busting a move on the dance floor with Beck, or was that a tequila-induced dream?"

I wince at the memory and glance away guiltily before shoving another spoonful of cereal into my mouth. I was really hoping she wouldn't remember that part of the evening.

If only it had stayed as innocent as dancing. My face heats as I recall the way Beck set me on the desk and spread me wide, licking me until I orgasmed.

When I fail to respond, she takes another step and jabs a finger at me. Her eyes lose some of their haziness. "Yeah," she mutters, "you two were *definitely* dancing. His hands were all over you. And you, *ya little hussy*, were totally enjoying it."

Oh, God...

This isn't a topic I want to delve straight into at nine o'clock on a Sunday morning. In fact, I don't want to think about it ever again. For reasons I can't explain, I am ridiculously attracted to Beck. Even though he is all kinds of wrong for me, my feelings have yet to dissipate. Every time I catch sight of him, my heartbeat skitters, and the muscles in my belly contract.

He's the last person I want to feel this way about.

His words from last night ring unwantedly in my head.

Your days of running from me are numbered.

Was he serious?

I'm not even sure what that means. Hopefully, nothing.

Alyssa waves her hand in front of my face. "Hello? Earth to Mia. Come in, Mia."

I snap out of those disconcerting thoughts. "Sorry," I mumble.

"Please tell me I wasn't hallucinating. Because if that's the case, I really *am* going to lay off the booze."

"No," I admit, "we danced together." I'm reluctant to give her further details. The last thing I need is Alyssa rooting for a relationship that is doomed to fail before it even starts.

Last night was a bad decision on my part. We need to leave it at that.

You know what this situation calls for?

A change in topic.

I raise my brow and turn the tables. "Is there anything *you* would like to tell me about?"

"Huh?" Her face scrunches.

"I saw you at the bar with Colton."

She blinks away the confusion as her expression hardens. "Can you believe that guy had the audacity to show his face after I purposefully went out of my way *not* to invite him?"

"Umm, maybe?" I pause. "Any interesting conversations?"

She moves to the armchair before slumping onto it and squeezing her eyes shut. "He wants to be friends," she mutters. "Don't worry, I was extremely clear about where he can shove his friendship."

I bet she was.

My lips lift into a smile. Once you've landed on Alyssa's shit list, there's no way off it. Poor Colton. He should walk away while he still can.

"Maybe that was the closure you needed to move on. Feel any better about getting it out of your system?"

Even though her eyelids remain closed, her lips tug down at the corners. "Surprisingly, no."

"I'm proud of you for giving him a piece of your mind. That took balls," I tell her.

She snorts. "As far as I'm concerned, he can shove those up his ass as well."

"Sounds like his ass is a crowded place."

Alyssa cracks open her eyelids and stares at me for a moment before we both burst out laughing. "Yeah, it does."

Chapter Fourteen

BECK

I glance at my phone and maneuver my way through the crowd of students traveling across campus like cattle. These people need to move their asses, or I'm going to be late. Class starts in less than five minutes, and walking in like I don't give a shit isn't the first impression I'm looking to make.

Once I reach Mitchell Hall, where the English classes are held, I take the stairs two at a time. Less than a minute later, I'm sliding onto a chair. With a huff, I pull out my computer and wait for Dr. Hayes to get class underway.

Devon Baker plunks his ass down next to me.

Great.

Like I need this distraction. Devon runs his mouth like he's getting paid by the minute. English isn't exactly what one would call a high-octane class. It will take every ounce of my focus to concentrate for a full fifty minutes.

With a grin, he fist bumps me. "Dude, I didn't know you were in this class."

"Last-minute change to the schedule." My advisor emailed me last week and dropped the bomb that Composition is a requirement for graduation.

So here I am.

And I'm not a happy camper about it either.

The thought of writing a bunch of papers makes me want to blow my brains out. And no, I'm not being overdramatic. I suck at writing. There's a reason I pushed this course off for years until I was able to forget about it. Unfortunately, my procrastination has now bitten me in the ass. When I grumbled about it to Coach, he told me he'd reach out to the professor and make sure she kept him in the loop as far as grades were concerned.

Talk about a double whammy.

Like I need that guy riding my ass all semester with a crop.

Needless to say, senior year isn't exactly off to a great start.

"I'm so freaking stoked about getting Hayes for this course," he says.

Seriously?

Those have to be the last words I expected to hear coming out of Devon's mouth.

He's one of those athletes who cobbled together a bunch of bullshit classes and slapped a major on it. He better hope his ass makes it to the NFL because I have no idea what else he'll do.

Before Devon can continue yapping, Dr. Hayes takes her position at the front of the classroom. I glance around and realize the lecture hall is packed to the gills. Since this is a required course, there's a mix of students. The freshmen are the easiest to pick out. They look all fresh-faced and eager to learn. The older ones, like me, look bored and want to get this over with.

"Hello everyone, and welcome to Composition!" This woman is a little too bright-eyed and bushy-tailed for a nine o'clock on a Monday morning. She needs to take it down a notch. Or maybe several. "My name is Rebecca Hayes, but you may call me Dr. Hayes."

A few people chuckle as she continues talking. I fidget as boredom sets in before sneaking a peek at my phone and wincing.

Three minutes.

Only one-hundred-and-eighty seconds have ticked by so far. How am I going to make it through this class for a full semester?

I force my attention to the professor as she delves into the requirements and expectations. A small part of me dies when she mentions a fifteen-page paper due at the end of the semester.

Fuck my life.

She might as well expect me to write a full-on book.

"Damn, but she's hot," Devon whispers, his eyes laser-focused on Dr. Hayes. "I've got a boner with her name written on it."

I scrunch my nose and glare. "Seriously, dude? I didn't need to know that. From now on, keep all dick comments to yourself."

"What can I say? It's the truth." He glances around the lecture hall. "Trust me, I'm not the only one with a chubby. Why do you think this class is so jammed packed?"

"Because it's a requirement." Duh.

"Did you check out her legs?" He doesn't wait for an answer. "Doesn't she make you hot for teacher?"

He snickers when I roll my eyes.

"She's fine."

Note to self—find a new place to sit.

I can't have Devon chirping in my ear all semester, or I'll end up failing the class.

"Bro, she's way better than that," he murmurs, salivating all over himself.

This guy is killing me. It takes effort to harness all of my concentration and tune out his noise. I don't understand why he's flipping out over this woman. Sure, she's pretty with blond hair cut in a sleek bob and deep brown eyes that sparkle with intelligence as they sweep over the lecture hall.

Most professors aren't exactly style icons. The word *dowdy* comes to mind. Although there's nothing frumpy about this woman. The black pencil skirt and white blouse she's wearing hug her generous curves. The first two buttons of her shirt have been left open, displaying a hint of cleavage.

All right, fine. I get it. She's a hot professor. But there's no way my mind can go there when I'm concerned about the workload she'll be piling on. Had I remembered this course was a requirement, I would have taken it last spring when I wasn't in season.

Now I'm fucked.

This class will bury me alive.

I clear that depressing thought from my head and zone back in as she says, "I'd like to introduce my teaching assistant." She points and smiles to someone sitting in the front row. My gaze follows her line of sight until a girl rises from her seat and turns to face the lecture hall.

A little zip of surprise sizzles through me when I realize it's Mia.

"Damn, she's hot, too." Devon rubs his hands together with anticipation. "This is going to be an awesome class."

I shoot him a scowl. "Shut the fuck up, Baker."

"All I'm saying is that she's hot." He holds up his hands and shakes his head as if he can't understand my irritation. "It's a compliment. Chicks love compliments."

I huff out a breath. "You really don't understand anything about women, do you? One of these days, some nice girl is going to kick your ass." My annoyance drains at that thought. "I only hope I'm around to see it happen."

"Please," he snorts, "the ladies love me. I have to fight them off with a stick."

Devon isn't wrong. The entire football team, even the benchwarmers, have their fair share of jersey chasers. It's a perk of being an athlete at Wesley. Most of these guys enjoy taking full advantage of it. It's easy for the attention to go straight to your head.

Both of them.

Once again, I focus on Mia.

Maybe this class won't be so bad after all.

Not that I wasn't expecting it, because it seems to be her modus operandi, but Mia has gone into avoidance mode. I'd hoped that we could level up our relationship after what occurred at Bang Bang, but that hasn't happened.

Which is fine.

She wants to be chased?

I'm game.

Chapter Fifteen

MIA

"I'll see everyone on Wednesday," Dr. Hayes announces, dismissing class for the day. Before the last word leaves her mouth, people scatter like rats trying to abandon a sinking ship.

I look around, careful to avoid eye contact with Beck. He's one of the few students who hasn't shoved their shit into their bag and taken off. I'd hoped that by ignoring him, he would get the hint and not wait around. It's not like we have anything to discuss.

We made out a week ago.

End of story.

Other than glancing at him when Dr. Hayes introduced me as the TA, I've kept my back firmly turned to him. Although that doesn't mean I haven't felt his gaze burning holes through me. It was all I could do not to squirm on my chair and peek over my shoulder.

Somehow, I resisted the urge.

Barely.

It's shitty luck that I've ended up TA'ing for Beck's class. What are the odds?

I've tried so hard not to think about the way he touched me at the club, but it's always simmering in the back of my mind. I'm ashamed to admit how many self-love sessions I've had regarding that incident.

I just need to get through the school year, and then we can go our separate ways. I won't have to worry about running into him around every corner. When my heart clenches at the idea of never seeing Beck again, I sweep the feeling aside and ignore it.

I give Beck a bit of side-eye only to find him taking his sweet damn time packing up his stuff.

Ugh.

Can't the guy do me a solid and move it along?

A nervous sweat breaks out across my brow as I try to delay the inevitable.

"Mia," Dr. Hayes says, "do you have a moment?"

And just like that, a lifeline is thrown.

Thank you, Dr. Hayes!

With a rush of breath, I haul the strap of my bag onto my shoulder before racing to the podium.

First semester of freshman year, I ended up in Dr. Hayes' Composition class. I've always enjoyed reading, but she helped me fall in love with the written word. Dr. H gave me the confidence I needed to let my creativity flow. After that semester, I registered for every course she offered at the university.

From beneath the thick fringe of my lashes, I watch as Beck and his friend—who I'm guessing is also a football player, because he's got that whole doesn't-have-a-neck thing going on—pack up their belongings before moving to the center aisle and heading toward the exit.

A relieved breath escapes from my lips when the door closes behind them. I was looking forward to working with Dr. Hayes this semester, now I'm dreading it.

The pretty blond professor snaps her briefcase shut before glancing at me. "Thanks again for taking this position at the last minute."

The graduate student who was originally scheduled to assist her ended up taking the semester off, so she asked me to fill in. There's really not much to the position. All I have to do is copy handouts and grade papers. If there are students who need extra attention, I'll meet with them.

"It's not a problem," I tell her. "I'm happy to do it."

At least an hour ago, I was.

Now? Not so much.

"How's the law school application process going?" she asks. "Did you finish them up?"

I shake my head. It's another thing on my to-do list. "Not yet. I'll be working on them over the weekend."

"If you want me to proofread anything, just text me. I'm more than happy to help." She smiles. "I can't believe you'll be graduating this spring! It doesn't seem like all that long ago you were in my freshman comp class."

My lips lift at the memory. "Tell me about it. The last couple of years have flown by."

"I'm so proud of you, Mia. You've done well at Wesley, and I have no doubt that you'll get accepted at every school you apply to." She reaches out and squeezes my shoulder. "You're going to do great things, I just know it."

Her words of praise leave a thick lump of emotion sitting in the middle of my throat. "Thank you, I appreciate you saying that."

"It's the truth. You've worked hard, and now it's paying off."

"I hope so." There's a fear in the back of my mind that I won't get accepted into law school, and I'll have to figure out a plan B.

"Everything will work out." She gives me a little wink. "We need more strong women in the world showing the boys how it's done."

I laugh and glance away. "I don't know about that." I've never considered myself a strong woman.

"With a great education, your options are limitless. Never sell yourself short."

"Thanks, Dr. H." Her words of encouragement mean a lot to me. She's someone I've always looked up to as a role model.

"You know better than that," she says with a mock frown. "When we're alone, you can call me Rebecca."

I nod.

"All right, we should get out of here. Unfortunately, I have an English department meeting to get to." She rolls her eyes. "Hopefully, there's still coffee left upstairs. Lord knows I'm going to need it."

I chuckle as she picks up her briefcase, and we head up the carpeted stairs to the exit.

After we push through the doors and into the corridor, Dr. Hayes says goodbye before turning toward the elevators that will take her to the fifth floor where the English offices are located. With one final wave, I pull out my phone and glance at the screen, noticing a few messages have popped up during class. As I take a step, a deep voice cuts through the quietness of the hallway.

"Hey, stranger."

I yelp in surprise and nearly bobble my phone when I find Beck leaning casually against the brick wall.

Turns out I wasn't nearly as successful in evading him as I'd originally thought.

Damn.

My gaze rakes over him, taking in every detail. I'm powerless to stop my physical reaction to him. My heartbeat picks up its tempo, and a million butterflies wing their way to life inside the confines of my belly.

I grab the strap of my bag and hug it closer as if that will protect me from him. "What are you doing here?"

"Just wanted to talk." He stares at me as if trying to sift through all of my private thoughts. "Seems like you're avoiding me again."

Doesn't he realize that I'm always trying to avoid him?

"Sorry, that's not the case. It's been busy. Speaking of busy," I take a hasty step away and point toward my salvation which comes in the form of an exit, "I really need to go."

The corners of his lips tilt upward as he lazily pushes away from the wall and saunters toward me. "Calm down, Stanbury. All I'm after is some conversation." There's a pause. "For now."

That's exactly what I'm afraid of.

"What do you want to discuss?" Before he can open his mouth, I blurt, "If it has anything to do with Composition, you should probably speak directly with Dr. Hayes. In fact, if you hurry, you can catch her at her office." I don't bother telling him that he won't find her there.

His lips tremble as if he's amused by my verbal diarrhea. "Sorry to burst your bubble, but you're the one I want to talk with."

"Oh." My shoulders fall.

"You kill me, Stanbury." A chuckle escapes from his lips. "Most girls can't get enough of me. And yet, you can't get away fast enough." He tilts his head. "I can't be the only one who sees the irony in that, can I?"

I shrug. "I guess you could always make it easier on yourself and find one of them instead."

He moves closer until his body towers over mine. "You're right, it would be a hell of a lot easier, but those girls don't interest me. You're the one I'm after."

His candor has me drawing in a breath.

"Wait a minute." His eyes dance with humor. "Have I actually managed to surprise you into silence? Can't say I thought that would ever happen."

It takes effort to shake myself out of the stupor I've fallen into. "Beck—"

"Go out with me, Mia." He pauses for a beat. "Give me another chance."

Is he joking?

No way.

Even though part of me wants to give in, my better judgment prevails, and I shake my head. "No, that's not a good idea."

"And why is that?"

"Because," I gulp down my rising nerves before forcing out the rest, "it's just not."

He presses closer until I have to crane my neck to hold his steady gaze. His voice drops. "I'm sorry for hurting you, Mia. Give me an opportunity to prove I'm not the same guy."

A chance like that would require me to put my heart on the line, and I'm unwilling to do that.

Not even for Beck.

Or maybe I should say, *especially for Beck*. He's the one guy who has the potential to cause untold amounts of pain.

"No." My breath catches at the back of my throat when he reaches out and traces the pad of his thumb against my lower lip. It takes everything inside me not to close my eyes and sink into his touch. Instead of doing that, I force myself to retreat, creating a sea of distance between us. My Beck-induced haze subsides, allowing me to think clearly again.

"It's better if we remain friends," I tell him.

His brows lift. "Are we friends?"

Maybe.

Sort of.

When I keep my lips pressed together, he grins. "I guess that's a good enough place to start." He slings his arm around my shoulder and hauls me close. "What do you say we have lunch together?" He gives me a wink. "As friends, of course."

"Um—"

No. Absolutely not. Every time I'm around this guy, I turn to putty in his hands.

"Excellent. I know the perfect place. You like subs, right?"

Not waiting for an answer, he steers me toward the doors that lead outside.

I groan.

What have I gotten myself into?

Better question—how do I get out?

Chapter Sixteen

BECK

Grinders R Us is the best coffeehouse on campus. It's where everyone stops to grab their daily dose of caffeine. Sometimes more than once. As I walk past the small brick building, a familiar profile catches my attention, and my footsteps falter.

There's been no movement on the Mia front. It's been a week since I asked her for a second chance and talked her into having lunch with me.

All right, maybe *forced* would be a better word for it.

No matter what I do, I can't seem to make headway with this girl. I've dropped by her apartment unannounced.

She's not there.

Or so Alyssa tells me.

I've tried hanging around after class, but she's cagey. Sometimes she heads up to Dr. Hayes' office.

I'm getting desperate.

Getting?

Ha!

You trucked by desperate a couple of years ago.

It takes a moment to snap out of my thoughts and to realize that

I'm pressed up against the picture window, fogging up the glass like a serial stalker who's left his van running fifty feet away.

As I take a quick step from the coffee shop, her gaze flits to the window and locks on mine. The smile curving her lips falters.

Busted.

Not knowing what else to do, I lift my hand in a tentative wave. That's when I notice she's not alone. There's a guy parked across from her.

Jealousy rushes through my veins as I straighten to my full height. Before I can get a game plan together, I'm yanking open the door and flying through it. Mia's dark eyes widen when she sees me barreling toward her.

If I honestly thought she didn't feel *something*, I'd cut bait and move on. But the girl melts every time I lay my hands on her. And if that's not hot, I don't know what is. Am I really supposed to walk away from that kind of attraction?

I don't think so.

When I'm close enough, I catch the tail end of their conversation.

"I was thinking if you're free this Friday, we might..."

His words trail off when he realizes that Mia's attention has become snagged by something else. Or maybe I should say—*someone else*.

The guy sitting across from her glances at me. I see the moment recognition sets in. His whole face lights up like he won big bucks on a scratch-off. "Hollingsworth, my man! How are you doing?"

"I'm good." His overly friendly demeanor has me searching his face, wondering if I know him. Although, I'm pretty sure I don't. Let's face it, this campus revolves around football. People recognize me everywhere I go. "How about you?"

He grins, vibrating like a puppy with excitement. "I'm awesome!"

Now that pleasantries are out of the way, I stare at Mia. "Hey."

"Beck," she murmurs as heat stings her cheeks.

Her attention never deviates from me. Which is exactly where I like it. The guy she's with doesn't seem to notice. What an idiot.

Before I can say anything else, he gushes, "That was a fantastic game last weekend. You killed North Carolina. There's no way you guys won't take home a championship this year!"

"That's the plan." Normally, I can talk all day long about football. Everything from the last game we played, who landed on the injury list, stats, to the upcoming draft. You name it, I can shoot the shit about it.

But right now?

Football is the last thing on my mind. It's not even a thought in my head.

"Hey, you want a coffee or something?" Her date jumps up from his seat like a Jack-in-the-box.

When Mia opens her mouth—most likely to protest—I cut her off.

"Thanks, I'd love one." I dig around in my pocket for a couple of bucks.

He throws up a hand and shakes his head. "No way, Hollingsworth, it's on me!" And then he's gone.

I have to say, getting rid of him was easier than expected. Once he takes his place at the back of the line, I settle on his seat.

Mia's eyes flash with irritation. "What do you think you're doing?"

I point to the chair as if it's obvious. "Sitting."

"I mean, here." She pauses before adding, "With me."

"I'm keeping you company while your boyfriend fetches me a coffee."

"He's not my boyfriend," she mutters, looking away.

A wide smile spreads across my face. "Good to know."

"It wouldn't matter if he was, because you and I aren't getting together."

"Never say never."

"I'm saying it, Beck." She enunciates the word. "*Never*. It's a firm *never* from me."

I shrug and push onward, undeterred by her negativity. "Stranger things have happened."

"Not that strange." She huffs out an exasperated breath. "Let's get back to the original question. Is there a reason you stopped by?"

"Actually," an idea pops into my head, and I run with it, "there is. I thought we could drive home together next weekend."

Confusion flickers across her face. "What's next weekend?"

"It's my parent's twenty-fifth anniversary party, remember?"

She winces. "It must have slipped my mind. Between school and applications, it's been busy."

"You're still going, right?" Everything in me stills as I wait for her answer.

"Yeah, I promised my parents I would."

Excellent. It works out well because next weekend is a bye week for the team, so we don't have a game. I'm looking forward to getting off campus and taking a breather. Even if my parents are throwing a massive shindig, at least Mia will be there. And maybe I'll have a chance to put my hands on her and seduce her over to the dark side.

"What do you say? Want to share a ride and reduce our carbon footprint at the same time?"

She bites her lip and diligently avoids eye contact. "That's probably not a good idea."

"Why not? You don't want to leave the earth a better place for the next generation?"

The corners of her mouth hitch into a faint smile before she presses her lips together, and it disappears.

"Wait a minute," I point to her face, "was that a smile?"

She shakes her head. "Nope."

"Yes, it was," I say with exaggeration. "I saw your lips twitch."

"It was a muscle spasm. Nothing more."

"I don't think so."

She shrugs.

I settle against the chair. This little exchange is going better than I expected. "How about we agree to disagree?"

"Fine." She clears her throat. "I'm all about eliminating our carbon footprint. It's riding with you that I'm dubious of."

"And why is that? Are you afraid you might succumb to my devastating charms?" I give her a wink. "Don't worry, I'll do my best to fight you off."

She rolls her eyes. But they're still simmering with humor, which is a good sign. It's sure as hell better than her usual reaction. So, I'll take it.

I lower my voice. "FYI—if it helps, I'll let you touch me as much as you want."

"Beck..." she murmurs, dropping her gaze to the coffee cup in front of her.

Unable to help myself, I place my fingers under her chin and lift it, so she has no other choice but to look at me. "What?"

"We talked about this."

"Did we?" I wait a beat. "And what did we decide?"

"That we're better off as friends."

"Yeah, about that," with my fingers still gripping her chin, I lean in and press closer to the table, "I've given it some thought and decided to nix that idea."

Her mouth opens.

"Here's your coffee!"

The spell is broken when an oversized container of java is placed in front of me. "Hope you like cream and sugar."

Damn, that line moved quicker than I thought it would. Mia jerks out of my grasp, and I reluctantly settle on the chair as my hand drops to the table.

"Great, thanks."

"My pleasure, Hollingsworth!"

When he takes a chair from a nearby table, dragging it next to Mia, I rise to my feet and grab my drink. "I should probably get moving, but thanks again."

"Anytime." His voice turns a little wistful. "Sure you can't stay for a while?"

"Sorry." I jerk my thumb toward the door. "I've got class."

His face falls. "Maybe another time."

I glance at Mia and wonder what the hell she sees in this clown. This guy's interest should be focused on her, not me. What a dumbass.

"Think about my offer and get back to me," I tell her.

"That's not necessary, I'll drive myself," she says quickly.

I shrug as if it's no big deal. "You know where to find me if you change your mind."

"I won't."

Yeah, that's exactly what I'm afraid of.

Chapter Seventeen

BECK

"Is there anyone who hasn't outlined their paper yet?" Dr. Hayes asks at the end of class. Her dark gaze slides over the sea of students before coming to rest on mine.

Between my football schedule and cracking the books, I've been buried. I've jotted down a few ideas, but it hasn't progressed any further than that. I'll admit to dragging my feet on this. Have I mentioned how much I hate writing papers?

With the fiery passion of a thousand burning suns.

I really need to pull the trigger and get some words on paper. It's already mid-September. The semester is flying by, and football will only ramp up in intensity the deeper we get into the season. Most of the professors at Wesley are pretty cool when it comes to allowing me to hand in assignments a few days late or rescheduling a test if it conflicts with an away game.

And why shouldn't they be?

Everyone knows that the football program brings in the big bucks. And big money means that these professors can fund their research projects. It's a mutually beneficial relationship. No one wants to bite the hand that feeds them.

Devon elbows me in the ribs. "Dude, professor hottie is totally checking you out."

"Huh?" I try not to pay too much attention to what comes out of Devon's mouth. It's ninety-percent bullshit. Both on and off the field.

"Dr. H, dumbass. She's been checking you out the entire hour."

Sometimes I wonder if Devon has taken one too many hits to the head. Concussion testing has clearly failed him.

"You are seriously one lucky bastard," he continues when I fail to show the appropriate amount of enthusiasm. "Dr. H is the scholarly version of Jessica Simpson. And we all know how I feel about her."

Unfortunately, we do. I was hanging out at his house last year and walked in on him spanking the monkey to thoughts of her. It was a permanently scarring experience. I can never un-hear those groans again. Even thinking about the incident makes me shudder.

As soon as Dr. Hayes dismisses us for the day, I pack up my computer and immediately beeline toward Mia. My plan is to leave after practice on Friday evening, and I want to make sure she hasn't changed her mind about hitching a ride.

I know there's not a snowball's chance in hell of that happening, but I gotta ask, right?

Plus, it's another opportunity to talk to her. And I'll take whatever opening I can find.

"Beck," Dr. Hayes calls out, "would you mind sticking around for a quick chat?"

Damn.

The look of relief that floods Mia's face as she scampers from the room hits me where it counts. Right in the old ego.

"Sure, no problem." I swing around and head back to the front of the room.

Dr. Hayes flips through a few papers before glancing at me as the lecture hall empties. I never really noticed it, but Devon is right. She does bear a strong resemblance to Jessica Simpson with her blond hair, deep brown eyes, and curvy body. I shake that thought from my mind and focus on what's being said. The sooner I can get this over with, the quicker I can get out of here.

Maybe I can catch up to Mia.

Not that she'll wait around.

"I wanted to check-in and talk about the progress you're making on your paper," she says.

Well, shit.

I shift my weight and come clean. There's no point in lying. "I haven't started writing it yet, but I've narrowed down the topics."

She raises a brow. "All right, I suppose that's a start."

I flash her a grin, and my muscles loosen. "I've been meaning to get moving on it." Actually, I was hoping Mia could give me some direction. That's part of her TA job, right?

"Let's start with your top two choices and see if we can get you on the right path."

"Sure." I grab my notebook from my backpack before flipping through the pages. "The first topic has to do with the long-term effects of concussions on football players." I glance up to see how that subject has resonated. When she nods, I continue. "And the second is compensating athletes at the college level."

With a thoughtful look, she tilts her head. Her bangs slide over her eyes, and she lifts her fingers, tucking a thick lock of hair behind her ear. "Hmmm, those are both interesting choices."

Relief flows through me that she's on-board with the themes I'm considering. "I'm not sure which one would work better."

"There's a lot of research available regarding concussions and helmet testing. So, my advice would be to go with that one."

"Yeah," I admit with a nod, "I was thinking the same thing."

Great.

When I shove my notebook into my backpack, Dr. Hayes lays her hand on my forearm. Surprised by the contact, my movements falter. I glance at her fingers before staring at her in question.

"Don't run away yet." Her lips curve into a smile. "I spoke with Coach Taylor last week. He mentioned how important it is for you to keep your grades up, so you don't get benched." She steps closer. "I told him I would work closely with you to make sure that doesn't happen."

"Thanks. I appreciate it."

Her gaze stays pinned to mine. "I have to admit that I'm always impressed with the athletes we have on campus. It's not easy to balance academics along with athletic responsibilities. That's a lot of stress and pressure to deal with."

A strange prickle of unease blooms in the pit of my belly, but I quickly brush it away. Under normal circumstances, when a woman touches me and stares at me like I'm a juicy steak, I'd assume she was flirting, but that can't be. Dr. H is my professor.

"It's nothing I can't handle."

I'm oddly aware of her fingers draped across my forearm. It's like they're burning a hole through my flesh. When I remain silent, she flashes another smile and leans toward me. The way she angles her body gives me a straight shot down her blouse. I have to be a good ten inches taller than her. Even though I'm not trying to peek down the front of her shirt, it's hard not to notice the generous swells of her breasts.

"Just know my door is always open if you need help with English or any other subject. I'd be more than happy to help you."

Umm...

"Thanks." I pause, wishing she would remove her hand. "If anything comes up, I'll let you know."

"Please do." The way she continues staring only heightens my unease. "I've worked with several athletes over the years, and it's always been a rewarding experience for both of us. I wouldn't have a problem reaching out to your other professors and asking for extended deadlines on your behalf. Most are accommodating, especially if they know a student is working closely with a colleague."

This has to be the strangest convo I've ever had with a teacher.

Not to mention, most uncomfortable.

I can't decide if she's talking strictly about academics or not.

Either way, this conversation has left a strange pit sitting in my gut. I'm probably reading something into the situation that isn't there. Dr. Hayes is a beautiful woman. My guess is that she doesn't need to troll her classes to get laid. She's probably got guys lined up around the block.

I'm definitely making a mountain out of a molehill.

When she lifts her hand, the unease dissolves and leaves me feeling like an idiot.

"Why don't we plan on getting together later next week, and we'll discuss your progress. That way, I'll know you're on track." Her lips lift. "How does that sound?"

"Sure, that works."

"My goal is to give you the necessary tools you need to be successful. Not only at this university but in life."

"I appreciate your help." I'm a dipshit for questioning if there were ulterior motives at play. Dr. Hayes is just being friendly. She obviously goes above and beyond for her students.

"If you have any questions, my contact information is on the syllabus."

"Yup." I hitch my backpack higher onto my shoulder before taking a step in retreat.

"Here, just a minute." She grabs a small pad of paper and a pen before scribbling something down. Then she tears the page off and holds it out to me. "That's my cell number. Usually, it's only available to my grad students, so please don't give it out."

I take the paper and look at her name and number. "Thanks."

"It's the quickest way to get ahold of me."

I glance at her before stuffing the scrap into the front pocket of my jeans.

"If you have any questions, shoot me a text. Even if it's to talk or unload. All right?"

"Yeah," I mutter, feeling weird again, "thanks."

She picks up her sleek black briefcase. "Well, I need to get to my office. I'm meeting with a group of graduate students to work on their thesis."

"Okay." I inch away from her. The more distance I put between us, the better I feel. I lift my hand into a wave. "I'll see you on Friday."

She winks. "If not sooner."

I jerk my head into a nod.

And then I'm gone, taking the carpeted stairs two at a time before pushing out through the lecture hall doors into the empty corridor.

Once I'm there, I expel the breath from my lungs, not realizing I'd been holding it.

Am I nuts, or was that woman coming on to me?

My guess is that I'm losing it. There is no way Dr. Hayes was flirting.

It's all in my head.

It has to be.

Chapter Eighteen

MIA

I park the Jeep in the circular drive and grab my duffle bag before heading up the wide stone steps in front of the house. The door is unlocked, which means someone has to be home. Once inside the two-story foyer, I call out, "Hello?" I pause and wait for a response. When silence greets me, I raise my voice and bellow, *"Mom? Dad? Are you home?"*

"In the kitchen, honey," Mom yells back. "I hope you're hungry."

Is that a joke?

I'm always hungry.

Especially for a homecooked meal.

I set my bag next to the front door before heading through the hallway that leads to the kitchen. Mom is at the oversized marble island chopping vegetables. A smile lights up her face when she sees me. I give her a quick kiss and hug before beelining to the fridge and pulling out a bottle of water. Happy to be home for a few days, I settle on the stool across from her.

"How was the drive?" she asks.

"It was fine." I pause for a beat before adding, "Although my Jeep made a few weird noises when I started it up. But it went away and didn't give me any other problems."

"Hmm." Her brows beetle together. "Make sure to mention it to your father when he gets home."

"When will that be?" I untwist the cap and lift the bottle to my lips, taking a long swig.

"Tomorrow morning." Even though the smile remains intact, it doesn't quite reach her eyes. "He's been out of town the last few days."

"Where did he go this time?" It feels like my father spends more time on business trips than he does at home. The man needs to take it easy. Whenever I mention it, he tells me that he loves his job and has no intention of slowing down anytime soon.

"New York, maybe." Mom lifts her shoulders. "That man is always on the go. At this point, all of the cities blur together."

"One of these days, he's going to have a heart attack." It's something I think about all the time. I don't want to lose anyone else. "He needs to stop working so hard and enjoy his life."

"You're preaching to the choir, honey. I keep telling him the same thing," she murmurs, focusing on the carrots and celery she's chopping, "but you know how he is."

Yes, I do. He's a workaholic, and I'm not sure if that will ever change.

"Your father's birthday is coming up soon," she says, "and I've been thinking about booking a cruise for us."

I perk up. "That's a great idea!"

She glances at me and quirks her lips into a tentative smile. The sadness that is always present in her eyes vanishes. "It's been years since we took a vacation." Looking thoughtful, she pauses before shaking her head. "It must have been before..." Pain flashes in her eyes, and she quickly glances at the vegetables on the cutting board.

"I know, Mom," I say softly. "Don't ask him, just book it."

She worries her lower lip. "You really think I should do it?"

"Definitely. That way, he'll be forced to take the time off."

"True," she sighs. "I'll give it some thought."

I rise to my feet. "Do you need any help with dinner?"

"Nope, it's all under control." She looks at the clock on the stove. "It should be ready in an hour."

"Okay. I'm going up to take a bath and relax a little." I love my apartment at school, but I miss my jetted tub.

"Take your time, honey. We can eat whenever you're ready." She dumps the veggies into a sauté pan. "Maybe we can rent a movie and hang out tonight. Or did you make other plans?"

"I'm all yours." A low-key evening with Mom is exactly what I need.

She smiles, and the last wisps of sadness disappear from her eyes. "I wasn't sure if you'd want to get together with a few friends and go out."

"No one is around, they're all at school."

"I'm sure Beck is back." She gives me a look chock-full of speculation. "I wondered if you two would drive home together."

"He asked," I admit reluctantly, "but I said no."

"How come?" She uses an oversized wooden spoon to push around the vegetables in the pan. "Beck is such a lovely boy."

First of all, he is *definitely* not a boy.

And second—

"No one on the face of this planet has ever referred to Beckett Hollingsworth as *lovely*."

She throws a look over her shoulder as her lips tremble upward. "Oh, I don't know about that. He's pretty darn lovely to look at, don't you think?"

My mouth drops open. "Oh my God! Did you seriously just say that?"

"I did," she chuckles. For the first time in forever, there's a light-heartedness to her. It's nice to see.

"You know," she continues before I can recover, "I've always thought he had feelings for you."

"Mom," I groan, embarrassment licking at my cheeks, "he does not. Trust me on this. Beck has more girls sniffing around him than he knows what to do with." Which is exactly why I keep shutting down his advances.

Fool me once, shame on you.

Fool me twice, and I deserve everything I get.

Ignoring me, she muses, "Remember how protective he was when you two were kids? That boy always sat next to you on the bus." A distant look enters her eyes as if she's tumbled back in time. "I always felt better knowing he was looking out for you."

Of course, I remember. It's probably where my infatuation with Beck stems from.

"He really is a sweet boy. Maybe a little misunderstood. I wish his father wouldn't be so hard on him."

I scrunch my nose. "You think Archie is hard on Beck?"

"Yes, I do. He treats Ari like the heir to the kingdom. I'm sure it was difficult for Beck to grow up in his older brother's shadow. Everything came so easily to Ari. School, athletics, popularity. He never had to work for any of it. And Beck," she shrugs, "he's different. Sometimes it seems like no matter how hard that poor boy tries, he will never please Archie." She glances at me. "When Brianna was alive, you both had your own interests. We tried to cultivate them without making you girls feel like you were in competition with each other."

That's true.

Brianna was a gifted artist. She loved to draw and paint. Even though she did well in school, math was always a struggle. Academics came easier to me. And picking up a tennis racket felt like second nature. My parents attended art shows and tennis tournaments. They never made us feel like one was more favored or important than the other. We each had our own talents, and when one of us did well, they always applauded it.

Now that I think about it, I guess what Mom is saying isn't wrong. Archie *does* treat his older son like the heir apparent. He's always crowing about Ari's latest accomplishments. And Beck is an afterthought.

A kernel of pity blooms inside my chest.

Does it bother Beck that Archie lavishes so much attention on his brother?

How could it not?

"Anyway," Mom says, drawing me back to our conversation. "Beck seems to be doing well for himself."

"Yes, he is." I fall silent as Mom's words swirl through my mind. It takes effort to push all thoughts of Beck away, but that's nothing new. "Okay, I'm going to head upstairs for a bath. I'll be down in a bit."

"Sounds good, honey." I take a few steps toward the hallway when she says, "Oh, I forgot to mention that I picked up a dress for you to wear tomorrow. You're going to love it."

"Thanks, Mom."

"Let me know what you think. It's draped over the chaise in your room."

"Will do," I call over my shoulder before jogging up the stairs.

Fifteen minutes later, I'm soaking in a frothy tub of bubbles. With my head resting against the porcelain edge, I close my eyes and let the tension leak from my body. I hate to admit it, but I can't stop thinking about what happened at the club. The way Beck set me on the desk and...

Yeah.

What is it about him that makes me lose total control?

Even thinking about the way he buried his face between my legs sends a tidal wave of arousal crashing over me. The pleasure he's capable of is like nothing I've ever experienced before. Is it any wonder I find him so damn addictive?

An uncomfortable ache throbs to life between my thighs as I shift in the warm water.

Don't do it.

Don't you dare touch yourself and think about him.

With my eyes closed, my fingertips trail across my breasts before carefully circling around the puckered tips. Hot licks of need spike through me. It's one thing to have Beck bring me to my knees and quite another to touch myself while conjuring up an image of him. If I were smart, I would ignore the heat swirling through my core, but I can't.

I'm too turned on.

My hand disappears beneath the sudsy surface until its able to stroke over the lips of my pussy. When my fingertips brush over my clit, I groan and spread my legs wider. One image of Beck with his face pressed against my core and his tongue dancing across my silky flesh is all it takes to push me over the edge. My muscles spasm as I moan out my orgasm. My fingers keep moving, stroking over my clit until I've wrung every shudder from my body.

The moment my mind clears, I groan. Only this time, it has nothing to do with pleasure.

What the hell is wrong with me?

Frustrated with myself for this infatuation that refuses to die, I suck in a breath and sink beneath the surface until my entire body is submerged.

Beck is a weakness I can't afford. I keep waiting for him to lose interest and move on, but that has yet to happen. What I know is this—if I'm not careful, he could break down every last one of my defenses, and I'm afraid it's only a matter of time before that happens.

Chapter Nineteen

MIA

I stare in the gilded mirror propped against the far wall of my room before twisting and turning, trying to assess myself from every angle. When I saw the gorgeous gray garment Mom had mentioned last night, I'd thought it was a dress. But it's actually two separate pieces. The top is beaded and sleeveless with a high neck. The skirt is a tulle concoction that flutters around my knees.

There is no way I would have picked out something like this for myself. And yet, it fits me perfectly and transforms me into a fairy princess. Once dressed, I move to the vanity and apply a bit of silvery eyeshadow that glitters and shiny lip gloss before twisting my hair into a sleek bun at the top of my head.

By the time I grab the small silver sequin clutch that has a stash of makeup along with my phone, Mom and Dad are waiting downstairs in the entryway.

Archibald and Caroline's anniversary party begins promptly at six o'clock and is being held at their estate. I peeked out the living room window a few hours ago, and there was a small fleet of trucks parked in front of the Hollingsworth mansion. Caroline is known for throwing elegant and sophisticated parties.

Mom is wearing a chic black shift dress that accentuates her trim figure. Diamonds drip from her ears and decorate her neck. Dad looks handsome in a black suit with a crisp white button-down and purple tie.

"I knew that dress would fit perfectly," Mom greets in a smug tone as I walk down the staircase. "You look stunning."

"You're an absolute vision, honey," Dad pipes up before pocketing his phone. He's worse than a teenager with his electronics. You would think the stock market depended upon Daniel Stanbury knowing every little hiccup.

I fluff the tulle with my hands as I arrive at the bottom step. "Thanks, Mom. It's a beautiful dress."

"Remember," she admonishes, "you make it beautiful, not the other way around." She gives me a little wink before tugging me close and dropping a kiss on the top of my head.

I glance at Dad, happy we're all together for a change. Mom and I had a great time last night curled up on the couch watching movies and eating popcorn. We laughed and talked about everything. Except Beck. After my little self-love session, I was relieved she didn't mention him again.

Dad walked through the door two hours ago, arriving home late. When I asked how the trip went, he shrugged and said as well as could be expected. Mom's face fell when he mentioned leaving again at the end of the week.

How will their marriage get better if he's never around to work on it?

I'm tempted to pull him aside and tell him that, but I'm not sure it's my place. They're the ones who need to fix their marriage, not me.

"We should probably head over," Dad says.

Mom grabs the small silver-wrapped gift sitting on the table near the door.

I glance at the pretty box in her hand. "What are you giving them?" I have no idea what you buy for the couple who has everything.

"A five-hundred-dollar spa gift certificate." She flashes me a smile. "I was thinking they could indulge in a couples massage."

Mom is so good at these things. "I bet they'll love that." I know I would.

"Yeah," she says a bit wistfully, "who couldn't use a bit of pampering from time to time?"

Note to self—tell my father to buy her that for Christmas.

As Dad reaches for the brushed nickel door handle, his phone buzzes with an incoming call. He quickly nips it from his pocket. One look at the screen has his brows knitting together.

"For goodness' sake, Daniel, you just returned home." Mom's voice bristles with impatience. "Can't we enjoy one evening without work interruptions?"

Not that I blame her for being irritated, but her remarks leave me flinching with unease.

"Sorry," Dad mutters, not bothering to take his gaze off his cell. "I need to take this call." He glances up with a contrite smile. "It shouldn't take more than ten minutes, then I'm all yours." He presses the phone to his ear and opens the front door, quickly ushering us outside. He mouths, "You two go, and I'll be over as soon as I wrap up this last piece of business."

Mom's lips flatten into a tight line. It's clear that she's fed up with his behavior. "You have ten minutes before I send Archie over to drag you to the party."

Relief washes over his features as he gives her a quick peck on the cheek. Once we cross over the threshold, the door closes behind us.

I glance at Mom to see if she's all right. "You need to book that cruise ASAP," I say quietly. "Getting him away for a week is the only way he'll take a break."

"Yeah," she mutters, sounding unconvinced, "I'll call the travel agent on Monday and see what we can do."

As we step off the brick pathway onto the lawn that connects the two properties, the heels of our shoes sink into the grass. At eight-thousand square feet, I always thought our house was massive, but the Hollingsworth mansion is double that. It's palatial. Mrs. Graham, the housekeeper, should hand out a baggie of breadcrumbs to visitors so they don't get lost.

As we arrive, there's a line of cars pulling into the circular drive before guests hand over the keys to guys dressed in white button-down shirts and black slacks. The valets take the vehicles and park them along the end of the street. Once we reach the front door, it opens before we can raise a fist to knock, and we're immediately ushered inside by Mrs. Graham. A waiter in a crisp-looking tux is stationed strategically near the front entrance with a silver tray of crystal flutes filled with champagne.

We grab a glass of the golden bubbly liquid before walking through the massive entryway toward the kitchen. Guests mingle in every corner. Mom and I greet a few people before making our way outside to the patio. A large white tent has been erected in the backyard. Since it's early fall, and the temperature is seasonable, the flaps have been tied back. Tables with stunning pink and white flower arrangements dot the interior. Crystal chandeliers hang from the ceiling of the tent. Sleek white seating areas are grouped together. All the decor is done in shades of pink with silver accents. It's all very elegant.

On the far side of the tent is a parquet dance floor. A stringed quartet plays classical music. Mom mentioned that later tonight there will be a DJ and dancing.

Even though there must be at least a hundred people present, my attention is immediately snagged by Beck, who looks handsome in a suit and tie, as he loiters at the bar with one of his cousins.

His fingers are wrapped around a thick crystal tumbler filled with amber liquid on the rocks. My breath becomes wedged at the back of my throat as his gaze drifts over the crowd before settling on mine. When heat leaps to life in his eyes, all I can think about is the way I touched myself last night in the tub.

I shove the memory from my mind before a blush can rise to my cheeks. A hum of unwanted attraction sizzles through my blood. My hand flutters to my lower belly to settle the horde of butterflies trying to wing their way to life.

No matter how patient I've been, these feelings never seem to dissipate. If anything, they've only grown stronger. I'm wondering if my attraction to Beck will ever fade.

It's almost a relief when Archibald and Caroline join us. When Archie asks where Dad is, Mom rolls her eyes and tells him about the business call. Even though I try to focus on their conversation, my interest is drawn to Beck. I'm hyperaware of his every move. The way his focus stays trained on me sends a surge of shivers careening down my spine.

It's only when Mom elbows me gently in the side that I snap to awareness. Her lips twist into a smile as she nods toward Beck's father. "Archie was asking how classes are going this semester."

Heat fills my face as I refocus my attention. "Sorry." I shake my head and lie through my teeth. "I was admiring the decor."

"You might have been admiring something else," Mom says under her breath before taking a sip of champagne.

Her mumbled comment sends another wave of heat flooding through me. It takes effort to keep the smile plastered across my face as I return the elbow. I do my best to ignore her as her shoulders shake with silent laughter.

Archibald and Caroline take a moment to glance around at their hard work.

"It was all my lovely wife. She spent the last couple of months planning this party, and it turned out beautifully."

Beck's mother beams at the compliment.

"Everything is gorgeous," I tell her, relieved that no one other than my mother noticed the reason for my distraction. If this is how the rest of the evening will go, I'm in trouble. I bring the flute to my lips and swallow down the bubbly liquid.

Caroline glances around the festivities with a satisfied expression. "I think we all know this is a dry run for when I finally have a wedding to plan."

That simple comment sends the champagne down the wrong pipe, and I sputter. Tears sting my eyes as a wide palm lands on the spot between my shoulder blades.

"Your parents can't take you anywhere, can they?"

Still coughing, I whirl around to find Ari, Beck's handsome older brother. A wide grin curves his lips. Before I'm able to react, he pulls me into his arms for a hug.

"Long time no see, squirt," he whispers in my ear.

Throughout college and the first year of law school, Ari came home during the summers and interned at his father's practice. This year, he received a prestigious clerking position with a law firm near Stanford. I haven't seen him since last Christmas.

"Good to see you, too," I laugh, squeezing him tight. "I missed you this summer. The office wasn't the same without you."

"I'm almost afraid to ask who your standing lunch date was." Before I can answer, he says, "Please tell me it wasn't Mark from accounting."

I burst out laughing as the knot in my belly loosens. "What do I look like, a glutton for punishment?" Mark is a nice guy, but that doesn't mean I want to spend my entire lunch break learning about the nitty-gritty world of payable and receivable accounts. The lunches where he tagged along with us only solidified the notion that I made the right decision not to pursue a career in accounting.

Caroline shoots my mother a sly smile. "They make an adorable couple. Don't they, Julia? Maybe there'll be a wedding in the near future, after all."

A gurgle of surprise rises in my throat as Ari tugs me even closer. "Looks like there's some plotting and scheming underfoot."

Unsure how to respond, I press my lips together and remain silent.

From the corner of my eye, I watch as Beck joins our group. His lips are drawn down at the edges, and I fidget beneath the heat of his stare.

Unsure how to extract myself from this uncomfortable situation, I lift the flute to my lips and guzzle down the champagne before wiggling the stem. "If you'll excuse me, I need a refill."

"Someone's thirsty," Ari chuckles. "Would you like me to get you another?"

I slip easily from his hold. "No, thanks." And then I'm off, sliding through the crowd with a relieved breath.

When I was a kid, I used to think Beck was Ari's mini-me. They both have the same dark wavy hair, bright green eyes, and athletic build. Now that they are older, the differences are more perceptible. The breadth of Beck's shoulders is a little broader, his chest is a smidge wider, his arms bigger and more muscular.

There is such a strong family resemblance that it would seem natural to be attracted to both. But I'm not. When Ari had pressed me close, I'd felt nothing. My pulse didn't skitter. The muscles in my belly didn't contract. My core didn't flood with arousal.

It's a disconcerting realization.

Needing a breath of fresh air, I hand my flute to a passing waiter. Instead of grabbing another drink, I rush from the tent. As much as I want to avoid Beck for the rest of the evening, I realize my time is running out. He won't allow me to elude him indefinitely. One thing I realize about my neighbor is that when he wants something, the guy goes after it with a single-minded determination.

And what he wants, is me.

Chapter Twenty

MIA

So far this evening, I've been able to evade Beck's evil clutches.

Barely.

He's spent all of his time stalking me through the party like I'm prey. It's exhausting to get embroiled in conversations as I keep a cautious eye out for him. The guest count has swelled, and a lot of them are family or close friends, so Beck has been dragged into countless exchanges.

His frustration is palpable.

It's kind of amusing.

If my luck continues to hold until the end of the night, I'll be able to slip away without him laying his hands on me.

By now, the party is in full swing. The quartet has been replaced by a DJ, and everyone is on the dance floor busting a move. Even Archie and Caroline are out there enjoying themselves. I search the crowd until my focus settles on Mom and Dad.

Shocker—Dad has his phone in his hand and is staring down at it. His thumbs are moving over the screen like crazy. Mom stands a few feet away with a hollow look in her eyes as she lifts the champagne to her mouth and finishes the glass.

Pursing my lips, I shake my head.

What is wrong with him?

Why can't Dad take a few hours away from work like he promised? I'm tempted to march over and grab the phone from his hands. Maybe then he would smarten up and pay attention to his wife.

As I take a step toward them, my feet grind to a halt when Beck sidles up to my mother with a fresh glass of champagne.

Like she needs that.

They converse before her gaze sweeps over the surrounding area. I quickly duck behind a potted plant, watching as she shrugs and shakes her head.

Damn. That was close.

"Who are we hiding from?" a voice whispers in my ear.

I yelp and jump in surprise. Thank goodness I'm not holding a drink. It would be all over the front of me.

I spin around and glare at Ari before smacking his arm. "What are you doing sneaking up on me like that? You nearly gave me a heart attack."

He crouches next to me and uses one hand to part the floppy leaves before staring through them. "You didn't tell me who we're hiding from. Is it Mark from accounting?"

"Oh God," I groan, "is he here?"

"Yup. I had an incredibly tedious conversation about the gross profits of the firm and what overhead could be cut if we're looking to improve it. Here are my thoughts on the matter—his position should be the first to go."

His comment brings a smile to my lips.

"Don't worry, if you're avoiding Mark, God's gift to the accounting world, he's," his words drop off before he says with a shitload of humor dancing in his voice, "*oh*, I see who has you cowering in the corner."

"I am not cowering!" When I poker up to my full height, the top of my head knocks into Ari's chin, and he staggers back a step before grabbing his jaw.

"Ow! Damn girl, that hurt!"

I cover my mouth with both hands and suck in a sharp breath. "I'm so sorry! I didn't mean to do that!"

He swipes his tongue across his teeth and winces. "I think you might have chipped a tooth."

"*No!*" I groan, embarrassed to have caused such damage.

He straightens and drops his hands. "Just kidding."

My shoulders collapse in relief as I shake my head and glare. "You're such a jerk."

Instead of responding to my comment, he says, "Uh-oh, looks like you've been made."

I glance at the spot across the tent where Beck and my mother have been conversing. Ari is right. As we speak, Beck is bulldozing his way through the crowd with a determined look on his face. A few people reach out, trying to detain him, but he's either not paying attention or deliberately ignoring them.

"I've got to go!" I squeak, taking a step toward the flaps of the tent. If I'm quick enough, I can disappear and make myself scarce.

Before I'm able to escape, Ari reaches out and grabs hold of my hand. "Oh no, you don't. How about we add some gasoline to the fire?"

"Huh?" I blink.

What the hell does that mean?

"Come on, let's dance."

I throw a cautious look over my shoulder at Beck as his brother drags me through a crowd of people. As we make our way to the dance floor, the music changes from an upbeat, fast-paced song to a slow one. Ari carves out a small space for the two of us before wrapping his arms around me and tugging me close. His cologne wafts around me, but it doesn't make my senses go haywire.

From the corner of my eye, I watch Beck settle at the edge of the dance floor with a scowl as he shoves his hands in the pockets of his suit pants.

Is Ari trying to make his brother jealous?

I glance at him. "Why are you doing this?"

A grin flashes across his face before he lowers his mouth to my ear. "What do you mean? I'm trying to help you out," he says innocently. "Seems like you want my brother to get the hint that you're not interested."

A rush of nerves scamper across my skin as I peek at Beck, only to realize he's disappeared from where he had taken up sentinel.

When I remain silent, Ari says with a chuckle, "Or am I wrong about that? Either way, the ball's in your court, squirt. I guess it's up to you to make the next move."

I nibble at my lower lip. This is what I wanted, right? For Beck to move on and leave me alone.

Except...

Relief isn't rushing through me the way it should be. And the sense of loss I feel is enough to swallow me whole.

I groan, knowing exactly what I have to do.

Chapter Twenty-One

BECK

Tonight has officially ended up in the shitter. I'd been looking forward to spending time with Mia away from campus, but that hasn't happened. It doesn't take a genius to realize that she's been avoiding me all evening.

For fuck's sake, she was hiding behind a potted palm.

No girl has ever gone to such great lengths in their quest to evade me.

It's official. My ego has been completely annihilated.

And then there's Ari, that rat bastard. Every time they were together, his arm was tucked around her waist. I'm this close to wrapping my hands around his neck and squeezing the damn life out of him.

Exactly when did he become so interested in Mia?

I can compete with a lot of guys, but not my brother.

Out of the two of us, Ari is the better man. There isn't anything he hasn't tried and succeeded at. High school, football, college, law school. Nothing fazes the guy. He comes, conquers, and then leaves.

If I didn't love him so damn much, I'd be annoyed.

My father can't sing his praises loud enough. At least the old man has one son who will do him proud in life. We all know it won't be me.

Unable to stomach the sight of them dancing, I swing away and cut through the crowd before beelining for the exit. On my way out, I snag a bottle of beer from the waiter. The area surrounding the tent is packed with guests. I glance at the house, wondering if it's possible to seek refuge in there, but it's ablaze with lights. Through the windows, I see more people milling around and chatting. They're everywhere. Escape doesn't seem possible.

If one more person asks about football or the draft, I'm going to throw myself in the pool. I'm talked out. I want to be alone and brood.

"Hey, Beck!" my uncle shouts from twenty feet away, "we haven't had a chance to catch up. How's the season going?"

I shake my head and cup my hand around my ear. "Sorry, can't hear you."

He waves his arm and says loudly, "Get over here, kid!"

I point to the house. "I need to check on something for Mom. I'll catch you later."

When he turns away, I breathe a sigh of relief and head in the opposite direction, ducking behind the tent to the far end of the property. Lights have been strategically placed throughout the yard and pool area. The further I venture from the tent, the more engulfed by darkness I become.

With a bottle of beer clutched in my hand, I collapse onto one of the chairs arranged around the brick firepit and stretch my legs out in front of me. I twist off the cap and bring the bottle to my lips before taking a swig. It's cold and refreshing, but does nothing to ease the growing ache in my chest.

The thought of Mia and Ari together makes me sick to my stomach. I've been focused on her for so long. Sometimes it seems like forever. How am I supposed to forget about her and move on? Is that even possible?

I guess I'm going to find out. If there's one lesson I've learned, it's that you can't force someone to like you.

It's a bitter pill to swallow.

The noise of the party fades as I slouch on the chair and stare at the bright pinpricks of light that dot the clear night sky. Maybe I'll hide out here for the rest of the evening. It's not like anyone will miss me.

"Is this chair taken?"

I jerk out of my misery only to find Mia staring at me.

Even though my heart constricts, I shrug and wave a hand. "Be my guest."

Carefully, she tucks her skirt beneath her before settling on the white Adirondack chair next to mine.

"Where's Ari?" I wince at the bitterness that shoots out of my mouth.

Jeez.

Jealous much?

I might have known this girl my entire life, but she still has the strange ability to twist me up into little knots. It's the most ridiculous thing, and yet, all I want to do is be around her. She's a brightly shining sun I find myself gravitating to.

Her eyes flicker to mine before darting away as her fingers twist nervously in her lap. "He's in the tent dancing with your grandmother."

"That sounds about right. Now that Nana has a brand-new hip, she's back to shaking her booty like it's the seventies."

A tiny smile tips the corners of her lips. "I have to admit, she's got some enviable moves. Everyone has formed a circle around her while she out-twerks your brother." Mia pauses before adding, "My guess is that she's had a few drinks."

"Probably more than a few," I chuckle. "Nana Betty loves her gin and tonics with a twist of lime. I used to make them for her all the time when I was a kid."

"I remember."

We fall into silence as Mia stares at her fingers.

Why is she here? She's done everything humanly possible to avoid me this evening. And now, the moment I stop chasing her, she seeks me out? It makes no damn sense.

No matter how old I am, I will never understand girls.

They're like the Bermuda Triangle.

Or a Rubik's Cube.

Totally unsolvable.

When I can't stand another moment of silence, I ask, "Why are you here? Shouldn't you be partying it up?"

With Ari.

The guy she's obviously interested in.

My lips twist with resentment as I pick at the bottle label with my thumbnail. There's no doubt about it, I am in full-on sad bastard mode. She should leave before I jackhammer to an all-new low and embarrass myself any further.

From the corner of my eye, I watch her fingers become more erratic. If I didn't know better, I'd suspect my presence made her nervous. But that's wishful thinking on my part.

"I wanted to talk to you."

Me?

Really?

"Oh?" I can't imagine why. Is this where Mia drops the bomb that she's filing a restraining order against me? Nothing would surprise me at this point. "What about? Seems like you've been working really hard to avoid me all night." Not to mention, the last couple of years. It might have taken me a while, but I finally got the memo.

Message received loud and clear.

Even though it's dark, a blush hits her cheeks.

"You're right," she admits. "That's exactly what I've been doing."

Woah.

What's going on here?

An actual acknowledgment?

I sit up a little straighter on my chair. "Are you going to tell me why?"

The sounds of the party fill the air between us, and I wonder if she'll answer the question.

"I don't want to be hurt again."

Fuck.

She's talking about what happened between us after our senior year of high school. I took her virginity and told her that I wanted more. Then my dad got in my head, and I backed out.

"I'm sorry, Mia. I never meant to hurt you." I shake my head. "When I asked you out, I was serious." I glance away and admit, "But I chickened out. Most of the time, I don't think I'm anywhere near good enough for you."

"Why would you say that?" she murmurs, voice filled with disbelief.

A bitter chuckle escapes from my lips. "How could I not? You're amazing at everything, and I'm," I shrug, "me."

"*Beck*," she whispers.

I grow restless under the heaviness of her gaze. As much as I don't want to have this conversation, it needs to be said. "It's the truth. You could do so much better than a guy like me." I've struggled with ADHD my whole life. The disappointment my father feels has chipped away at my self-esteem over the years. Maybe that's not the image I project to the world, but it's how I feel deep down inside.

A strangled groan leaves my lips as I realize how much I've revealed. Now she'll think I'm a pathetic loser. All I'm doing is making Ari look better. It's the story of my life.

I drag a hand over my face and focus on the trees that creep at the edge of the property. Embarrassment bubbles up inside me like a geyser.

What the fuck was I thinking?

Maybe if I ignore her long enough, she'll leave. Nothing about this evening has worked out the way I thought it would. I'm ready for it to be over. Mia has spent years avoiding me. It shouldn't be too difficult to do the same until graduation.

From the corner of my eye, I watch as she rises to her feet.

Thank fuck.

A dozen bottles of beer, and maybe I'll forget this conversation ever took place. I'm not one to get blackout drunk, but right now, it's the best plan I can come up with.

Instead of returning to the party, she closes the distance between us. It's only when she lowers herself to my lap, that I stare at her in surprise. My hands settle on her waist so she won't tumble off my thighs as her arms slide around my neck.

"Do you remember what you asked me two weeks ago outside Dr. Hayes' classroom?"

She's so damn close that her warm breath drifts across my lips. Barely am I able to concentrate on the question she poses.

"Beck?" Humor tinges her voice.

I blink and wrack my brain. Two weeks ago? Outside Hayes' classroom?

Oh...right.

Mia had used her stealthy avoidance tactics to thwart me, but I'd loitered around and waited for her.

"You asked for a second chance," she reminds softly.

Yup, that's right. And she shot me down before I could blink.

"I remember," I mutter, wondering where she's going with this.

She presses closer. The light floral scent she's wearing wraps around me. I suck in a deep breath as need pulses through my body.

"Ask me again," she whispers.

A little zip of electricity sizzles through my veins. I search her eyes, trying to sift through her thoughts in the darkness. Is this some kind of joke? Are all of my parent's guests planning on jumping out and laughing hysterically when I ask this girl out again only for her to reject me?

Nerves settle in the pit of my belly. "Will you give me another chance?"

Her mouth brushes over mine. Back and forth, she caresses my lips until I'm close to losing it.

"Yes."

With a frown, I drag myself away. "You're not fucking with me, are you?"

The corners of her lips quirk. "No, I'm not."

"You sure?"

"Yes," she laughs, "I'm sure."

"All right then." Every muscle in my body loosens. "Carry on with what you were doing."

Instead of waiting for her to come to me, I press my mouth against hers. As soon as she opens, my tongue slips inside. Mia's arms tighten around my neck. That's all it takes to get lost in the taste of her.

"It's nice to see you two have finally worked out your issues," a smug voice says from behind us. "I was beginning to lose hope."

Son of a bitch.

I pull away from Mia enough to twist around and glare at my

brother. "Get out of here before I kick your ass." Even though Mia is perched on my lap, I press her protectively against my chest.

"Don't worry, I'm going." He chuckles before throwing his hands up in the air. "I don't even get a thank you for pushing you two crazy kids together?"

I snort as Ari disappears as silently as he arrived on the scene.

For a moment, I stare at Mia. "So, what now?"

She purses her lips and pretends to ponder the question. "You kiss me."

"I can do that," I murmur, not needing to be told twice.

Chapter Twenty-Two

MIA

"Okay," Dad peeks around the hood of my Jeep, "try starting it again."

I turn the key, but nothing happens. Not even the clicking sound that means the engine is trying to turn over. Dad grumbles before straightening to his full height. I open the door and hop out, coming around to the front.

With our heads bent together, we stare at the engine.

"Any ideas?" I ask, already knowing the answer. Neither one of us understands a damn thing about cars, except how to drive them.

Dad scratches the side of his head, looking perplexed. Ask him anything about the stock market or assets and equity management, and he can give you a dissertation that would bore you to tears.

Ask him about cars, and he's as silent as a church mouse.

"Nope," he says cheerfully, "I got nothing." He puffs out his lips as he continues staring. "I guess the next step is to call the garage and have it towed."

My shoulders collapse. This Jeep is my baby, and I hate being without it. It was a gift for my sixteenth birthday. Hands down, best present I've ever received. I don't want anything to be seriously wrong with it. Someday I'll need to buy a new car, but I hope it's not anytime soon.

"Give me a minute to grab my keys, and I'll drive you to school."

As Dad jogs up the stairs to the front door, Beck pulls his shiny black Ford F-150 into the driveway and parks alongside my lifeless Jeep.

The tinted window disappears to reveal Beck in the driver's seat. His gaze bounces from the Jeep, with its hood popped open, to me and then Dad, who has stopped on the porch. "You need a jump, Mr. Stanbury? I've got cables in the back."

"No, I don't think it's the battery, the damn thing won't even turn over. I'll call for a tow, and then take Mia to school. Even if we get it started, I wouldn't feel comfortable letting her drive it. The mechanic will have to check it out first."

Beck nods as if that makes perfect sense. "I'm heading to Wesley. Mia is welcomed to hitch a ride. There's no reason for you to spend two hours in the car."

Dad runs a hand through his silvered hair. Uncertainty flickers across his features as he shifts his weight and considers the offer. "You sure you don't mind?"

Beck shakes his head before shooting me a smirk. "Nah, we live in the same building. It's not a problem at all."

Dad turns to me with a hopeful expression on his face. "Are you good with that, honey?"

"Sure, it'll save you the trip." Even though I'm trying to play it cool, nerves tingle at the bottom of my gut.

As soon as the first word slips from my mouth, Beck is throwing open the door and jumping out of the truck. "Are your bags in the backseat?"

I nod as he opens the passenger side door and grabs my duffle bag before walking around to the back of his vehicle.

Once he slams the door, he turns to me. "Ready to go?"

I blink in surprise. "Um, yeah."

Dad closes the distance between us and draws me in for a hug. "I'll text you tomorrow and let you know what's going on with the Jeep, and then we'll figure out how to get it to you."

"Let me know when it's ready, Mr. Stanbury. I can drive Mia home."

"Thanks." Dad reaches out to shake Beck's hand. "I appreciate all your help."

"Sure thing." Beck sends a wink my way. "That's what neighbors are for, right?"

"Yeah." Dad stares at us as if realizing something is different about our interaction and isn't sure what to make of it. "All right, drive safe."

With our goodbyes out of the way, Beck walks around to the passenger side and holds the door open.

I raise my brows. "My goodness, quite the gentleman."

His lips quirk with humor. "This is me attempting to sweep you off your feet with impeccable manners." He presses a quick kiss against my lips. "Is it working?"

I shoot a cautious look at my dad to see if he noticed the affectionate gesture. Thankfully, he's already on the phone with the tow company. Beck grins, seeming to know what I was thinking before securing me inside the truck.

I might be willing to give Beck a shot, but that doesn't mean I'm anywhere near ready to share that news with my parents.

With a smile on his face, Beck settles next to me. My mind spins as he turns the key and starts the engine before pulling the truck into gear.

"Wave to your dad, sweet pea. He looks concerned about your welfare."

I force my hand to rise as we pull out of the circular drive.

Beck is right. Dad is standing with his hands planted on his hips, frowning as the truck drives away. I have no idea what his reaction would be if he knew I was getting serious with our neighbor.

Although my guess is that he wouldn't be pleased.

As a child, Beck was hell on wheels. Constantly challenging authority and pushing the limits until someone snapped. His youth is dotted with rash indiscretions. That behavior continued well into high school.

Has he settled down over the years?

Grown and matured into the kind of guy I can trust with my heart?

That remains to be seen. It would be impossible to ignore all of my reservations, but I'm cautiously optimistic.

Last night, while dancing with Ari, I realized that I've been running from Beck because he scares me. My feelings for him scare me. They've never wavered, only intensified, and that scares me more than anything. Those thoughts swirl through my mind as the highway stretches out in front of us, and the city grows more distant in the rearview mirror.

Beck glances at me before reaching out and snagging my fingers with his larger ones, giving them a gentle squeeze before dragging them to rest on his thigh. "I won't hurt you again, Mia. I promise."

I glance at him, surprised he's able to read me so easily.

Does that scare me even more?

You bet your damn ass it does.

Chapter Twenty-Three

BECK

I rap my knuckles against Dr. Hayes' office door.

"Come in," is the muffled response from the other side.

As I push open the door and poke my head in, she glances up from her desk and smiles. Papers are spread out all around her. "Thanks for stopping by. I wanted to check-in with you regarding the progress you've been making." She pauses for a beat. "Please tell me that you've been working on the paper."

I crack a smile. "Yeah, I have."

"Good. I was worried after our last conversation. It seemed like you were dragging your heels about delving in."

"You're right, I was," I admit. "It's a little overwhelming."

She wags a finger at me. "You athletes are all alike."

I really hope not. School might not come easy, but that doesn't mean I don't work at it.

As I get ready to slide onto the chair parked across from her desk, Dr. Hayes rises to her feet and points to the small couch against the far side of the office. "Would you mind if we sit over there?" She arches, thrusting the fullness of her breasts against her silky white tank. My gaze skitters away, landing on the navy sweater draped across her chair. "My back has really been bothering me." She closes the distance between us. "That's what grading papers for several hours a day will get you."

"I bet." I hustle over to the couch, which is more of a glorified loveseat. There's no way two people will fit comfortably on it, especially when one of them weighs in at two-hundred-and-twenty pounds.

I drop onto a cushion and keep my attention focused straight ahead. Her thigh brushes against mine as she settles next to me. All of those uncomfortable feelings she stirred in me the last time we spoke come rushing to the surface.

It's not like there has been anything blatant about her behavior. But still...

I don't like the way it makes me feel. I shift restlessly, wishing there was more room between us. It feels like she's practically sitting on my lap. It's awkward.

"How has your week been going?" she asks, unaware of the thoughts circling through my head.

I glance at her from the corner of my eye. "Good."

"You're a man of few words, Beck Hollingsworth," she chuckles. "The strong silent type."

That would be because you make me uneasy.

Even though I don't say it out loud, the words are perched on the tip of my tongue. Any moment I'll blurt them out.

Dr. Hayes flips through her notebook until she lands on a page with my name scribbled on top of it, along with a few notes. She shifts her body until she's able to face me. Our thighs are no longer touching, but our knees are pushed together. I remain still, so we don't brush up against one another any more than we have to.

I glance at her face, trying to get a read on her thoughts. Her expression is open and friendly, that of a concerned professor. There's nothing about her demeanor that would lead me to believe she's aware of the discomfort she's causing.

"Let's talk about the sources you've come up with and where you are in the process of drafting your outline."

I blow out a steady breath, and the tension filling my muscles dissipates.

"There are a lot of studies out there regarding concussions and contact sports, so finding research material hasn't been an issue. I've already gathered six different sources." The more I talk about what I've found, the more comfortable I become. "One problem I'm running into is that there's so much information, I'm having a difficult time narrowing down my focus and organizing it."

"Sometimes having too much information can be as problematic as not finding enough." Her lips lift. "Think about your thesis statement and try to stick with information that supports the main points you're trying to convey." She gestures toward my backpack. "If you have your outline, I'd love to take a look and give you some direction."

"Sure, let me grab my computer."

"Great." She relaxes against the couch and crosses one leg over the other. Her skirt rises a few inches up her thigh.

I pull out my laptop from my backpack and fire it up. Once the document pops up on the screen, she scoots toward me. The soft curve of her breast brushes against my bicep.

I clear my throat and stare pointedly at the screen. "Would it be easier for you to read if I give you the computer?"

"Nope," she presses closer, "this is fine."

Silently, she scans the document. Every once in a while, she'll point to a word or section. When she does, something hard and pointed drags across the bare skin of my arm. I'm really hoping it's not her nipple, but what else could it be?

When she glances at me, I'm startled to realize how close her face looms. A couple of inches at best.

"Have you started writing your first draft?" Her attention falls to my lips.

"Umm, yeah," I mutter.

She continues staring. "Do you want to pull it up?"

"Sure." I refocus on the computer. Every time I hit a key, my arm rubs against her boob. Finally, I get the document pulled up and jerk the screen toward her. I want to get this over with and get the hell out of here.

Dr. Hayes makes a humming noise deep in her throat as she reads over the draft. "This is great. You're definitely on the right track."

"Awesome." I snap the laptop closed with more force than necessary and shove it in my backpack.

Hallelujah, we're done. I can leave.

As I'm about to spring to my feet, she places a hand on my thigh. My gaze drops to her fingers in surprise.

"Let's plan on meeting up again next week. I know how easy it is to get off-track, and I want to make sure you're continuing to make steady progress."

"Oh." Well, damn. That's not what I wanted to hear.

"I see such potential, Beck. I'd love the opportunity to tease it out of you. I really believe you could benefit from a little one-on-one instruction."

"I don't know if I can work that into my schedule," I mumble, unsure what to say. One-on-one instruction is the last thing I want from her. My gut is telling me it's not English she wants to tease out of me.

Dr. Hayes squeezes my thigh before lifting her hand away. The moment I'm free of her touch, I pop to my feet.

"Beck?"

It's only after I freeze that I realize I've stopped directly in front of her face. Her eyes are level with my junk, and it seems like she's staring straight at it before she glances up.

"If you need anything, you can always text me."

No, thank you.

Instead, I force myself to say, "I'll be sure to do that."

And then I flee from her office like the hounds of hell are nipping at my heels.

As I crest the second-floor landing of the library, my gaze sweeps over the tables strategically placed near the anthropology and sociology section, but I don't immediately notice Beck.

I'm about to pull out my phone when a high-pitched giggle draws my attention to a girl lounging on top of a study table. I'm not able to see who she's talking to, but my guess is that it's a guy. I know flirty behavior when I see it.

Dismissing her, I glance away and continue searching for Beck. Maybe we were supposed to meet on a different floor or section. When another laugh erupts, I glance at her again. She shifts, and I catch a glimpse of dark wavy hair.

I don't need to see any more to know she's talking to Beck. I step to the side, and his handsome features come into view. The strawberry-blond-haired girl perched on the table leans over, giving him what I assume is an unobstructed view of her cleavage.

Jealousy bubbles up inside me like a geyser before I quickly stomp it out. I'm not one of these girls who want to spend every spare moment of her time fending off other females. I also don't want a guy who will flirt with every vagina he comes across.

This is precisely why I was reluctant to give Beck another chance.

It hasn't even been a week since I agreed to go out with him, and already he's chasing after other chicks?

No, sir. That won't be happening on my watch. We can snuff this out as quickly as it sprang to life. Thank God he showed his true colors before I could become any further invested. I'm not even going to confront him. He can screw himself.

I'm out of here.

As I take a hasty step in retreat, ready to stomp down the stairs, Beck glances over and catches sight of me. A wide smile lights up his face as he waves me over like he wasn't caught red-handed with another girl.

Does he really think I'm going to be all right with this behavior?

Hell, no. He messed with the wrong chick. I'm not one of his bubble-headed groupies who will put up with anything for the chance to be with him. I hitch my backpack up higher on my shoulder before stalking toward him.

Not once does Beck's attention deviate from me. As I reach the table, I open my mouth to blast him into next week.

He beats me to the punch. "Hey, babe. Missed you."

His fingers tangle around mine before he tugs me closer. Thrown off by the affectionate greeting, I trip over my own feet and stumble toward him. He slides one hand into my hair before bringing my face to his and kissing me. It's nothing more than a fleeting caress, but it's enough to stir something deep inside me.

What the hell is going on here?

Confusion swirls through me as I glance at the girl on the table. She grins and continues swinging her long legs.

Shouldn't she be upset that Beck is making out with someone in front of her?

None of this makes sense.

Only then does it occur to me that maybe—*just maybe*—I got the scenario wrong.

Beck keeps a tight grip on my fingers as if unwilling to let me go. "Callie was keeping me company while I was taking a break."

I clear my throat and force out an introduction. "Hi, I'm Mia. It's nice to meet you."

Can you imagine if I hadn't kept my jealousy under wraps and lost it? Even the thought is enough to embarrass me.

Callie flashes a full-wattage smile that nearly blinds me with its intensity. I'm tempted to smack this girl for being so damn perfect with her bouncy hair and amazing body.

"I'm Callie." She swivels toward me. "Beck has been telling me all about you."

"Really?" As if I needed any more evidence that I jumped to the wrong conclusion.

"Yeah," she enthuses. "There are going to be a ton of disappointed girls on campus when they learn Beck is officially off the market."

Officially off the market?

Is that what's happened?

I give Beck a bit of side-eye to get his take on the matter. He grins as if amused by my reaction.

"I should probably take off." Callie hops gracefully from the table. Her perfect breasts jiggle enticingly with the movement. I sneak a peek at Beck to see if he's watching. I mean, how can he not be? Her breasts are big and bouncy. I'm almost entranced by them, and I'm not into girls.

Instead, his gaze stays trained on me. A little hum of awareness zips through my veins. It's almost as if Callie and her gravity-defying boobs aren't on his radar.

"I've got a ton of homework to finish up. I'll see you in class, Beck." She turns to me and waves. "Nice to meet you!"

Beck gives her a chin lift as I return the sentiment.

Once she's gone, I mutter, "Callie seems nice."

"Yup, she's cool. She cheered freshman year and then quit." He shrugs. "It was too much of a time commitment."

Cheerleader. I could definitely see that. She's peppy.

When I attempt to pull my hand free so we can get to work, he tugs, and I tumble onto his lap. His hands band around my waist to hold me in place.

He cocks his head as a smile simmers around the edges of his lips. "You thought I was flirting with her, didn't you?"

"Nope." I shake my head. "Never crossed my mind." There is no damn way I will admit that to him. Even if it is the truth.

His grin widens until I'm tempted to smack him. "I'm serious about being with *you* and only *you*. I don't have any interest in other girls."

I glance away. Whatever this is between us is moving at lightning speed. Am I ready for that?

"Mia," he whispers, recapturing my attention. "You don't have anything to worry about."

There is so much sincerity overflowing from his green eyes that it's impossible not to believe him. "Okay."

"I've waited a long time for this. I'm not going to fuck it up."

How can I possibly resist a guy who says something like that to me?

Even though we're in the library, I press closer and lower my lips to his. It's all too easy to lose myself in the taste and feel of him.

After a handful of moments, he groans and pulls away. "If you keep that up, we won't get much work done."

It might be worth it.

"Stop looking at me like that," he whispers. "You have no idea what it does to me."

I inhale a shaky breath. He's wrong about that because it does the same to me.

Studying.

Right.

We need to get to it. I'm supposed to be helping him with his paper. When I attempt to rise from his lap, his hands stay wrapped around my waist.

"One more kiss," he growls.

A smile curves my lips as they settle over his. This time, I try not to get lost in the feel of him, but it's not easy. When I pull away, our faces stay close, his breath becoming mine.

"I was thinking, if your Jeep is ready by the weekend, we could take off Saturday after the game." He pauses. "And I could take you out."

My breath catches at the idea. "On a date?"

He presses another kiss against me. "Yup, we're talking dinner and the whole shebang."

His smile is contagious. "Now you've piqued my interest."

"Good. It goes a little something like this—I'll pick you up and take you to a nice restaurant, and then afterward, we'll find a secluded spot to make out for a while. We can pretend we're back in high school again."

I laugh, loving the sound of that.

"Maybe we should practice the making out part to be sure we get it right." I add shyly, "We can head back to my place after we're done working. Alyssa won't be home for a while."

"Nope," he says firmly. "All messing around will have to wait until after the date. We're going to do this right."

My heart melts into a puddle of goo.

What's this guy doing to me?

A grin flashes across his face. "What?"

I shake my head and trace his lips with my index finger. "You're not the guy I thought you were."

"I'll take that as a compliment."

When my finger dips inside his mouth, he bites down gently, and I gasp before pulling it out.

"Nothing is going to mess this up," he murmurs.

A little bubble of happiness bursts in my heart. I really hope he means everything he's saying. Because this Beck, the one he's slowly revealing to me, is someone I could fall for. Even though the idea of putting my heart in his hands is a frightening one, I'm no longer sure I have a choice in the matter.

"We should probably hit the books." I need to focus on something other than the emotions crashing around inside me.

With one last kiss, I slide from his lap and settle on the chair across from him. Beck emails me a copy of his outline along with the rough draft for comp class. It takes about twenty minutes to look it over, add suggestions with the editing tool before sending it back to him. Then he gets to work, sifting through his research and working on his paper.

Before I realize it, two hours have slipped by.

"How did your meeting with Dr. H go?" I ask before stretching my muscles.

"Fine, I guess." Something indecipherable flickers in his eyes, and I'm not sure what to make of it. "She said everything looked good."

"From what you've shown me, you're on the right track. Once you finish up with the rough draft, the process should move faster." I pause before adding, "Consider yourself lucky that you didn't get Dr. Templeton for this class. He's so boring and long-winded. Dr. Hayes is amazing. Don't you love her?"

He glances away, and his smile fades. "Yeah, she's okay."

Just okay?

Everyone on campus adores Dr. H. Beck is the first person I've run across who hasn't sung her praises. She goes above and beyond for her students. She's always trying out new teaching methods to keep her class fresh and interesting.

I tilt my head and try to puzzle out why there's been such an abrupt shift in his demeanor. It's like a mask has fallen over his features.

"Did something happen?" I ask. Although, I can't imagine what that could be.

"I don't know." He shrugs and fidgets with his pen. "I'm not sure."

"What do you mean?"

Beck shoves away from the table and folds his arms across his chest. I try not to get distracted by the movement. God bless, but he has amazing biceps.

I'm pulled out of my perusal when he says, "She's nice. Friendly." There's a pause, and his voice drops. "Maybe a little *too* friendly if you catch my drift."

Huh?

I shake my head. "*Too friendly?*" No one has ever complained about Dr. H being *too* friendly. In fact, that's what makes her such a great teacher. Every month, she hosts a book club meeting for students at her house. There are appetizers, drinks, and intellectual conversation where everyone is free to express their opinions.

Seriously, who does that?

There's not another professor on campus who is more beloved than her.

So, I'm uncertain what Beck is driving at.

"I don't know," he mutters, clearly frustrated by his inability to express his thoughts. "Maybe it's all in my head. Forget I said anything about it."

If there's a problem, I want to know what it is. I reach out and lay my fingers over Beck's before giving them a squeeze. "No, tell me."

He huffs out an exasperated breath before pressing closer to the table. "I've met with her twice now, and each time, it feels like she's coming on to me."

What?

No way!

It takes everything I have inside not to burst out laughing. It's the look on his face that forces me to keep the sound buried deep inside.

He's serious.

He believes this is happening.

"Okay," I say carefully, wanting to get to the bottom of this. "What has she done to make you feel so uncomfortable?"

He withdraws his fingers from mine and grows restless before glaring at something in the distance. "I don't know." He jerks his shoulders. "It's the way she stares and talks to me. She keeps touching me." He bites his lower lip. "When I was in her office, she sat way too close on the couch. Her boob was pressed against my arm. It was weird." A dull red color settles in his cheeks.

"Anything else?" I prompt, waiting for something that is more of a smoking gun.

"She gave me her cell number and told me to text anytime."

"I've had her number for years," I tell him.

When he presses his lips together and doesn't say anything more, I continue, wanting to put him at ease. "I've always found Dr. H to be super friendly and affectionate. I've been in her office a lot of times, and we always sit on the couch when we talk. We've grabbed coffee together. Maybe she shouldn't be so physically demonstrative," I shrug, "but that's just who she is. Most students don't have a problem with it."

I'm not sure if I'm making the situation better or worse.

"So...you think I'm overreacting?" he asks.

Definitely.

But I don't have the heart to tell him that. Instead, I say, "I think you've misinterpreted her actions. If she realized her behavior made you uncomfortable, she'd be upset." I search his eyes, hoping I've laid his concerns to rest.

"I don't know," he mutters. "Maybe you're right."

My lips lift at the corners. "Trust me, I am. She's being friendly. Nothing more."

His face clears as he nods. "All right. You know her better than I do."

When he stretches, flexing his arms, my mouth turns cottony, and all thoughts of Dr. Hayes are instantly forgotten.

He grins as if he knows exactly how he affects me. "You ready to get out of here?"

"Yup." I pause for a beat. "Are you sure I can't convince you to give me a sneak peek of what the *make-out* portion of the evening will entail?"

Heat flares to life in his eyes. "Sweetheart, if I gave you a preview, you wouldn't want me to stop."

A thrill of anticipation shoots through me because he's right. Since we've gotten together, we've held off on sex. We're taking this relationship slow. That being said, I'm all but dying to get my hands on him.

And vice versa.

The wait is killing me.

But it's worth it.

Beck is worth it.

Chapter Twenty-Five

BECK

Nerves prickle at the bottom of my gut as I park my truck in Mia's circular driveway and cut the engine. This is the same nauseous feeling I get in the tunnel, waiting to run onto the field before a game. Like I'm going to puke. I have no idea why taking Mia out on a date feels like such a big deal, but it does. All I know is that I want everything to be perfect.

I grab the flowers from the front seat and take the wide stone steps two at a time before ringing the bell. The sound echoes inside the cavernous entryway. I run a hand over my button-down shirt and khakis one last time.

Wait a minute—are the khakis and dress-shirt overkill? Maybe I should have kept it casual. I'm not looking to spook her.

Damnit.

It's too late to do anything about it now.

Why did I think this was a good idea?

After a few agonizing moments that feel like an eternity, the door swings open, and Mia stands on the other side of the threshold. That's all it takes for the doubts filling my head to disappear.

Neither of us say a word as her lips lift into a hesitant smile.

This.

This is exactly why I wanted to take her out.

My gaze rakes over her from head to toe. She's wearing a black sweater that hugs her breasts and a short, dark-wash jean skirt paired with black tights. Her hair hangs in loose waves that frame her face and tumble around her shoulders.

My mouth waters. It takes every ounce of self-control not to reach out and yank her into my arms.

"Hi," she says, breaking the silence.

"You look beautiful." It's the only thought running through my head.

"Thanks." She ducks her chin as color blooms in her cheeks.

Sometimes I don't think Mia has any idea how gorgeous she is.

She points to my hand. "Are those for me?"

I glance at the flowers before shaking my head. How the hell could I forget about them? It took at least twenty minutes to pick out the perfect bouquet at the florist.

I thrust them toward her. "Yeah, sorry."

She takes the colorful blooms before burying her face in them. "They're beautiful. Thank you. No one has ever brought me flowers before."

It makes me doubly glad that I made the effort.

She nods toward the kitchen. "Let me put them in a vase, and then we can leave."

I shove my hands in my pockets as she silently pads down the hall. I hear the faucet run, and then she's back, carrying a crystal vase in her hands before setting it on the table in the entryway.

She slips her feet into black heels that make her legs look even longer.

How the hell am I supposed to keep my hands to myself all night?

I clear my throat and those thoughts from my mind as I rock back on my heels and glance around. "Are your parents home?"

Mia shakes her head before grabbing her purse. "Nope. Mom went to visit her sister, and Dad left on Thursday for another trip."

That's probably for the best. I have no idea how Dan would feel about me dating his daughter. He likes me well enough as the son of his friend and neighbor, but am I good enough for Mia?

Probably not.

But like she said, we're taking this relationship slow. I won't worry about jumping over that hurdle until I clear this one.

"All set?" I ask.

"Yup." She closes the door behind her as we head to the truck. When she reaches for the handle, I brush her hand aside and open it. Once she's safely secured inside, I close the door and jog around to the driver's side before sliding onto the seat and starting up the engine. A few moments later, I'm pulling from her drive and heading out of the subdivision. I wave to the guard in the gatehouse before we hit the main road.

"You never mentioned where we were going." Her fingers tangle together in her lap.

It's difficult to believe she could be nervous. I reach out and grab her fingers, wrapping my hand around them.

"I made reservations at Marco's. It's an Italian restaurant on the other side of town." I glance at her. "Have you ever been there?"

"It's one of my dad's favorites. We used to go there all the time when I was a kid." Her eyes grow distant. "I can't remember the last time we had dinner there."

"They have the best eggplant parmigiana."

"The spaghetti and meatballs are good, too," she adds with a smile.

I nod in agreement. Marco's is one of those restaurants where you can't go wrong no matter what you order. It makes me doubly glad I picked that place to take her. Other than group dates when I attended prom and homecoming, I've never taken a girl out on a date before.

I pull the truck into the crowded parking lot and cut the engine. We exit the vehicle before heading inside to the hostess station. The ambiance is upscale, and the lighting is dim. The dining room is cavernous with high ceilings that give it a spacious feel.

It's the perfect place for a first date.

If I play my cards right, it'll be one of many.

I'm almost tempted to pat myself on the back for a job well done, but I'll save that until after I drop her off. Although, so far, we're off to a good start.

The hostess grabs two menus and seats us at a white cloth-covered table in the main dining room near the stone fireplace. I make sure to pull out Mia's chair before taking a seat across from her. A waitress stops by and fills our water glasses as we peruse the menu.

"Any idea what you're going to order?" I ask.

A thoughtful expression flickers across her face as she shakes her head. "There are so many options to choose from. It all looks amazing." She glances at me. "Maybe the lasagna."

"Yeah, that sounds good," I agree, "but I'm going for the eggplant."

As she continues to study the menu, I glance around the dimly-lit room before my attention gets snagged by a couple tucked into the corner. I blink and refocus my eyes to make sure they're not playing tricks on me. When the man shifts, I get an unobstructed view of him. My heart kicks up its tempo as he leans across the table and locks lips with the woman seated on the other side.

There's no mistaking the guy.

It's Dan, Mia's father.

What's most disturbing is that the woman he's with is not his wife. She looks nothing like Julia. There's no way to even confuse the two.

What the hell?

Didn't Mia say that her father was out of town for business? If that's the case, what is he doing here with another woman?

I drag a hand over my face, knowing this is going to blow my whole night apart.

"Instead of lasagna," Mia murmurs, still staring at the menu, "I'm going to try the lobster stuffed ravioli."

Fuck.

Fuck.

Fuck.

When I fail to respond, she glances at me. "What do you think?"

"Oh, ah..." Even though I have no idea what to do, I realize staying is not an option. At some point, Mia will notice her dad, and I can't allow that to happen.

"You know what? We should go somewhere else." When her eyes widen, I add hastily, "Some place better."

"You want to leave?"

I wince at the shock lacing her voice. "I want our first date to be special, and this isn't going to cut it."

She lays the menu down in front of her. "I can't tell if you're being serious or not."

"Dead serious," I say nervously. "Let's go."

As Mia opens her mouth to pelt me with questions, our server arrives at the table with a smile plastered across her face.

"Hello, my name is Kimber, and I'll be your waitress for the evening. Have you ever been to Marco's? If not, welcome!" Her gaze bounces between us. "The chef has created several specials this evening—"

"We won't be staying," I interrupt.

Mia's eyes bulge, looking like they might fall out of her head. Kimber, our perky waitress, stares at me with an equal amount of surprise.

"Beck, I don't—"

"Sorry for the inconvenience." I bolt to my feet like a lunatic. This whole evening has burst into a fiery ball of flames. I'm not sure if I'll be able to recover from this catastrophe. But what other choice is there?

I can't allow Mia to catch sight of her father.

"Ready to go?" She stares at me in bewilderment as I extend my hand.

"Ummm..."

"Great, let's get out of here!"

Mia glances at our waitress as if she might be able to explain my odd behavior. When I don't retract my hand, she tentatively lays her fingers in mine and carefully rises from the chair. Not wanting her to see Dan, I scoot my body to the side and block her view.

It's all I can do to hustle her ass out of here as fast as humanly possible. If I haven't destroyed my chances with her, maybe we can find a different restaurant and start this date over again. We can pretend this never happened. Although, that's probably wishful thinking on my part.

Thirty steps, and we'll be in the clear.

I swipe my hand across my brow and realize I'm sweating. This has turned into a real shitshow. I tighten my grip around her fingers and drag her from the table. She makes a squeak of protest before stumbling to keep pace with me. Once we reach the entryway where the hostess station is located, the pressure in my chest loosens, and I can once again breathe.

That was a close one, but I did it. I hustled her out of there before any damage could be done.

Mia tugs on my hand. "We can't leave!"

Why the hell not?

"I forgot my purse at the table." She points toward the main dining room.

Goddamn it.

I'm tempted to leave it behind and chalk it up as a casualty of the evening.

"Wait here," I growl with more force than necessary, "and I'll grab it."

Her brows slam together as her mouth pops open in protest.

"Please," I plead, "just wait here." I stalk away before she can argue. As I arrive at the table, I glance at Dan from the corner of my eye. He's still staring at the woman across from him as if he doesn't give a damn that they're in a public place where anyone could see him cheating on his wife.

With a scowl, I shake my head.

If his daughter wasn't with me, I'd march over there and ask him what the hell he's doing. Instead, I swipe Mia's black purse from the table and spin on my heels before grinding to a halt.

Mia stands frozen at the entrance of the dining room. With wide eyes, she stares past me. Her mouth hangs open as shock fills her face.

Fuck.

That, unfortunately, seems to be the word of the evening.

I look over my shoulder, but Dan is oblivious to the fact that his daughter is at the same restaurant as his side piece. Her father's attention is focused on the blonde sitting across from him. Their hands are clasped, and the besotted expression on his face speaks volumes. There's no way to misconstrue what's playing out.

I close the distance between us until I can slide an arm around Mia's waist. "Come on," I say gently, "let's get out of here."

She stays rooted in place. Her focus never deviates from the couple on the other side of the room.

"Mia?" I lower my voice, trying to reach her. "We need to go."

"You knew about this?" Hurt seeps into her voice.

The accusation arrows to my heart before exploding upon impact. I shake my head. "No, I noticed them after we sat down."

"That's why you wanted to leave." She nods as if a puzzle piece has fallen into place, and my odd behavior now makes sense. Her shoulders sag beneath the weight of this knowledge.

"Yeah." There's no longer a reason to hide the truth.

A sheen of wetness coats her eyes as I steer her toward the exit. "Come on."

"Should I say something?" She sucks her bottom lip into her mouth as she contemplates the question.

What the hell is the protocol for a situation like this?

Damned if I know.

"No, let's get out of here. You can think about it and then decide what to do."

As I secure her inside the cabin of the truck, a sigh escapes from my lips. It's a relief to be out of the restaurant. The more distance I put between her father and us, the better off she'll be.

I glance at Mia only to find her staring pensively out the windshield. Pain radiates from her in heavy waves. Unsure how to comfort her, I reach out and snag her fingers before squeezing them.

Even though I suspect the answer, I still ask, "Are you hungry? We could go someplace else to eat."

She shakes her head. "No, just take me home."

Once I pull into her drive, I put the truck in park and angle my body toward hers. If I could take away her pain, I would do it in a heartbeat.

Silently she reaches for the handle.

As she pops it open, I ask, "Do you want me to come in?" I tack on before she can get the wrong idea, "To talk?"

She shakes her head. "Thanks, but no. Right now, I want to be alone, so I can figure out what to do."

"You don't have to do anything," I tell her. "Whatever is going on is between your mom and dad. It has nothing to do with you."

"I know." With a heavy sigh, she steps out of the vehicle. "I'm sorry about tonight, Beck. I appreciate the effort you put into planning our date."

I force a smile to my lips, wishing there was something I could do or say to make the situation better. When I remain silent, she jerks her head into a nod.

"Bye," she says before slamming the door.

I watch as she walks up the stone stairs and lets herself into the house. Her gaze fastens on to mine, and I raise my hand to wave before she disappears inside.

This date has turned out to be an epic fail. Not in a million years did I ever expect our night to end like this.

Chapter Twenty-Six

MIA

Unable to sleep, I stare sightlessly at the ceiling. No matter how much I try to block out what I saw at Marco's, I can't. The image of my dad having an intimate dinner with a strange woman refuses to be buried.

Even though I know what I saw and how I felt in the moment, part of me wonders if it's possible I could have misconstrued the relationship. Was it a dinner between friends? Or colleagues?

From across the restaurant, I could see the besotted look in Dad's eyes as he stared at the blonde across from him. How long has it been since he looked at Mom that way?

I sift through my memories, going back years, but can't come up with a definitive answer. If Dad ever looked at Mom like that, it was before Brianna died.

Beck's words ring unwantedly throughout my head.

This has nothing to do with you.

He's right, it doesn't. This is between my dad and mom, but still... seeing him with another woman feels like a betrayal to our family.

How could he do this?

After everything Mom has been through, how could he inflict more damage?

I turn onto my side and curl up in a tight ball under the covers as a wave of nausea crashes over me. This isn't the kind of secret I can keep from Mom. She has a right to know what's going on. The thought of telling her makes me sick to my stomach.

I glance at the clock on the nightstand. It's after midnight, and I'm no closer to finding sleep than I was two hours ago. Maybe I should go downstairs and make a cup of tea.

As I throw off the covers, there's a tap against the windowpane. I pause as my heart thumps a painful beat against my ribcage before squinting into the darkness. The breath rushes from my lungs as Beck's features materialize on the other side of the glass. I hurry across the room and unlatch the lock, shoving open the window.

"What are you doing here?" Relief and happiness swirl inside me at the sight of him.

He stares at me from the thick tree branch he's perched on. "I wanted to make sure you were all right. What happened earlier was brutal."

"You could have texted or come to the front door."

"It's been a while since I climbed your tree." He shrugs as a smile lifts his lips. "Kind of seemed like a grand romantic gesture. Don't you think?"

I shake my head and unsnap the screen from the window before pulling it off and leaning the metal frame against the wall. "You're crazy."

"Only for you." Beck balances his weight on the branch before levering himself through the window. He lands gracefully on the floor before popping to his full height and dusting himself off. I quickly slam the window closed and clip the screen back into place.

"Are you doing okay?" He closes the distance between us until he can tug me into his arms. "I was worried."

Unable to help myself, I melt against him before burying my face in his chest. I have no idea why his presence is so comforting, but it is. "I'm all right. Still in shock, I guess."

He wraps his arms around me, pressing me closer before dropping a kiss on the top of my head. "Have you made any decisions?"

I huff out a breath and mumble, "I called him."

"Really?" Beck pulls away. "What happened?"

"It went straight to voicemail."

"Oh." He draws me to him again before tucking me beneath his chin. I hate to admit how perfectly we fit together.

"Dad texted five minutes later. He said he was in the middle of a business dinner and would call in the morning."

"Un-fucking-believable," Beck mutters.

Anger floods through me before pooling in my voice. "I was so tempted to text back and ask how dinner with his whore was."

"Shit, Mia..." he whispers against my hair before squeezing me tighter.

A fresh wave of tears stings my eyes. "Can you imagine the look on his face if I had done that?"

"I'm so sorry, baby. I wish I had hustled you out of there before you caught sight of them."

I burrow my face against Beck before inhaling a big breath of him. The woodsy scent of his cologne settles something deep inside me. "You have nothing to be sorry about. *He* does."

A humorless chuckle falls from my lips when I remember sitting down to dinner at Marco's. "I'd thought you had changed your mind about us going out. All of a sudden, you were acting weird and trying to drag me from the table."

"Nothing could be further from the truth. I'd been looking forward to dinner since I asked you out. I'm sorry our night got ruined."

"Yeah," I say softly, lifting my head from his chest. "Me, too." Maybe I haven't wanted to admit it to myself, but I'd been looking forward to this date. Probably more than I should have. I'm trying to be cautious and smart and take things slow, but Beck is making that difficult to do.

He lowers his face until his lips can graze mine. The moment we make contact, all the noise rioting in my brain goes silent. Beck angles his head as his mouth roves gently over mine. When my lips part, his tongue slips inside to dance with my own.

My palms glide over his chest until they're able to lock around his neck and pull him closer. Somehow this kiss mutes all the pain vibrating deep inside me, and for that, I'm grateful. I don't want to think anymore.

I just want to feel.

And *this* feels amazing.

I pull away enough to whisper, "Stay the night with me?"

"Is that what you want?"

"Yes." After everything that's happened tonight, it's what I need.

"Then I'll stay."

Chapter Twenty-Seven

BECK

Before Mia can untangle herself from me, I scoop her into my arms. She squeaks in surprise as I carry her to the bathroom before depositing her onto the long stretch of marble countertop. Silently she watches as I close the plug on the white porcelain tub and run the water.

Once it's at the right temperature, I swing around to face her. "A bath will help you relax."

She bites her lip. "Are you going to join me?"

"Nope." I shake my head. "This is for you."

When the tub is almost filled, and steam is rising from it, I position myself between her legs. I gather up the material of her pink tank top and carefully pull it over her head before dropping it to the floor. She sits before me in tiny white shorts with pink hearts stamped across them.

I reach out and cup the soft weight of her breasts, squeezing the fullness. Her nipples pebble against my palms before I release them and trail my fingers down her ribcage until I reach the elastic band of her shorts. I hook my thumbs beneath the material before dragging them down to reveal even more sun-kissed flesh. She lifts her backside so I can slide the thin cotton over her hips and down her thighs. The shorts get added to the small pile on the floor.

She makes such a pretty picture sitting naked in front of the mirror. This girl doesn't understand the power she holds over me. She could have had me on my knees years ago.

I lean forward, kissing one breast before nipping at the hardened tip. Then I give the same treatment to the other. The whimper that falls from her lips has my cock stiffening with need. I have to remind myself that what I'm doing isn't for me, it's for her.

I lick a hot trail down the middle of her ribcage to her bellybutton before sinking lower. My hands slide to her inner thighs, opening them gently until my mouth can settle on her pussy. When I swipe my tongue over her opening, Mia groans and arches her back. My hands slide from her thighs over her hips until I can cradle her backside with my palms. I bury my face against her heat, laving her sweetness with my tongue.

The goal is to make her forget about everything she saw tonight. Even if it's only for a few moments. I want the pleasure to overtake the pain.

When she's dancing on the edge, I pull back, not wanting her to spiral out of control. With one last kiss against her lower lips, I rise to my feet. Mia's head is tipped back, and her eyes are closed.

"Do you like that?" I press a kiss against her mouth before scooping her up and cradling her against my chest.

"Mmm." Her eyelids flutter open as she lifts her lips to mine for another kiss.

The moment my mouth settles on hers, our tongues mingle. She purrs before slipping her arms around my neck and tugging me closer.

I'm breathing hard and close to coming in my boxer-briefs when I pull away. "You should enjoy your bath before it gets cold."

The dazed look filling her eyes is like a punch to my gut.

I lower her into the tub until she's settled against the sloped porcelain. A sigh of contentment slips free as her body sinks into the steaming water.

"Do you want it hotter?"

"No." Her eyelids feather closed. "It's perfect."

My gaze roams over her naked body.

When we were kids, she was all long limbs, knobby knees, and elbows. It was around seventh grade when Mia's body changed. Her breasts and hips filled out. Every time I saw that short white tennis skirt against her tanned thighs, I would sport wood. Or I'd catch a glimpse of her in the hallway at school. The way her shirts stretched across the soft curve of her breasts left my mouth watering.

Even thinking about it now makes me groan.

I really need to get out of here and stop staring at her until I can get a better handle on myself. As I head for the door, her eyes crack open.

"Where are you going?" she asks sleepily. She's in full relaxation mode, and that's exactly where I want her.

"I'll be back in a minute. Just enjoy yourself."

I disappear from the bathroom before she can ask further questions. Once in the hallway, I cross over the catwalk and move down the staircase before heading to the kitchen. I grab a mug from the cabinet and fill it with filtered water from the fridge before setting it in the microwave. While the water is heating, I search the cabinets for tea. As I come across a box of chamomile, the microwave buzzes.

Perfect timing.

I grab the mug and seep the bag in the hot water.

When I return to the bathroom, steam has permeated the air, and Mia is lying against the rim of the tub with her eyes closed. I settle next to her with the mug in my hands.

Her dark eyelashes flutter. When she sees me, her lips lift into a satisfied smile.

"I brought you something."

She sits up and takes the mug from my fingers. "You made tea?" Surprise dances in her eyes.

I shrug. "It wasn't a big deal."

She glances at the drink before releasing a sigh. "You're making this awfully difficult."

Not understanding the comment, my brows draw together. All I'm trying to do is make her feel better. Maybe I'm doing a piss-poor job of it. "What do you mean?"

"I'm trying to hold myself back." Her gaze flicks to mine. "I don't want to get too excited about this." There's a pause before she adds, "*About you.*"

Not that I blame her for it, but I hate that she feels the need to protect herself from me. It makes me wonder if I'll ever be able to earn her trust.

"I'm not that guy anymore." I reach out and trail my fingers along the curve of her jaw. "I'm trying to prove that to you."

She sinks into my touch. "You're doing a good job of it."

"Guess I need to keep it up." That's all I can do.

Mia brings the mug to her lips and takes a sip before setting it on the edge of the tub. "Thank you."

"You're welcome." I pause before adding, "Whatever you need from me, all you have to do is ask, and it's yours."

Her body sinks beneath the surface of the water. When she's fully submerged, she widens her legs until she's completely exposed. My gaze drops to her spread thighs before skimming up her body to settle on her face.

"Tell me what you need, Mia." My voice turns rough with pent-up arousal.

She remains silent as I trail my fingers through the water. Carefully, I circle one breast until the nipple tightens before doing the same to the other. A sigh of pleasure escapes from her.

"Is this what you wanted?"

She shakes her head.

My fingers drift lower, swirling around the indentation of her belly button before moving downward and feathering over her lower lips. She widens her legs as I circle my thumb around her clit. Her body grows restless beneath my touch.

"Feel good, baby?"

"God, yes."

Not once do I dip my fingers inside her tight sheath. I continue tormenting her, driving her closer to orgasm. She bites her lower lip to stifle a whimper.

"Need more?"

"*Please.*"

I slip one finger inside her body. As I pull away, her inner muscles tighten, and a whimper of protest falls from her mouth. I circle her clit a few more times before sinking deep inside her. She finds a rhythm and gyrates against my hand. Her body tightens as her muscles convulse around me. The pleasure that falls from her lips has my cock throbbing with need. I don't think I've ever wanted anyone more than this girl.

Once her orgasm dissipates, I lean over and take her mouth with my own.

"I love watching you fall apart," I whisper against her lips.

Her eyes flare as color flags her cheeks.

"You know what I love even more?" I ask.

The dazed expression clears as she shakes her head.

"When you orgasmed on my tongue at the club. Your pussy got so fucking wet. I wanted to lap it all up."

When her mouth falls open, I grin before plunging my tongue deep inside her sweetness. How will I ever get enough of her? It doesn't seem possible. As much as I'd like to sink inside her body, that won't be happening. This is about Mia's pleasure, not my own.

This is the first relationship I've been involved in. Everything before this was a string of meaningless encounters. There was never a reason to hold back or take things slow.

But Mia is different.

She's the first girl who has ever mattered. What we have, what we're attempting to build together, is more than physical. I don't want her to think it's based on sex.

"Why don't you finish your tea before it gets cold, and then I'll help you out."

She lifts the mug to her lips and takes another sip. "I'm done."

I grab a plush navy towel from the rack before holding it out so she can step into it. She rises gracefully to her feet as water sluices down her body.

How is it possible that she's this perfect?

As she stands before me, I drag the towel over her damp skin, starting first with her shoulders. Once they're dried, I stroke up and down her arms. I move behind her, swiping at the long line of her spine before dropping to my haunches and running the towel over her rounded cheeks.

I press a kiss against each perfect globe before sweeping the plush material over her legs. When no moisture remains, I place my hands on her hips and turn her, so she's facing me. It's gently that I stroke the area between her thighs. She groans as the cloth slides back and forth with enough pressure to create friction.

Her hands grip my shoulders as her eyelids feather shut and her head lolls back. By the time I'm done, her pussy is more wet than before I started. I remove the towel and lean closer, pressing a kiss against her clit. My tongue swirls around the tiny bundle of nerves. Then I dry her belly and ribs before circling the plush material over her breasts. Her nipples tighten as I swipe over them. When I'm finished, I pop to my feet, sucking one hard bud into my mouth before lavishing the same attention on the other.

"I think we're done here."

"That's unfortunate." Her cheeks are stained with color, and her eyes are heavy-lidded.

I chuckle before scooping her up into my arms and carrying her into the other room. Gently, I place her in the middle of the queen-size bed. Her gaze stays locked on mine as her thighs fall open.

Fuck, but she's beautiful.

Pink.

Soft.

Inviting.

Those are the only words that rush through my brain.

I kick off my shoes and yank the back of my T-shirt, pulling it over my head before tossing it to the floor. The athletic shorts and boxers are the next to go as I shove them down my thighs until the material is puddled around my feet.

I crawl onto the bed and up her body. Her legs wrap around my waist, cradling my thick erection against her softness. All it would take is one thrust of my hips, jand I could sink deep inside her body. Instead, I keep a tight leash on my control. She moans and rubs her slick heat against my hard length.

"Don't you want to be inside me?" she murmurs.

"More than anything," I breathe, "but tonight, I'm going to hold you in my arms."

Questions circle through her dark depths. *"Really?"*

"Yup."

"Naked?"

"Damn right."

"I'm glad you're staying," she whispers, tugging me closer.

"Me, too." The only thing that matters is that Mia is here in my arms.

That she's mine.

Or, at the very least, on her way to being mine.

And maybe I'm on my way to being hers.

Chapter Twenty-Eight

MIA

My sleep is deep and filled with dreams. Most, I can't hang on to. The one I find myself immersed in before waking is filled with Beck.

The sexy neighbor I've crushed on forever.

The guy I've avoided for the past seven years out of self-preservation.

Dreams and memories intertwine until they become one. I can't remember if he touched me last night or if it was all part of a delicious fantasy. Once I'm able to shake the last dregs of sleep, I stretch my limbs as the memories from last night crash down on me.

Beck climbing through the window.

Running a bath and stripping me bare.

Making me a cup of tea.

Orgasming.

Drying me off and carrying me to bed.

And then falling asleep in his arms.

I roll to my side only to find the space next to me vacant. Not only is the bed empty, but the sheets are also cold to the touch, which means Beck snuck out a while ago. Disappointment surges through me, threatening to swallow me whole. I flop onto my back and stare at the ceiling before tugging the sheet over my naked breasts.

Doubt creeps in at the edges and makes me question everything. Most of all, myself. More than anything, I want to believe in Beck. I want to believe that the pretty words he's strung together mean something. That his feelings are real.

Like mine are.

Not wanting to dwell on those troubling thoughts, I throw off the covers. As I'm searching for pajamas, Beck walks through the door carrying two plates. I'm slammed with the realization that he didn't pull a disappearing act.

The guy made breakfast.

Giddiness bubbles up in my chest like a geyser.

As soon as Beck sees me, a wide smile tips the corners of his lips. "Morning, sunshine. Sleep well?"

I rake a hand through my hair, knowing it's in disarray. "Yeah, I did." Probably because his arms were banded around me through most of the night.

He gives me a sexy little wink. "Me, too."

Naked, I crawl back onto the bed and tuck the sheet under my arms before reaching for a plate. "Hope you don't mind I made breakfast."

Is that a joke?

I stare at the dish in surprise. Chocolate chip pancakes with whipped cream and maple syrup. There're also three slices of bacon and a hash brown patty. This is exactly what my perfect breakfast consists of.

Is it a coincidence?

Questions dance in my eyes.

His lips lift as he points to the plate. "All of your favorites."

It takes effort to clear my throat along with the emotion that has become wedged in there. "I noticed." I shake my head, trying to get a handle on the situation. "How did you know?"

"Remember when our families used to go out for brunch together?"

Of course, I do. Picking out a dress for our Sunday morning get-togethers was agonizing. I usually ended up changing my outfit a bazillion times. Even though I swore up and down that I wasn't dressing with Beck in mind, that's exactly what I was doing.

"That was a long time ago," I murmur, mind cartwheeling.

"You ordered the same thing every time." His eyes darken to a deeper shade of green. "And you'd make these cute little noises deep in your throat when you ate the pancakes."

Heat slams into my cheeks because he's not wrong. I *love* chocolate chip pancakes, especially when drenched in whipped cream and syrup.

Yummy.

"I always looked forward to brunch with your family." His grin turns wicked. "Watching you devour your pancakes gave me major wood."

It's official—my face is on fire.

I can't believe he felt that way.

"Don't look so shocked." He taps the tip of my nose with his index finger and smirks. "It's always been you, Mia."

I never realized. Girls have been chasing after Beck since seventh grade. How was I even on his radar?

"I forgot something in the kitchen." He sets his plate on the night-stand. "Be right back."

Before I can open my mouth, Beck disappears through the doorway and into the hall.

Now that he's gone, I suck in a deep breath and try to wrangle all of my emotions back under control. But it's not easy. Every time I think I have a grasp on Beck, he does something that blows me out of the water.

He's not the guy I thought he was.

How could I have been so wrong about him?

I focus on my plate and use the side of my fork to cut through the fluffy pancakes. Chocolate oozes from where I slice through the stack. Beck saunters into the room with two glasses of orange juice.

My fork stalls midway to my mouth as I stare.

What's this guy trying to do to me?

He stumbles to a halt. "Is something wrong?"

Beckett Hollingsworth made me pancakes.

And a hash brown.

And bacon.

And brought me orange juice.

How could anything possibly be wrong?

It's all too right.

I shake my head and shove the forkful of warm fluffiness into my mouth before I say something I might regret. A soft moan escapes as my eyelids flutter shut. The pancakes practically melt in my mouth. Once I swallow them down, I open my eyes. "They're delicious. Thank you."

He stares intently at my lips before giving his head a little shake. "No problem," he mutters, grabbing his plate and settling on the bed next to me.

It's almost impressive the way Beck wolfs down his breakfast. I forgot what a big appetite he has.

I laugh and point to his clean plate. "Hungry much?" I've barely made a dent in my food, and he's already done.

He grins before patting his flat belly. "Starving."

"I could tell."

When I'm finished, Beck runs the plates down to the kitchen. Less than two minutes later, he's back and sliding into bed. He tugs me into his arms, and I nestle against his chest. When he runs his fingers through my hair, I close my eyes, enjoying the comforting touch.

"Have you come to any decisions about your dad?"

Ugh.

Until this point, I've been successful in shoving those unwanted thoughts to the back of my brain where I don't have to dwell on them. But I can't avoid the issue forever.

"Not really." Once we slid between the sheets last night and Beck wrapped his arms around me, I fell into a deep sleep. "If you were me, what would you do?"

He blows out a steady breath as his face grows serious. "I don't know," he admits. "We have different relationships with our fathers." His voice softens. "And your family has been through a lot more than mine."

Thoughts of my sister swirl through my head. Nothing has been the same since Brianna died. Most of the time, it seems like my parents are going through the motions of living their lives.

Although, the man I saw last night looked nothing like the Dad I know. He looked happier than I've seen him in a long time. Ten years younger, at least. Instead of having his face buried in his phone, he was actually paying attention to the person sitting across from him.

"Is it possible your mom is aware of the relationship?"

That thought never occurred to me.

"I don't know." It's difficult to imagine that my mother would knowingly sit home alone while my father screwed around on her.

"Maybe you need to give it more thought before you make any rash decisions. Like I said last night, what happens in their marriage is between them."

"Yeah," I mumble, feeling more confused than ever, "I guess."

Beck reaches out and tangles our fingers together. The moment our skin comes in contact, electricity zips through me. All at once, I'm aware of my naked state. And that he's only wearing boxers. A punch of arousal hits me in the core. Before I can change my mind, I toss the covers aside and crawl on top of him. Beck's eyes widen as I straddle his waist.

"Did I thank you properly for breakfast?"

"Umm..." When he gulps, it's enough to make my confidence soar. "Yes?"

My fingers slide through his hair as my lips hover over his. "You deserve another thank you."

His hands go to my naked back as I press him against the mattress.

"Mia," he groans.

I arch a brow, enjoying the strange power I seem to hold over him. It's a heady sensation. There's nothing but the thin cotton of his boxers separating my heat from his thick erection. All I want to do is grind myself against him.

Instead, I scoot lower, kissing his chest and stroking my fingers over the hard slabs of his muscles. I've dreamt about doing this for years. My tongue swipes over his nipples, sucking first one and then the other into my mouth.

A sigh escapes from Beck as he tunnels his fingers through my hair.

I slide lower, kissing my way to his rock-hard abs before arriving at the elastic band of his boxer-briefs. I slip my fingers beneath the material, sweeping them back and forth against his warm flesh. I've caught glimpses of his cock, but never this up close and personal. I tug at the boxers until his boner springs free.

His dick should come with a warning label—*object larger than it appears.*

I glance at him and smirk. "Impressive."

Beck releases a strained chuckle. "Thanks. I take great pride in it."

I refocus my attention on him before stroking my fingers over his erection. "You should." Wanting him naked, I slide the boxers down his hips and over his thighs before tossing them to the floor.

His cock is hot to the touch and feels like silk-covered steel. I'm enamored by the feel of him. With soft strokes, I pet him, running my fingers down the length before carefully palming his balls. Beck groans as I worship his body. Moisture beads at the slit of his erection, and I lean down, swiping my tongue over it. There's just a hint of saltiness.

He releases a deep guttural sound that vibrates in my ears and restlessly shifts his hips.

When I repeat the gesture, he growls, "Damn, baby, that feels good."

Surprisingly, I'm enjoying this as much as the chocolate chip pancakes. I can't get enough of him. Luckily for us, we have hours to explore one another before heading back to school later this afternoon.

As I lean down, ready to take him in my mouth, there's a noise from within the house. I poker up and twist around toward the open bedroom door. "Did you hear that?"

Before Beck can answer, a voice calls from downstairs—

"Mia? Are you up yet?"

Dad.

Oh, God.

Beck meets my wild-eyed stare with a version of his own. *"Dad?"* I squeak, heart pounding harshly against my chest.

"Of course," he laughs, his voice getting closer as he climbs the staircase. "Who else would it be?"

I leap from the bed and stumble, all but crashing against the door to slam it shut. Beck rolls off the edge and jumps to his feet. He grabs his boxers before staggering sideways as he yanks them up his legs.

"Get in the closet!" I whisper-yell, grabbing my robe from the chaise and tugging it on so I'm no longer naked.

I can't believe this is happening.

What the hell is he doing here?

There's a rap of knuckles against my bedroom door.

I run my fingers through the tangled length of my hair before forcing myself to walk to the door and pull it open. I paste a smile on my face when I find Dad on the other side.

"I thought you were out of town until tomorrow." The lie leaves a bitter taste in my mouth, but it's the best I can come up with under the circumstances. Resentment and anger swallow the nerves that had been rushing through my body only moments ago.

"Change of plans," he says with a shrug. "The conference ended early, so I thought we could grab breakfast before you leave for school. Sound good?"

Images from the restaurant last night roll through my head. A million questions sit poised on the tip of my tongue. It's all I can do to keep them trapped inside.

Unable to look him in the eyes without exploding, I glance away. "Um, yeah. Give me a few minutes to get ready."

"Great, I'll meet you downstairs."

I watch him retreat before turning toward the staircase. When he disappears from sight, I close the door and lean against it before squeezing my eyes tight.

How am I supposed to sit across from him and act like everything is normal? As if he hasn't blown my world apart?

"Hey, are you all right?"

I open my eyes and find Beck standing in front of me. He cups my cheeks before tilting my face toward his.

"Not at all," I whisper.

"Then don't say anything. Give it some time."

"I'm not sure I can do that." I glance away before shrugging. It feels like the weight of the world is resting on my shoulders. "I guess we'll see how it goes."

His thumb strokes over my bottom lip.

"Do you want me to come with?" He searches my eyes. "Because I will."

Warmth spreads through my chest that he would even consider putting himself in that uncomfortable situation. Even though the offer is tempting, I shake my head.

"Are you sure?" His lips lower before brushing across mine. The movement is sexy and comforting all at the same time.

"It'll be better if I go by myself."

"If that's what you want." He presses a kiss to my mouth before murmuring, "Let me know when you return from breakfast, and we'll head back to school."

"You don't need to wait."

"I'm not leaving without you." He smacks one last kiss against my forehead before his hands fall away from my face. "You better get dressed."

Dread settles at the bottom of my belly as I grab panties and a bra from the dresser and pull them on before heading to the walk-in closet and picking out jeans and a sweater. Not bothering with my hair, I grab an elastic band and pull it into a simple ponytail.

As I walk toward the door, I glance at Beck as he lounges on my bed. "You'll sneak out after we take off?"

"Yup."

"All right." I have to force myself to leave the room. "I'll see you soon."

"I'll be waiting."

As I descend the staircase, I spot Dad sitting on the antique bench in the entryway. His face, as usual, is buried in his phone. My feet grind to a halt as I'm slammed with a thought.

Is he texting the woman I saw him with last night?

All the calls and texts he's received before shuttering himself away in his office for hours on end whirl through my head. Work was always the excuse he gave for the countless trips he took.

Was it all a lie?

The realization makes me nauseous.

I don't want to view my father as anything other than the man I've loved with all my heart since I was a little girl. But how can I do that with everything I know and suspect?

When Dad glances up and catches me studying him, he stuffs his phone in his pocket and rises to his feet. Carefully I search his face for any trace of guilt, but there is none to be found. Somehow that makes the situation worse.

"You slept late," he says with a smile, eyes crinkling at the corners.

I shrug. "Just tired, I guess."

"I'm glad you got a chance to rest up." There's a pause. "Did you take the Jeep out and make sure it was running all right?"

"No, not yet." The Jeep is the last of my concerns.

"Okay, I'll grab the keys from the kitchen, and we can get moving." He's already walking through the hall when he asks, "Any place, in particular, you want to go?"

Even though I have no idea if Marco's is open for Sunday brunch, I'm tempted to throw the suggestion out there. Instead, I say, "How about The Honeybun?"

"Sure, I could go for that." After a moment, he returns to the hallway with a furrowed brow. "Did you already eat? There are pans and dishes on the counter."

Oh.

My mind cartwheels, grasping for an explanation that will make sense. It would be all too easy to lie and say I made myself breakfast for dinner last night. But I'm loath to do that. Lying has never come easily to me. Especially when it involves my parents.

"Yes," I force the words from my mouth, "I ate earlier."

"Oh." His head is turned as he stares at the sink. I know what's coming next. I can almost see the wheels spinning in his head.

"Is someone here with you?" he asks hesitantly.

I blow out a steady breath and straighten my shoulders. "Beck is upstairs."

It's almost comical the way his brows shoot up across his forehead and into his hairline. If this were any other conversation, his reaction would make me laugh.

"Beck?" Shock weaves its way through his words. *"Hollingsworth?"* He waves his hand toward our neighbor's house. *"From next door?"*

I wince as his voice continues to escalate.

"Please tell me that he stayed in a guestroom."

Again, I could lie. It would be the quickest way to end this uncomfortable conversation. Dad probably wouldn't believe me, but it's doubtful he would push the issue. We would pretend that I didn't have sex with Beck and move on with our lives. But there's no reason for me to do that. I'm twenty-one years old. Who I sleep with is none of his business.

"No. He stayed with me." Those five words are like a lead weight that sits uncomfortably between us.

"I don't understand any of this," he mutters, plowing a hand through his hair. "Are you two seeing each other?"

"Yes, we are."

Confusion swirls through his eyes. "How long has this been going on for?"

"It's a relatively new development."

He blows out a steady breath as his broad shoulders collapse. "I have no idea what to say about all this."

"You don't need to say anything."

"Is your mother aware of what's going on?"

I shake my head. "No, we haven't told anyone yet."

Tentatively, he steps toward me. "As much as I like Beck," there's a pause, and I steel myself for what will come next, "he's not the right guy for you."

I echo with disbelief, *"He's not the right guy for me?"*

His frown deepens into a scowl. "Come on, you know *exactly* what I mean. Beck doesn't have a serious bone in his body. His life is football. Other than that, he parties and sleeps around. I don't understand why you would be interested in someone like that."

My mouth falls open. "Dad! That's not true!"

He closes the distance between us. "That kid has always been a troublemaker. I used to feel bad for Archie and Caroline, always having to clean up his messes."

"That was in high school," I grit out. "He's changed. People are capable of it."

"Has he really changed that much?" Dad snorts and rolls his eyes. "Because I find that difficult to believe."

"Yeah, he has. Maybe you need to look at the person he is today instead of judging him for the one he used to be."

"Oh, please," he mutters. "Archie says he still gets into trouble."

I shift my weight and glare, frustrated with this conversation. "Have you ever considered the possibility that Archie is as biased as you are?"

He presses his lips together before jerking his shoulders into a shrug. An uncomfortable silence settles around us before a puff of breath escapes from him. "The last thing I want to see is you get hurt. Beck isn't the type of guy to be faithful."

Ha!

That's rich.

How can he look me in the eyes and say that?

Dad pokers up to his full height. "What's that supposed to mean?"

I flinch and realize the words have unintentionally slipped from my mouth.

"Mia?"

My heartbeat hammers in my ears until the sound is all I'm cognizant of. He stares as if he no longer recognizes me. What he doesn't realize is that the feeling is mutual. "I saw you last night, Dad."

He doesn't so much as blink. Not even a flicker of guilt enters his dark eyes. His lack of response is almost enough to make me question what I saw.

When he remains silent, I repeat myself, louder this time. "I was at Marco's last night and saw you having dinner with a blond woman."

Dad laughs, but the sound is forced. "You're mistaken, I was in Cincinnati."

He's lying. I know what I saw. He was at the restaurant. His dishonesty this morning is almost as hurtful and disappointing as catching him with another woman was last night. He'd rather create doubts in my mind than own up to his own shady actions. I never expected this kind of behavior from him.

It only hardens everything inside me.

"Stop lying. Beck is the one who spotted you, Dad. He didn't want me to see, so he tried to hustle me out of the restaurant. But I saw you anyway." I fold my arms tightly across my chest. "Would you like me to call him down here?"

His jaw tightens as anger flashes in his eyes. "That won't be necessary."

My voice drops as I shake my head. "You were never out of town, were you?"

"No."

Even though I was expecting the answer, it still hits me like a sucker punch.

As painful as this line of questioning is, I push on. "Who is she?"

The anger dissipates from his eyes as sadness creeps in. "Does it really matter?"

Of course, it matters.

"You've been cheating on Mom." My eyes pop wide with disbelief. "So yeah, it kind of matters."

"She's a colleague," he begrudgingly admits.

Un-fucking-believable.

"How long has this been going on for?"

"A while," he mutters, looking away.

What does that mean?

A few weeks?

A few months?

A few years?

Longer?

It makes me sick to my stomach, and I find myself unable to continue. My belly churns, and for a moment, I wonder if I'll throw up. My arms drop to my sides as if they weigh a thousand pounds. "How could you do this to Mom?"

"I never meant for it to happen." His shoulders slump. "I—"

"That doesn't matter!" I cry with frustration. "You've been sneaking around and having an affair with another woman! Not only have you lied to Mom, but you've also been lying to me!"

"My personal relationships have nothing to do with you." He plows a hand through his hair. "You don't understand what it's been like since Brianna died."

"Really?" How can he say that? "I know *exactly* what it's been like! You're not the only one who lost her! Mom lost a daughter, and I lost my only sister! We *all* lost her, Dad, it wasn't just you!" Tears sting my eyes as anger boils in my blood. "How dare you use Brianna as an excuse for your infidelity!"

Heat slams into his cheeks as he winces. For the first time since his affair has been dragged into the light, he looks ashamed. "I'm not using her as an excuse," he mumbles.

"That's *exactly* what you're doing." I'm so disgusted by this conversation that I don't even want to look at him.

"Losing her was more than any of us could endure, and we all dealt with our grief differently."

"Did you ever consider," I shoot back, "that we should have dealt with it together instead of splintering apart the way we did?"

"Her death was so painful." His eyes grow distant. "Sometimes, it felt as if the grief was more than I could deal with."

I know, but still...

"What about Mom? Does she have any idea what's going on?" Maybe Beck is right, and she's aware of Dad's infidelity. If that turns out to be the case, I'm not sure how I'll be able to look at either of them the same way again.

He shakes his head. "She doesn't know."

"You have to tell her, Dad. You have to make everything right. This can't continue."

Emotion flickers in his eyes before his gaze darts away.

A sliver of dread snakes down my spine as an uncomfortable silence stretches to the breaking point. "You *are* going to end this, right?" Panic and disbelief weave their way through my voice.

He drags a hand over his face. "The situation is more complicated than you can understand."

"You know what I understand?" Before he can respond, I continue, voice rising with every word. "That you made vows to Mom, and when Brianna was taken from us, you took the easy way out and had an affair. *That's* what I understand."

The sound he makes when he swallows is audible. "I need to think about what's best for everyone."

What the hell does that mean?

A strangled laugh slides from my lips. "You know what would be best for me? If my family stayed intact." My voice fills with anger. "I think Mom would agree with that, don't you?"

When he presses his lips together and remains silent, I'm struck with a heartbreaking realization. It's as painful as a two-by-four slamming into the back of my head.

"You have no intention of ending this affair, do you?" The words might be arranged in the form of a question, but it's not.

We both know the answer without him having to verbalize it.

"It's complicated," he repeats weakly, as if that makes it better.

"No," I snap, losing my patience, "it's not. You have a wife. A woman you've been married to for over twenty-five years. Explain what's complicated about it?"

The acidic taste of bile rises in my throat.

His reluctance to end this relationship makes me realize that it's not a casual affair. Even though I had purposefully dropped the issue a few minutes ago, I now feel the need to press for an answer. "How long has this been going on?"

"A while."

"A year?" I spit.

He stares mutely.

My voice escalates. *"A few years?"*

His stubborn silence sends a wave of nausea and anger crashing through me.

"This is your chance to do the right thing," I grit out. My hands tighten into useless fists that hang at my sides. Disappointment and exasperation churn in my gut. I don't think I've ever felt this disgusted with anyone in my life. Let alone, one of my parents.

How is this issue not cut and dry?

Not once has he shown an ounce of remorse or offered to end his affair. And that's frightening. This woman—whoever she is—means something to him.

Possibly more than we do.

Unable to stomach the sight of my father, I swing around and force myself up the staircase. Putting one foot in front of the other feels like a Herculean effort. When I'm halfway up, I pause and glance down at him. He hasn't budged from the foyer. "If you don't tell her, I will."

Spitting out those words feels like the equivalent to dropping a bomb.

It's appalling that I have to threaten him.

He jerks his head into a tight nod but offers nothing more.

As I stare at my dad, I realize he's not the man I thought he was.

How could he be?

The father I've revered since childhood would never hurt the people he loves the way this one has.

This man is nothing more than a stranger.

Chapter Twenty-Nine

MIA

"I can't believe you didn't tell me what was going on!" Alyssa shoves me in the shoulder, and the force sends me careening into a random guy on the walking path.

My hands grasp his chest for purchase as he holds my upper arms to steady me. Heat fills my cheeks. "I am *so* sorry!"

The guy grins, making no attempt to release me. "It's not a problem."

Alyssa grabs my arm and yanks me free. "Sorry, bud, she's taken."

He shrugs. "That's too bad."

Alyssa snorts before dragging me down the path.

"I'm going to kill you," I mutter through clenched teeth.

"No, you're not." She doesn't sound the least bit concerned by the threat. "You love me too much to do that."

"Hmmm," I scrunch my face and contemplate the statement, *"do I?"*

"Yup." She links her arm through mine as we continue walking. "Anyway, back to the original convo we were having before you rather clumsily threw yourself at that guy."

When I glare, she grins and keeps yapping. "I can't believe you kept this from me!"

"It wasn't like that," I try to explain. "It just happened."

"Please, girl. The Mia and Beck saga has been years in the making. It didn't just," she makes air quotes with her fingers, *"happen'*. This courtship has been moving at glacial speeds."

She might be right. All I know is that I don't want to discuss the Beck situation until it picks up traction.

Giving Alyssa a little taste of her own medicine, I shoot back with, "It's not like you've been entirely forthcoming about Colton."

It's almost comical the way her face goes blank. "That's because there's nothing to tell."

I narrow my eyes and search hers for the truth. "Are you sure about that?"

"Positive." It's airily that she announces, "Colton Montgomery is part of my past, not my future."

I have my suspicions as far as Alyssa's ex is concerned, but that's all they are at this point. *Suspicions*. As I open my mouth to delve deeper, my phone rings.

The music from my ringtone has my belly doing a painful flip. Every time my cell makes the slightest noise, dread nearly swallows me whole, and I hold my breath until I'm on the verge of passing out.

I dig through my bag in search of my phone. After a few moments of rooting around, my fingers lock around the slim cell. Nerves prickle along my flesh as I glance at the screen.

Mom.

Alyssa jostles me in the shoulder. "Aren't you going to answer that?"

"Yeah." I force out the air that has become trapped in my lungs before sliding my thumb across the green button. "Hey, Mom."

Silence greets me from the other end. I'm about to repeat her name when she clears the thick emotion from her throat. That's all it takes for me to realize she's spoken to Dad. In some ways, it's a relief that I won't have to break the news to her.

"Mom? Are you all right?"

Alyssa waves a hand in front of my face. When I glance at her, she mouths, "What's going on?"

"I'll tell you later," I whisper. "Sorry."

Eyes filling with concern, she nods and points to the fine arts building on the horizon. "I need to go."

I wave as she takes off. Even though my one o'clock class starts in less than five minutes, I head toward a bench situated under a tree before settling on it. There's no way I can push off this conversation until later.

When the line remains silent, I say, "Mom, talk to me."

She sniffles. "Have you spoken to your father?"

I don't want to lie, but I don't necessarily want to admit the truth either. It seems like it would only make matters worse.

"No," I wince and force the fib from my lips, "not recently."

Tears clog her voice, and it makes me furious all over again that Dad has inflicted so much pain. Mom doesn't deserve this. If there's any kind of silver lining to be found in this situation, it's that they can start fresh and repair the damage to their marriage. Maybe even be stronger for it.

"He left." A sob breaks free from her. "He packed his bags last night and walked out."

Shock crashes over me like a wave as I stare sightlessly at the students bustling across campus.

When I remain silent, she says, "Mia? Did you hear me?"

It takes effort to shake myself from the mental fog that has descended. "Yes, I heard."

She cries quietly on the other end of the phone, and my heart breaks all over again. There's nothing I can say or do to comfort her. Rage rushes through every part of my body.

"I can't believe this is happening," she whispers.

"I'm so sorry." It takes effort to keep my voice level and not curse his name. "Did he say why he was leaving?"

The sound of her tears falls faster. "He's in love with someone else." Disbelief and confusion drip from every word. "He said that our marriage has been over for a while."

It's as if the air has been knocked from my lungs, and I can't breathe. I can only sit on the bench gasping as people walk by laughing and chattering, oblivious that my world has imploded,

Is he really walking away from us?

It seems impossible.

"Do you want me to come home?" I ask. "I could leave after my next class and stay the night."

She sucks in a shuddering breath before blowing it out. "I appreciate the offer, sweetie, but you need to stay there. It's important that you focus on your classes."

I snort out a laugh, knowing there's no way I'll be able to do that.

"Are you going to talk to him? What about seeing a counselor?" I pause before adding in a hopeful tone, "Maybe he'll change his mind."

"I have no idea what I'm going to do." Bitterness gathers in her voice. "But if he doesn't want to be married to me, then I damn well don't want him back."

I rub my temple and consider the next step. "It might be a good idea to talk with a lawyer and get some legal advice."

"Oh." A heavy silence falls over us. "Yeah...maybe I'll do that."

At a loss for words, I say, "I'm sorry, Mom."

"Me, too, sweetie. Your dad was right about one thing. Nothing has been the same since Brianna died." Grief and sadness fill her voice. "Maybe I shouldn't be surprised by this, but I am."

It's true that nothing has been the same for our family. We pretended to pick up the pieces of our lives and move forward, but that was a façade. Instead of dealing with the pain of her loss, we buried it. Dad delved into work and started an affair while Mom drank too much and shopped.

And me?

I set out to be the perfect child so they wouldn't miss the one they lost. I tried to shine as if that would be enough to overshadow her death.

In hindsight, it sounds stupid.

How could that possibly fill the void Brianna left behind?

My sister died seven years ago, and sometimes it feels like the wounds are as fresh and painful as when it happened. We've all been tiptoeing around our grief instead of facing it head-on.

"Call if you need anything, Mom. I can come home anytime."

"I'll be fine, don't worry about me."

We disconnect, and I stay seated on the bench, staring at the phone in my hand.

"Mia?"

I glance up only to find Beck staring at me. His brows are drawn together as if he can't figure out what I'm doing. "Aren't you supposed to be in class?"

"Yeah."

He settles beside me before searching my face. "What's going on?"

"Mom called." Tears fill my eyes. "Dad packed his bags and left."

Beck stares in surprise before wrapping his arm around my shoulders and tugging me close. "I'm so sorry." He presses his lips to the top of my head. "Are you all right?"

I shrug, still feeling dazed. After my conversation with Dad Sunday morning, maybe I should have expected this outcome, but I really thought he would do the right thing. How could he choose her over us?

How could he do that?

"Is your mom okay?"

"No. She's been blindsided. I offered to come home, but she didn't want me to."

"If it'll make you feel better, I can call my mom and have her check on Julia."

It's not a bad idea, but I'm not sure if Mom wants anyone—let alone our neighbors and friends—to know what's going on.

As I consider the offer, I bite my lip and shake my head. "No, not right now. I'll call her when I get home later."

He nods and squeezes me tight. "Let me know if there's anything I can do to help."

"Thank you." When I lift my face, he brushes his mouth against mine.

"You know I would do anything for you, right?" he murmurs between kisses.

The corners of my lips tremble upward. A few months ago, I could have never imagined trusting Beck enough to lean on him for emotional support. And yet, here we are. In a few short weeks, he's become one of the most important people in my life.

The irony isn't lost on me that the one man I thought I'd always be able to depend on has flaked, and the one I would have never dared open my heart to is proving himself to be someone I could fall in love with.

Chapter Thirty

BECK

A small knot of tension sits at the bottom of my belly as I rap my knuckles against Dr. Hayes' partially open office door. She glances up from her computer screen and smiles before waving me in.

"Thanks for stopping by." She pulls off her glasses and sets them on the desk next to her coffee cup. "I read over your latest draft and have a few suggestions." She leans back in her chair. "I thought it would be easier for us to discuss them in person rather than emailing back and forth."

"Sure, no problem."

"Great. Want to get started?"

I nod.

As I take a step toward the desk, she waves to the tiny loveseat. "Let's sit on the couch, it'll be more comfortable."

Comfortable for who?

Certainly not me.

My step falters as I clear my throat and search for an excuse. I'm trying to keep as much distance between us as possible. "My computer is kind of heavy. It might be better to set it on the desk while we work." I'm grasping at straws. My computer weighs a pound or two at the most.

Her lips twitch with amusement. "The coffee table will be just fine."

Damn.

Mia's words swirl through my head.

She's friendly.

She isn't coming on to you.

She's one of the most beloved professors on campus.

You've misinterpreted her intentions.

Dr. Hayes rises from her desk and slides past me while I stand rooted in place. When her body brushes against mine, my anxiety levels spike.

It's all in my head.

I'm being too sensitive.

Once she's settled, I glance longingly at the office door before forcing myself to close the distance between us. My lips flatten when I realize she's positioned herself smack dab in the middle, not leaving much room on either side.

When I hesitate, she pats the cushion beside her, and I have no other choice but to sit down. I squash my six-foot frame as close to the armrest as possible and keep my attention focused straight ahead as I set the computer on the coffee table and fire it up.

Any distance I had purposely left is eaten up when she scoots closer.

With our thighs pressed together, she pulls out her notes and glances at the computer screen before pointing out where more clarification is needed. For the next thirty minutes, we meticulously move through the body of the paper. Mia has been helping me to edit when she has time, so it's not a total mess. As we work side-by-side, my muscles loosen. Other than our bodies pressed close, she hasn't done anything else to make me feel uncomfortable.

It's a relief to realize that Mia was right. I'm an idiot for thinking this woman was coming on to me.

Dr. Hayes wraps up her critique by saying, "Keep working, and we'll meet up again next week to check your progress. If you follow the suggestions I've made, there's no reason you can't get an A on this paper, and frankly, in this class."

An A?

Pigs flying out of my ass seem more likely than that. I've never received an A on a paper in my life. Sometimes it was all I could do to eke out a B.

"Why is that so funny? I'm being serious." She points to the computer. "This is shaping up to be a great paper. One I look forward to reading."

Now *that* makes me laugh.

I shrug and shake my head. "Writing has never come easy to me." Even though I was dreading this meeting, it's obvious there was never anything to be concerned about. "I appreciate you spending so much time with me."

"Helping students realize their full potential is one of the most rewarding aspects of my job." She shifts, and our knees touch. "It's one reason I'm so passionate about my work." Her hand flutters to mine before covering it.

My gaze drops to our clasped fingers. "Well, um, thank you, Dr. Hayes."

"When we're alone, you can call me Rebecca."

"Right." This meeting has taken a turn for the awkward. I don't care if she's touchy-feely or not. I don't like it. Now that the paper has been wrapped up, all I want to do is escape.

When I attempt to retract my fingers, her grip tightens, halting my movements.

"Beck—"

I glance up and realize her face is much closer than before.

"I had hoped you would take advantage of my offer to work one-on-one with you. Kind of like a mentor." She tucks an errant lock of hair behind her ear. "There is so much I could teach you, if you would let me."

Relief rushes from my lungs when she lifts her hand from mine. Instead of pulling away, it settles on my thigh, where it rests danger-ously close to my balls.

Friendliness is one thing.

This is something altogether different.

"Um—"

Before I can say anything more, she's on her knees between my legs. Her other hand drops to my thigh before she slides both toward my junk.

Hunger flashes in her eyes before settling on my lap. "I've been very patient about waiting for you to get the hint. So, I've decided to take matters into my own hands." As those words leave her lips, her fingers wrap around my cock.

Holy shit!

"Dr. Hayes," I choke out as a strange paralysis takes over. I can't move. My muscles feel locked in place.

"Rebecca," she corrects, tongue darting out to smudge her lips. "Call me Rebecca."

"I'm not—"

There's a knock on the office door. My head jerks up as it opens in slow motion.

"Dr. H—"

Oh, fuck.

Mia.

I would recognize her voice anywhere.

"Now's not a good time!" the professor shouts, but it's too late.

As Mia falters over the threshold, her wide gaze locks on mine before sliding to the woman between my outstretched legs. I quickly knock her hands away, hoping the situation doesn't look as damning as I imagine it does.

"I, um, sorry," Mia mumbles before taking a hasty step in retreat. Hurt and shock swirl through her dark depths before she quickly slams the door closed.

The thick wood reverberates on its hinges as silence settles around us.

"Well, that's not good." Dr. Hayes rises gracefully to her feet before running a hand over her pencil skirt. "Luckily, Mia is my teaching assistant, so it shouldn't be too difficult to smooth this over." Instead of looking embarrassed, a smile curves her lips before a chuckle escapes. "Did you see the look on her face? I think we shocked the poor girl."

We?

I don't think so.

I sure as hell wasn't a willing participant in this.

Not bothering to answer, I bolt to my feet and snap my computer shut before shoving it in my backpack.

"Next time, we need to make sure the door is locked." She gives me a little wink before sliding behind her desk and sinking to her chair.

There won't be a next time.

"I need to go," I mutter. All I can think about is finding Mia and explaining what happened.

With my backpack slung over my shoulder, I leave the office and jog through the hallway to the elevators. Bypassing them, I take the stairwell, sprinting down five flights before reaching the ground floor. I push through the metal door into the lobby but don't see Mia's dark head anywhere.

A few guys from the football team are shooting the shit outside Mitchell Hall. When they call me over, I wave them off and run past. My heart skips a beat when I see her striding about twenty yards ahead of me. I hasten my pace, pushing through the people on the path. A few grumble before glancing at me. When they realize who I am, they shut their mouths.

"Mia!" I call out when I'm close enough, "wait up!"

She doesn't glance over her shoulder, but I know she heard me because she picks up her pace, as if trying to escape. There's no way in hell I can allow that to happen. When I'm within striking distance, I reach out and wrap my fingers around her upper arm to stop her. The moment I make contact, she whips around and bares her teeth.

"Don't you dare touch me!" she hisses. Anger vibrates from every cell of her body. I don't think I've ever seen her so enraged.

"Mia, give me a chance to explain!"

When she attempts to jerk her arm from my hold, my grip tightens.

"If you don't let go," she growls, "I'll scream."

Fuck.

No matter how much I want to tell my side of the story, I can't force her to listen. Reluctantly, I release her arm. I'm almost taken aback by the fury and disgust swirling through her eyes.

"It's not what it looked like." My heart slams harshly against my ribcage until it feels like it might explode.

A humorless laugh falls from her mouth. *"Really?* Because it looked like Dr. Hayes was moments away from giving you a blowie."

I wince as her voice increases in decibel with each syllable. A few students walking past, turn and stare with curiosity.

"She asked me to stop by her office so we could go over my paper." My tongue darts out to moisten my lips. "Everything was fine, and then she was on her knees."

"And you didn't push her away?" Her brows jerk up with disbelief.

"It all happened so fast." I plow a hand through my hair.

"You sat there and let her touch you," she accuses.

"No!" I shake my head. "I—"

"What?"

"I don't know," I whisper, wishing she would calm down and give me a chance to explain. My thoughts are all jumbled together, and I'm not making sense. It looks like I have something to hide when nothing could be further from the truth. "I tried to tell you that she was hitting on me."

"Yes," she snorts, "it really looked like she was forcing herself on you."

"Maybe it didn't look that way, but that's exactly what happened!"

She searches my eyes for a long moment before shaking her head. "I don't believe you."

My shoulders collapse in defeat. I'm not sure what more I can say to make her understand the situation. When Mia retreats, it feels like there is a yawning chasm sitting between us. Reaching her no longer feels possible.

I take a hesitant step in her direction, only wanting to bridge the growing distance between us. "Mia, I said that I would never hurt you, and I meant it."

"I'm such an idiot for believing in you." Tears well in her eyes. "You're no better than my father."

Her words are like poisonous darts that pierce my flesh. All I've tried to do is prove that I'm not the guy I used to be, and I've failed.

"You know that's not true," I murmur through the pain that blooms in my heart.

What could I have done differently?

I wasn't lying when I said it all happened so fast. For a moment, it had felt like I was paralyzed, powerless to stop Dr. Hayes from touching me. For a guy my size, it's ridiculous that I couldn't stop a tiny woman from laying her hands on me.

Shame and guilt bubble up inside, nearly swallowing me whole.

"I can't do this with you," she says, interrupting the thoughts that churn in my head, "I need to go."

When I reach out, she backs further away as if she can't stand the thought of me touching her.

"Please, don't leave like this." It feels like Mia is slipping through my fingers and there's not a damned thing I can do about it. "Can we talk later?"

She shakes her head and straightens her shoulders. "No, you've hurt me for the last time."

Before I can say anything else, she spins away and heads for the walking path that cuts through campus. Instead of going after her, I remain rooted in place. Chasing Mia will only push her further away.

I plow a hand through my hair, knowing there might not be a way to fix this.

It's altogether possible that I just lost the only girl who ever mattered to me.

Chapter Thirty-One

MIA

I hop out of my Jeep and smooth down my skirt before hurrying into El Toro, a popular Mexican restaurant in town. Under normal circumstances, this is one of my favorite places to eat. The chicken enchiladas are to die for.

But today?

I don't really have much of an appetite.

Mom drove down so we could have lunch together. It's been a couple of days since Dad dropped his bomb, and I've been checking in to make sure she's doing all right.

So far, so good.

As I arrive at the hostess stand, I see Mom has already been seated at the back of the restaurant near the window. There's a huge margarita sitting in front of her. When the hostess leads me to the table, I give Mom a quick hug before settling on the chair across from her.

"Hi, sweetie," she says. Her gaze drifts over my floral-colored blouse and red skirt. "You look nice."

"Thanks. You do, too." I'm relieved to see that she hasn't fallen apart. I was worried she would be dressed in sweats. Not that I would blame her. Instead, she's looking fashionable in a black knee-length skirt and a pale pink blouse. Diamond earrings drip from her ears, and a matching tennis bracelet is wrapped around her wrist. Her black Chanel Jumbo Flap Bag sits on the table next to the window.

Mom picks up her glass and takes a healthy sip before setting it down. "This is quite good," she marvels. "Would you like one?"

Day drinking?

I shake my head. "No, I have a class in two hours." Not that people don't show up after having a few drinks, but still. It's never been my thing.

"Tell me what's going on in your life." She pauses before adding, "Sometimes it feels like all we do is talk about your father. I'm tired of it."

For a moment, I consider spilling the beans about Beck, but then I realize she didn't know we were seeing each other in the first place, so what would be the point?

"There's nothing new to report." It's probably for the best I never got around to telling her. Our relationship lasted a hot minute before it crashed and burned spectacularly.

I should have trusted my instincts instead of believing Beck was capable of change. It's disheartening to realize that my dad was right.

Mom purses her lips and searches my eyes. "Hmm, now why don't I believe you?"

I'm saved from further questions when our waitress arrives on the scene. Since I already know what I want to order, I don't bother perusing the menu. It's what I get every time I'm here. Chicken enchiladas with beans and rice.

Yum.

Their mole sauce is freaking delicious. I could eat it by the spoonful. All right...so maybe I've done that once or twice.

Mom orders a chicken burrito and finishes her margarita before requesting another. I'm a little surprised by how quickly she sucked the sugary drink down.

After Brianna died, Mom was no stranger to having a few glasses of wine in the evening. During particularly rough patches, she'd polish off a bottle on her own. Numbing the pain with alcohol was one way she coped with her grief. I don't want her using it as a crutch to deal with the implosion of her marriage.

Once again, it makes me furious with Dad for yanking the rug out from under her feet.

The waitress leaves, and I nudge Mom's glass of water toward her.

When I can't stand another moment of the simmering tension, I say, "I know you don't want to talk about everything that's going on, but are you doing okay?"

She hoists a fake smile. "Of course, honey. I already told you there's nothing to be concerned about. It'll all get sorted out."

"I can't help but worry." I reach across the table and lay my hand over hers. "I want to help you through this, but I'm not sure how."

"I'm sorry." She stares at our clasped hands, and tears fill her eyes. "You should be worrying about senior year, not me."

"You have nothing to apologize for," I say, startled by her outburst of emotion. "You didn't do anything wrong." My voice grows steely. "Dad is the one who left without attempting to work through your issues." It's as if he struck a match, threw it in a puddle of gasoline, and then walked away when it turned into a raging inferno. It still blows me away that he could do this.

"It's my fault." When a tear slides down her cheek, she quickly swipes it away. "After your sister died, I checked out. I've spent the last couple of days going over everything in my head and what bothers me most is that I wasn't a better mother to you."

Her words leave me feeling as if there's a vise constricting my chest so tightly it's impossible to suck in full breaths.

"Don't say that, Mom. You did the best you could."

"It's the truth." She releases a sigh and stares out the picture window we're parked in front of. It's a gorgeous day. The sun is shining brightly, and the sky is a deep cornflower blue filled with puffy white clouds that drift lazily by. It feels like the kind of day where nothing could be wrong in the world, and yet, my mother's life is in tatters.

Not just hers. Mine, as well.

Even though I've tried to push all thoughts of Beck from my mind, I can't help but dwell on the scene I walked in on. For a moment, I had wondered if I'd stumbled into the wrong office. It didn't seem possible that Beck would be sitting on the couch, legs outstretched while Dr. Hayes knelt between them.

It was pretty damn obvious what was about to go down.

Her.

Ugh. I just puked in my mouth.

Even though I told Beck we were done, he's been calling and texting non-stop. I finally blocked his number. There's nothing he can say to make this right. The thought of them fooling around behind my back makes me sick to my stomach.

Mexican for lunch no longer seems like such a good idea.

I blink back to the present when Mom says, "I fell apart after Brianna died, and I never recovered."

None of us did.

"Mom, we don't have to talk about this if you don't want to."

She dabs her eyes with a napkin. "Maybe if I'd been able to move on, this wouldn't have happened. Your father and I wouldn't have drifted apart."

I lean forward, closing some of the distance between us. "This isn't your fault. Did he ever tell you that he was unhappy?" When she shakes her head, I continue. "Instead of talking about what was really going on, he threw himself into work and—"

"His secretary?"

A wave of shock washes over me. "*That's* who he's been seeing?"

She nods and shrugs. "I'm not proud to admit this, but I parked outside his work the other day and watched them walk out together. They were holding hands. Then he helped her into the car, and they left."

Mandi?

He's been having an affair with his secretary?

That's such a cliché, it's almost embarrassing.

I don't know what to say other than, "I'm sorry, Mom."

"You know what burns my ass the most?"

That's a loaded question.

When I remain silent, she continues. "That I would buy her gifts every year for Administrative Assistant Day."

Yeah...I could see how that would chafe.

"Apparently, my gifts weren't good enough since she helped herself to my *husband* instead."

Yikes.

The waitress returns with my Diet Coke and Mom's margarita.

"Just in the nick of time," she mutters, swallowing down half of it in one thirsty gulp. "Have you spoken to him yet?"

I shake my head. Like Beck, he's reached out. And like Beck, I've avoided his calls and texts. There is nothing he can say or do that will change the disgust and disappointment coursing through me. If he wasn't happy in his marriage, he should have done something about it instead of sneaking around behind Mom's back.

"As furious as I am with him," she says, "I don't want to cause a wedge in your relationship. No matter what happens between us, he *is* your father, and he loves you."

It's almost a relief when our lunch arrives. Mom needs something solid in her stomach to counteract the tequila. She's been snacking on the chips and salsa, but it's not enough.

I use my fork to push around the beans and rice on my plate. "I'm not ready to talk to him right now. He didn't only walk out on you, he walked out on me, too."

She reaches across the table and snags my hand. "He left me, honey. Not you. He loves you more than anything."

That may be so, but I'm too angry to deal with him right now. It doesn't escape me that the only reason he came clean about the affair is because I caught him in the act. And even then, he chose to lie before begrudgingly admitting the truth. He could have also let me know about the decision he arrived at before talking to Mom so I could have been prepared, but he couldn't be bothered to do that either.

So, no...I'm not interested in speaking to him now that he's shacked up with his whore and living his best life. Maybe some time down the road, but not right now.

Mom points her fork at my plate. "You haven't eaten much. Aren't you hungry?"

I shrug. "Not really. Don't worry, I'll take it home for dinner."

She glances at her own untouched plate. "Yeah, me neither."

I'm concerned about her driving home, especially since she didn't eat much. "Do you want to come back to my place for a while?"

"No. I forgot to mention it, but I've decided to stay with Aunt Amy for a few days. She'll help me find a lawyer and walk me through the process. I'm feeling a bit overwhelmed at the moment."

Aunt Amy has three divorces under her belt, so she's an old pro at this. "I'm sure that will be helpful." I pause before asking point-blank, "Are you all right to drive?"

"I'm fine," she snorts and waves her hand. "It takes more than one and a half margaritas to knock me on my ass."

My lips bow up at the corners.

That's probably true.

When I've finished picking over my enchilada, I set my fork on the table. "I'm going to run to the bathroom before we leave."

"All right, honey. I'll pay the check."

"Thanks, Mom. Lunch was nice."

"Not really," she chuckles, "but I love spending time with you."

I shimmy around the table and wrap my arms around her shoulders. "Maybe we can do this more often."

"I would love that," she says, leaning into my embrace.

I run to the bathroom at the back of the restaurant. Once inside, I take care of business and wash my hands before applying a bit of lip gloss. As I'm about to head out, the door swings open, and I do a doubletake as Dr. Hayes walks in.

Everything inside me freezes.

"Mia! I wasn't expecting to run into you today." She pauses, carefully looking me over. "How are you feeling?"

Huh?

My brows slam together until I remember emailing her yesterday about the stomach virus I'd come down with. It wasn't a *total* lie. The idea of sitting in her class all the while remembering what she looked like on her knees between Beck's legs makes me want to throw up.

"Much better, thank you." When an uncomfortable silence settles over us, I clear my throat and inch toward the exit. "I should really get back to the table."

As I take another step toward the door, her fingers wrap around my wrist. I glance at her hand in surprise.

A hesitant smile curves her pink-stained lips. "Could we talk for a moment before you run away?"

I shake my head. "Now probably isn't a—"

"I won't keep you long." She steps closer. "I promise."

Good time.

Ugh. Talking with Dr. Hayes is the last thing I want to do. It ranks right up there with talking to my dad or Beck.

My shoulders slump as I mumble, "I guess."

Her hand falls away from my wrist. It's odd that she can stand here and act like everything is perfectly normal. As if I didn't see her getting ready to blow one of her students.

The guy who was supposedly my boyfriend.

Pain blooms in my chest before I quickly stomp it out. I refuse to give Beck another moment of my time. I've given him way too much as it is.

Her attention stays locked on me as she leans against the counter. "I wanted to apologize for what you walked in on the other day. It was highly unprofessional of me to engage in a personal relationship on campus."

I blink, knocked off balance by her apology because honestly, it doesn't sound like much of one. "Isn't it inappropriate for you to be involved with one of your students?"

Her smile never falters. "It was consensual."

The little bit of food I've eaten for lunch threatens to revolt. "Was it?"

"Of course. Do you think any twenty-one-year-old male in his right mind would turn down sex with one of his professors?" She shrugs. "Consider it a perk of my position," she laughs. "I keep getting older, but the guys stay the same age. It's fabulous."

Gross.

The conversation I had with Beck at the library a couple of weeks ago forces its way into my consciousness. He'd tried telling me that Dr. H had been acting a little *too* friendly, and I'd brushed off the conversation. A pit settles in my belly as I consider the possibility that

I was wrong. Maybe he wasn't as willing of a participant as I'd assumed.

As much as I don't want to discuss the topic, I have to get to the bottom of it. "How long has your relationship with Beck been going on for?"

"I wouldn't really call it a relationship." A smug smile plays around the corners of her lips. "More like a pursuit."

"On your part?" My breath becomes wedged in my throat as I wait for her answer.

She gives me a wink. "I love the thrill of the chase."

After I'd walked in on them in her office, Beck had once again claimed she'd come on to him. I wince, remembering my reaction. Instead of believing him, I had accused him of being a liar and walked away.

When another silence falls over us, Dr. Hayes reaches out to squeeze my arm. "I'm glad we could clear up this misunderstanding, Mia. I'll see you in class tomorrow?"

I blink out of those thoughts before shaking my head. "No, I'm sorry. It turns out I won't be able to TA for you after all."

"Excuse me?" She straightens as her voice fills with disbelief. "You're going to leave me high and dry for the rest of the semester because you walked in on a private moment behind closed doors?"

"No, that has nothing to do with it. The reason I can't work for you is because I've lost all respect for you. Ever since freshman year Composition, I've admired you. I thought you were someone worthy of emulating. But you know what? I was wrong. How can I look up to someone who uses their position of power to make sexual advances toward a student? What you did to Beck was sexual harassment, plain and simple." I cock my head and narrow my eyes. "You realize he could file a complaint against you with the university."

Her eyes bulge as her mouth drops open. "It was consensual," she whispers again.

"Is that what you tell yourself when you hit on guys half your age and make them feel like they have to trade sexual favors for grades?"

She makes a choking sound deep in her throat but remains silent.

"Yeah, that's what I thought." With nothing left to say, I push out of the bathroom and head to the table where Mom is waiting. My hands are shaking so badly that I have to press them together to make them stop.

Mom rises to her feet when she sees me. "Are you all right?" Her brow furrows as she searches my face. "You look awfully pale."

"I don't think the enchiladas are sitting well."

"Uh-oh." She wraps an arm around my waist and steers me through the restaurant. "We better get you home before they hit."

My lips lift. "Thanks, Mom."

I lean against her shoulder as we push through the doors and into the bright fall sunshine. Only then, do I suck in a shaky breath and force down all the emotions that churn dangerously inside me.

Beck was telling the truth, and I didn't believe him.

I groan with the realization that I probably threw away the best relationship I've ever had. And there might not be a way for me to get it back again.

Chapter Thirty-Two

MIA

"You really said that?" Alyssa gapes before shoveling the last of my enchilada into her mouth. It's been sitting untouched in the refrigerator for days. *"To Dr. H?"* she mumbles around a mouthful of tortilla, cheese, and chicken.

I swing away from her as she sits on the couch in our living room. "Yup."

"Damn, girl!" she hoots, slapping her thigh. "You are seriously my hero!"

I tunnel my fingers through my hair and groan. Days later and I'm still reeling from the encounter in the bathroom at El Toro.

"No, I'm not." I spin toward her again as I continue to pace. A mixture of nerves and nausea makes it impossible to sit still.

My bestie shakes her head. "Are you kidding me? Everyone on campus has heard the rumors about Hayes. It's about time someone called her out on her bullshit."

"I've heard the gossip, too," I admit, "but I never suspected there was any truth behind it." I blow out a slow breath. "If I hadn't seen it happen with my own eyes, I still wouldn't believe it." Which only makes me feel like more of an asshole because I sat there in the library and brushed off Beck's concerns. Then I called him a liar and pretty much told him to fuck off.

"What are you going to do? File a complaint with the university?"

"I don't know." My teeth sink into my lower lip before worrying it. "I need to talk with Beck. He's the real victim in all this. I'm not sure if it's my place to say anything."

"When are you going to do that?"

"I have no idea." I drop onto the leather armchair across from the couch. A mirthless chuckle escapes from my lips. "After the way I treated him, it's doubtful he'll ever speak to me again." I lift my fingers to massage my temples. A headache brews behind them. "And I can't blame him for that."

The look she gives me is full of pity. "Yeah, blocking him on your phone and all social media probably wasn't the best move. You kind of went nuclear on his ass."

I wince. Her assessment of the situation isn't wrong. I have no idea if there's a way to come back from this.

A soft knock on the apartment door has both our heads whipping toward the entryway.

Alyssa's eyes widen. "Do you think that's him?"

"Why are you whispering?" I glance at the door. "Do you really think he can hear us?"

She sticks out her tongue before jumping off the couch and jogging toward the door.

We're both surprised when she swings it open only to find Colton on the other side.

I crane my neck to see what's going on. Their voices drop, becoming hushed. Their heads are bent together as if sharing secrets, but that can't be. Alyssa hates Colton with the passion of a thousand burning suns. I strain my ears to hear what's being said but can't make out anything other than whispered tones.

Well, well, well...isn't this an interesting turn of events.

I'm tempted to sidle up to the pair and stick my nose where it doesn't belong. When Alyssa shoots a furtive glance over her shoulder, I don't bother to hide my interest in their conversation.

Wait a minute...is Alyssa *blushing*?

That can't be. The girl doesn't have a bashful bone in her body. Not only is this exchange becoming more fascinating by the second, but it's taking my mind off Beck and the disaster I made of our relationship.

She swings toward me. Her gaze darts around the living room, landing everywhere but on me. "So...we're going to grab something to eat."

"Really?" I point to the empty food container on the coffee table that she practically licked clean. "You inhaled an entire enchilada."

"I have a big appetite." Her eyes narrow. "Are you trying to food shame me?"

My shoulders shake with laughter. "Not at all."

If it's possible, more color seeps into her cheeks.

Damn, but I really need to find out what's going on between them. Because obviously something is. And the bitch hasn't mentioned one word.

Looks like I'm not the only one keeping secrets.

"I'll see you later," she mutters, swiping her purse from the credenza near the front door.

"Yes, we'll definitely—"

The sentence isn't even out of my mouth before she slams the door shut behind her, leaving me to my own devices.

I wave a hand at the empty doorway. "No, no, that's all right, I'll stay here," I call out, raising my voice to add, "thanks anyway for the invite!"

With a sigh, I allow my body to sink into the chair before staring at the ceiling. I need to figure out how I'm going to handle the situation with Beck. No matter what happens between us, I need to apologize.

There's a knock on the door as my phone chimes with an incoming text. I jump from the chair and glance at the message. It's from Alyssa.

Heads up.

My brows slam together.

Could she be more cryptic?

I need a decoder to figure it out.

Or maybe I can buy a vowel.

I pad to the front door and pull it open. My heart stutters before beating into overdrive at the person I find standing in the hallway.

"Dad." My fingers bite into the handle. I'm so tempted to slam the door in his face. Especially after the lunch with Mom. "What are you doing here?"

He's the last person I expected to find knocking on my door.

Make that the second last.

Looking strangely nervous, he shrugs and stuffs his hands into the pockets of his slacks. "I thought I'd stop by so we could talk."

"Oh...I wish you would have called first."

His lips ghost into a thin smile. "Maybe if you would have answered my calls, stopping by unannounced wouldn't have become necessary."

"Yeah," I mutter, "I guess."

When I don't budge from the doorway, he says, "Are you going to invite me in?"

Begrudgingly, I step aside, giving him room to pass. Once he's inside the tiny entryway, I close the door and head into the living room before dropping onto the chair. He follows me in, settling on the couch across from me.

He looks around the room, taking in all the little details that have been added. Both of my parents helped me move in, but he hasn't been back to see the finished product. "I like what you've done to the place, it looks nice."

"Thanks." I shift on the chair as an uncomfortable silence settles over us.

We both fidget, looking everywhere but at each other.

This is beyond awkward.

What sucks is that my father and I have always had a close relationship. He's the one who introduced me to tennis. When I was a kid, he would take me to the courts, and we would spend hours hitting balls and working on my serve. I have a lot of great memories of my dad that revolve around tennis. It's difficult to swallow that he blew it all to shit with one traitorous action. I'm not sure if it's possible for us to get back to that place again. The man sitting across from me doesn't resemble the one who filled those memories.

Nerves stretch tautly across my skin as he releases a sigh before dropping his gaze to his clenched hands.

"I'm sorry, Mia."

"For what?" Now that the shock of his visit has dissipated, fury rushes in to fill the void. I can't stop dwelling on my lunch with Mom and the anguish and humiliation he inflicted upon her.

"For lying," he says, "and hurting you. Most of all, I'm sorry you found out about my affair the way you did. I should have handled the situation differently."

My eyes narrow. "So...you're sorry for hurting me and that I found out the way I did but not for cheating on your wife and breaking up our family." Maybe I'm being a little harsh, but that's too damn bad. I refuse to make this easy on him.

His shoulders slump under the weight of my words, and suddenly, he looks much older than his forty-eight years. "I've been in love with Mandi for a long time." He searches my eyes before admitting, "And now that we don't have to sneak around, it's like a huge weight has been lifted from my shoulders. Everything is out in the open, and I'm no longer stuck..."

Did he seriously just say that?

It's only after his voice trails off that I realize my eyes have widened, and my mouth is hanging open.

"Wow." Slowly I shake my head. "I guess it all worked out for you, *Dad*."

"I didn't mean it like that," he says, attempting to backtrack. "It's just a relief not to be living a lie. The last two years have been stressful."

I bet.

His words are like a punch to the gut.

"You've been sleeping with this woman for two years?"

He jerks his head into a nod.

"That's it then?" I stare at him as a fresh wave of shock washes over me. "You're not going to try to fix your marriage?"

Guilt flickers in his eyes before they skitter away. "No. Our marriage has been over for a long time." He clears his throat. "I'm sure your mother would agree with that."

"It might have been nice if you'd had a conversation with her about it before you slept with someone else."

He hangs his head. "You're right. I shouldn't have allowed the situation to spiral so far out of control. I take full responsibility for that. After Brianna died, your mother and I drifted apart. When you left for college, I realized how unhappy I was in our marriage. I thought about leaving at that point, but your mother was still in such a fragile place. So, I waited and hoped things would get better." He shrugs helplessly. "But they didn't."

I press my lips together, refusing to say anything. If he's looking for sympathy, he won't get it from me.

"Is it so difficult to understand that I wouldn't want to spend the rest of my life in a loveless marriage?" He waits for a beat before continuing. "Your mother and I have become more like roommates than anything else. Old friends who are stuck together, making the best of a situation." He searches my eyes. "But the thing is, I love Mandi. She makes me feel young and hopeful again. This is my second chance at happiness, and I need to take it before it passes me by."

I'm rendered speechless by everything coming out of his mouth.

Who the hell is this guy because I sure as hell don't know.

"Mia? Did you hear me?"

I jerk back to our conversation and shake my head to clear it. "No, sorry." I'm on information overload. I can't process anything else.

He leans forward, and excitement leaps to life in his eyes. "When you're ready, I'd like to introduce you to Mandi."

He wants to introduce me to the woman he left my mother for?

The same woman he's been cheating with for two years?

I don't even know what to say. Wrapping my lips around words feels impossible. I can only sit and stare at him.

"She has two kids. They're still in middle school, but you're going to love them." He pauses, enthusiasm growing in his voice. "They can't wait to meet you."

I shake my head. "No."

Is he insane?

Or am I the one who has completely lost it?

I can't tell anymore.

He tilts his head. "No?"

"I'm nowhere ready to meet the woman you left Mom for, and I have no desire to meet her kids either."

Surprise flickers across his face before he mumbles, "Well, I didn't mean this very minute. I was thinking more like a month or two. Christmas is right around the corner, and I was hoping we could have everything smoothed over by then."

Nope, it's definitely him. He's lost his ever-loving mind. He'll be lucky if this is *smoothed over* by the following Christmas.

"Sorry to burst your bubble, Dad," I shove a hand through my hair, surprised I have to explain myself to him, "but I don't think that will happen."

Happiness drains from his eyes. "I guess you'll let me know when you're ready to be part of my new life."

You know what?

I have zero desire to be part of his *new life.*

In fact, he can take his *new life* and shove it where the sun doesn't shine.

How can he be so oblivious to the damage he caused?

It's like he wants to sweep it all under the rug and pretend it never happened so he can move on with someone else and start his *new life.* Meanwhile, Mom and I are trying to pick up the tattered pieces of our old one.

It's a relief when Dad rises to his feet.

"I suppose I should go." He shoves his hands into his pockets. "You probably have homework or studying to finish up."

I nod, unwilling to tell him any different.

Neither of us speaks as we walk to the entryway. The man beside me no longer feels like my father. He's nothing more than a stranger. Once we reach the door, he pulls it open and pauses. "You'll keep in touch?"

Even though it's a lie, I nod. Maybe, at some point in the future, we'll be able to get our relationship back on track, but it'll take time. Whether or not he realizes it, he's inflicted a lot of pain that I need to work through.

When he wraps his arms around me, I stand frozen, unable to return the embrace.

"Remember that I love you, Mia. None of this is your fault."

I suck in a sharp breath before gradually blowing it out. If I don't keep a tight rein on my emotions, I'll lose it. Not for one damn moment did I ever think I was to blame for the destruction of his marriage. The fault for that lies *entirely* with him.

Once Dad releases me, his lips lift into a smile. After he disappears down the hallway, I close the door and sag against it.

This has officially become the week from hell.

With a sinking heart, I realize it's not over yet.

Chapter Thirty-Three

BECK

The spiral I throw lands perfectly in Colton's hands. Whatever problem he had been struggling with earlier in the season seems to have worked itself out.

Thank fuck, because that's the last thing we need right now. We have four games under our belt and eight more to go. It's still early, but we have an undefeated record.

When Coach blows his whistle, signaling the end of practice, I unsnap the chin strap and pull off my helmet, letting it dangle from my fingers. Colton jogs toward me, meeting me as we head off the field.

Grinning from ear-to-ear, he holds out his hand for a fist bump.

"Looking good out there," I tell him. "Nice to see you got your groove back."

"Damn right I did, baby!" He flashes a grin as relief oozes from every pore of his body. "And not a moment too soon with the Alabama game coming up."

Already I know it'll be a tough one. Both mentally and physically. We're neck and neck with Alabama. After next Saturday, one of us will be first in the conference, and I'm going to do everything in my power to make sure it's us.

I'm glad Colton finally got his head out of his ass and into the game. I don't know what's changed, and I don't particularly give a crap. All I care about is that he's squared away. Seems ironic that as soon as Colton manages to pull it together, my shit falls apart. Although, I'll be damned if I let it mess with my game.

I keep telling myself that maybe, in the long run, it's better this way. For a long time, I thought Mia was the one. Turns out that's not the case. The bitch of it is everything had been going so well. I'd really hoped...

I shut down that line of thinking before it can spread like a contagious virus and infect my bloodstream.

Colton rams his elbow into my side, and I glare. "What the fuck, dude?"

He lifts his chin toward the bleachers. "What's Mia doing here?"

Huh?

My gaze sweeps over the stands before landing on her dark head in the second row.

"I don't know," I mutter, trying to ignore the way my heart lurches at the sight of her.

"Guess you're gonna find out," he says.

When she realizes I'm staring, she rises to her feet before moving down the cement stairs and stepping onto the track that circles the field.

Once we pull up to her, Colton stops and grins like a Cheshire cat. "Hey, Mia. Wasn't expecting to see you here."

The way his voice simmers with humor makes me want to knock him upside the head.

She smiles, but it's not a full-blown one that reaches her eyes. There's a wariness holding her back. "Hi."

Silence falls over us before she clears her throat. "Beck, do you have a moment to talk?"

You know what?

I don't need this bullshit right now.

Not with the upcoming games.

Not with the NFL Scouting Combine and Draft.

For years, I let this girl mess with my head, and I can't afford to do it any longer.

I always thought there might be a chance for us, but I was wrong. It took me awhile, but I finally got it through my thick head.

We weren't meant to be.

End of story.

That being said, do I have more time to waste on Mia Stanbury?

Hell, no.

"Sure."

Goddamn it.

Colton grins before taking off. "All right, bro, I'll see you in the locker room." And then he's jogging to catch up with Devon Baker. They disappear through the tunnel and into the stadium.

The team walks past, and a few guys slap me on the back as they head to the locker room. There's a lot of laughter and good-natured ribbing. Now that practice is over, everyone has perked up.

Sweat runs down the back of my neck before getting absorbed into the material of my jersey. I'm exhausted from two hours of drills. All I want to do is get out of these pads and hit the showers.

I squint against the sun as it dips behind the stadium. "What did you want to talk about?"

Mia wrings her hands as her gaze flits around the field. She looks like she's being devoured by nerves. Part of me wants to reach out and put her at ease, but I refrain from touching her. Instead, I keep my arms locked at my sides. She made it perfectly clear the last time we spoke that she wants nothing to do with me.

So, as hard as it is, I wait.

Her anxiety continues to rachet up as her tongue darts out to smudge her lips. I stare at her perfect cupid's bow of a mouth, unable to stop myself from tracking the movement. My dick twitches against my jock, and I shift impatiently, wanting to get this over with.

Why the hell is she here when all she's done is avoid me for the last couple of days?

I almost laugh. What the hell am I talking about?

Mia has spent most of her life trying to evade me. I should be used to it by now. After what we shared, I thought everything had changed.

Guess I was wrong.

It isn't the first time, and it won't be the last.

"I'm sorry, Beck," she blurts. "I owe you an apology."

My gaze jerks from her mouth to her eyes. Out of everything she could have said, that's the one thing I wasn't expecting. "What are you apologizing for?"

She sucks in a deep breath before steadily releasing it back into the atmosphere. "I should have believed you about Dr. Hayes."

I tilt my head and narrow my eyes. "What makes you so sure I *wasn't* lying?"

The question gives her pause, and her knuckles turn bone white as she locks her fingers together. "I spoke with her, and she admitted to hitting on you."

Well, color me surprised.

When I remain silent, Mia continues in a rush, "I walked in on a situation and jumped to the wrong conclusion instead of giving you a chance to explain, and for that, I'm sorry."

A thick lump of emotion settles in the middle of my throat. "Not only did you accuse me of screwing around with my professor, but you thought I was cheating on you. When I tried to explain, you shut me down and walked away." I step closer so she has to crane her neck to hold my stare. "You should have known better, Mia."

"I know," she whispers, her breath escaping in harsh pants, "I'm so sorry. Can you forgive me?"

"Ever hear the expression—too little, too late?" I continue to push into her personal space until we're so close that the tips of her breasts press against my chest pads.

"Yes." Her face falls as she nods. "Even if you can't forgive me, I needed to apologize for hurting you."

When she tries to retreat, I drop my hands onto her shoulders to keep her in place. My face hovers inches from hers.

"So that's it?" I pause. "All I get is a lame apology for breaking my heart?"

Her dark eyes fill with tears. "I don't know what else to say other than I'm sorry."

"Maybe you should start by telling me that you love me."

She blinks in confusion before her eyes widen. *"What?"*

I lower my mouth until it can ghost over hers. Goddamn, but I've missed her kisses. Actually, I've missed everything about this girl. The last couple of days have sucked. "Tell me that you love me."

When a whimper slides from her mouth, my cock stirs.

"I love you, Beck." Her attention stays focused on me. "Even when I didn't want to, I did."

Emotion explodes in my chest. "Say it again," I demand, needing to hear those three little words.

She smiles, and the tension haunting her eyes dissipates. "I love you."

As soon as my lips settle on hers, she opens until my tongue can slip into her mouth as I wrap her up in my arms. I pull away long enough to mutter, "Know what you're going to do next?"

A bemused expression settles on her face as she shakes her head.

"Unblock me."

Laughter bursts from her as she presses her forehead against my chest. "I'm sorry. I shouldn't have done that."

"Damn right, you shouldn't have," I grunt.

"It will never happen again."

"I'm going to hold you to that promise." I press another quick kiss against her. "Looks like you have a long night ahead of you."

She pops a brow. "And why is that?"

"Make-up sex." A grin curls its way around the edges of my lips. "And lots of it."

Silent laughter shakes her shoulders. "Is that so?"

"Yup." Before she can say anything else, I bend down, wrap my arms around her thighs and hoist her over my shoulder. She lands against me with a squeal before grabbing hold of my jersey as she dangles upside down. I reposition my hands, sliding one to her ass and the other around her legs to hold her in place.

Thankfully, this time, she's not wearing a thong. No one gets to see the goods except me.

"Beck!" she shrieks. "What are you doing?"

"That should be obvious. I'm taking you home where you can apologize in the privacy of my bedroom." The thought has my cock stiffening right up. "I hope you don't have plans for the rest of the night because you'll be otherwise engaged."

"Please tell me that you're going to shower," she laughs, "because you kind of stink."

She's right, I smell terrible. That's what a couple of hours of practice will get you. Man sweat, baby.

But now that she's mentioned it...

"That can be part of the making up you owe me. What do you think about that?"

"Only that I love you, Beckett Hollingsworth."

I squeeze her ass as we walk through the tunnel. "Right back at you, babe."

EPILOGUE

Beck

Three and a half years later...

"Mia Hollingsworth," the Dean of the Law School announces as she walks across the stage in her cap and gown.

I jump to my feet and stick my fingers between my lips, whistling like crazy. Mia grins as her gaze seeks mine out in the thick crowd of observers. "Way to go, Mia!" I holler at the top of my lungs. I don't give a rat's ass if she's embarrassed. She worked damn hard for this moment, and I want everyone and their mother to know how proud I am of her.

Speaking of mothers...

I wrap my arm around Julia and give her a squeeze as we share a grin. My parents occupy the seats next to her. On my left is Mia's father, Dan, and his wife, Mandi.

When Mia told me that she planned on inviting both of her parents to the graduation ceremony, I thought she was nuts. Or maybe drunk. She insisted everyone was in a better place now. Considering that a fight has yet to break out, she might be right. Three years seems to have mellowed Julia's bitterness toward her ex-husband.

And his home-wrecking new wife.

I won't lie, the first year was a rough one. Dan ended up paying through the nose in order to expedite the divorce proceedings. It turns out Mandi was preggers.

Yeah...

That news went over like a lead balloon with his daughter. And who can blame her for that? There was a long stretch of time where they didn't talk. It's only been within the last year that Mia reached out and rekindled their relationship. It's been slow going. We're talking baby steps. But they seem to be on the right path.

I glance at my mother-in-law. I'm happy to report that she's doing much better. With the settlement from Dan, she went back to school for interior design and is working full-time at a design house. Once the divorce proceedings were underway, she began therapy and is now in a more Zen place.

Believe it or not, Julia has even dipped her toe in the dating pond.

And the guy she's seeing?

Has absolutely nothing to do with finance.

For today, everyone has put their differences aside, and we're all getting along like one big dysfunctional family. If we're lucky, all these good vibes will last throughout lunch. No one wants to ruin this day for Mia.

Dad is working on opening another law office in San Francisco since that's where I was drafted as their backup quarterback. First-round, baby. Don't worry, I worked my way up to starting QB after my rookie season.

As soon as the commencement ceremony ends and the auditorium empties, we all head outside to wait for my wife.

Yup, you heard that right.

After a year of dating, I proposed and put a ring on it. Then, before Mia's third year of law school, we got hitched. And it's been wedded bliss ever since.

Just kidding. Nothing is perfect, but it's pretty damn close. I can't imagine my life without this woman filling it.

I search through the sea of faces until I find my wife. The moment she sees me, a huge grin breaks out across her face, and she runs, hurtling herself into my arms. When I swing her around, she giggles before pressing her lips against mine.

"Congrats, babe, you're officially a lawyer!"

Her face lights up with joy. It's the best damn expression. One I'll never tire of.

Sure, maybe it took us a while to get our shit together, but it happened. And what I mean by that is—I chased her until I wore her down, and she finally had no other choice but to give in and marry me.

That's a joke. The Grinders R Us visit aside, we all know I didn't stalk her...right?

Right?

Moving on. No matter how it worked out, Mia Stanbury—AKA Mia Hollingsworth—is officially mine, and I don't have any plans to let her go. If I'm doing my job right as a husband, she'll have me locked in for the long haul as well.

"I love you, Beck," she whispers before pressing her lips against mine.

I squeeze her to me and hold her close. "Right back at you, babe."

-The End-

Ready to delve into The Boy Next Door?
Get it here!
https://books2read.com/theboynextdoor2

ABOUT THE AUTHOR

Jennifer Sucevic is a USA Today bestselling author who has published eighteen New Adult and Mature Young Adult novels. Her work has been translated into both German (as well as audiobook format) and Dutch. She has a bachelor's degree in History and a master's degree in Educational Psychology. Both are from the University of Wisconsin-Milwaukee. Jen spent five years working as a high school counselor before relocating with her family. If you would like to receive updates regarding new releases, please contact Jennifer through email, at her website, or on Facebook. sucevicjennifer@gmail.com

Social media links-

www.jennifersucevic.com

https://www.instagram.com/jennifersucevicauthor

https://www.facebook.com/jennifer.sucevic

https://www.tumblr.com/blog/jsucevic

https://www.pinterest.com/jmolitor6/

https://www.wattpad.com/user/jsucevic

www.ingramcontent.com/pod-product-compliance
Lightning Source LLC
Chambersburg PA
CBHW051142190726
48290CB00006B/1948